Summer of the Fetch

Todd Fahnestock

DEDICATION

For Giles

Stay on these roads

CONTENTS

ACKNOWLEDGMENTS

First, I'd like to thank Chris Mandeville, my writing co-worker. She was there every step of the way for this novel, from the initial concept to final keystroke. You spurred me to write more.

Next, I'd like to thank my fabulous beta readers. The timeline was tight, and you raced through this book with fabulous feedback. You really came through for me!

- Aaron Brown
- Andy Grover
- Brian Wirtz
- Carle Greene
- Courtney Farrell
- Damien Kirk
- Georgine Traver
- Giles Carwyn
- Jenny Fitts Reynolds
- Katelin Barson
- Luna Leverett
- Tracy Nicholas
- Tara Henderson

A special thanks to Luna for her insights about Yosemite, and to Giles and Brian for their invaluable rock climbing beta.

I also want to acknowledge my amazing editor, Mandy Houk.

Lastly, I want to give a huge thank you to Rashed AlAkroka. You are a consummate professional, my friend, and you knocked this one out of the park. Thank you for your putting your amazing talents to work on the *Summer of the Fetch* cover. You're the best in the biz. I'm honored to work with you.

Mailing List/Social Media

MAILING LIST
Don't miss out on the latest news and information about all of
my books. Join my Readers Group

FACEBOOK GROUP

AMAZON AUTHOR PAGE

CHAPTER 1

I remember everything about the day I first saw the fetch. It was the spring of 1988, but the warming air whispered of summer. I remember the deep blue of the sky, the smell of the sagebrush, and the sun slowly sinking toward the horizon. I remember the window framing her, this magical creature who was going to change my life forever.

My mother had just died a week ago in a car crash, and my life as I knew it was over. All my hopes for the future were fading. I could only see one path in front of me now, and I waited for it like a criminal waits for his execution.

I sat alone on my bed in our house, clutching my acceptance letter to The Colorado College. I'd applied last fall with barely a hope to be accepted. I mean, I was a good student, but not a great one. I was taking two AP classes my senior year. My friends were taking four. They were going to places like Princeton and Brown. Except for Gage, of course. He hated "the Ivy League pukes," and he'd gotten his acceptance letter from CC weeks ago.

I'd been waiting for mine for months in tense anticipation. Now I had it, and I might as well light it on fire for all the good it was going to do me. I wasn't going to college anymore. My chance to attend, slim from the beginning, had dropped to zero. With Mom gone, I had no one in my corner. My dad would rather stick a fork in his eye than pay for what he called an "overpriced piece of paper."

I looked around at the white walls of my room. Curtains of light blue and white fluttered in the cool spring breeze. My room had always made me feel safe, but now it felt desolate. Once, we had all lived in this house: Mom and Dad and my head-banging older brother. But now it was just me, staring at the white walls, waiting for a phone call that had my stomach in knots.

A year ago, my family had burst apart. My parents had divorced. Dad took some stupid job in Malaysia and moved there with his new wife. My brother moved to California to work at UCLA as a janitor while he pursued his dream of becoming a rock star, and my mother and I stayed here.

Our house was perched on a rise on Florida Mesa, about ten minutes from the little town of Durango. I could only see three other houses from my window, and each was far away. They didn't stack houses right next to each other on the mesa like they did in town. It took a good two minutes of walking to reach our closest neighbor.

It was mid-May, about a week from my high school graduation. The days were mild, the nights cool, but I could feel summer coming. The Colorado sun shone down on the oak trees and fields outside my window, and every now and then a breeze would blow the scent of warming sagebrush through the window. It felt like, at any moment, I would catch a whiff of sunblock too, like someone outside was trying to grab a little bit of summer before it was actually here. Sunblock always made me think of the pool in town, which made me think of Tina Cartwright in a swimsuit.

Tina Cartwright... She was another hope that had faded. I'd wanted to ask her out for two years, and I never had. I'd been telling myself that I'd work up the nerve, maybe in the last week of school. Maybe over the summer somehow. Now I'd never have the chance.

The phone finally rang, and I jumped. I'd been expecting it

but I still jumped. Taking a deep breath, I picked it up, put it to my ear. I didn't say hello.

"Eric?" Dad's voice came over the line. Butterflies of fear batted around inside me.

"Yeah," I said.

"How are you doing?"

I'm totally fucked. How are you? I thought, but I didn't say that.

"You know," I said.

"How was the funeral? Good?" he asked.

How can a funeral be good?

"I don't know," I said.

He didn't seem to hear my answer. I don't think he really cared. He had a purpose, and nothing stopped my Dad when he had a purpose. He just moved on to the real reason for his call.

"So I've set up a ticket for you," he said. "It's just a hop to Stapleton. You'll switch planes there. Then you'll fly to Malaysia. Non-stop." He said "non-stop" like it was something to get excited about.

"I... I got my acceptance letter today," I said, and the butterflies went frantic. I knew what he was going to say, but just maybe I was wrong. Just maybe he'd see how important this was to me, and he'd care. He'd try to help me.

Dad went silent, and all I could hear was static on the line. "The college thing?" he finally said.

"Yeah. I-I can go. I got my letter."

"Eric, we talked about this. It's $12,000 a year. I'm not paying for that."

And there it was, exactly what I thought he'd say. He lived in a mansion in Malaysia—he'd told me three times now—with fancy cars and servants. But he wasn't going to spend a dime on "an overpriced degree you'll never use." He wasn't going to spend a dime on me.

The worst thing was that I hadn't needed his help before Mom died. CC had a great financial aid program, and I qualified because Mom made next to nothing. But now, that hope was dead. They'd take one look at my dad's yearly income and charge me full tuition.

And even if I sold everything I owned, I couldn't come up with $2,000, let alone $12,000.

"I don't want to go to Malaysia," I said. "I want to go to college."

Again, static silence over the line.

"We are not going over this again, Eric," he said. "You're coming here. You can't just live on your own."

"I could live on my own," I said. I felt like I wanted to explode.

"You're a kid, Eric. And you don't know anything about the real world. It's not like those fantasy books you read or that Mazes and Dragons game. The real world would crush you. You'd never make it."

"I could," I said so softly he probably didn't hear me. I hated that his words stung. Why couldn't he just believe in me? Why couldn't he say: *Hey, do what you want. Go make me proud. Inspire me.*

"The flight is at 10 a.m.—" he began.

"This is my life!" I blurted. "And I don't want to live in Malaysia. It's a bullshit place and you're just having some stupid year with a stupid company and your stupid..." I hesitated. "I mean...with your new wife," I amended lamely.

But I'd crossed a line. I felt it then, the switch. Dad's rage came on so fast.

"Now look," he said in that dark tone I'd known and feared my whole life. "You don't talk that way about Sandra."

"You didn't come to Mom's funeral," I said. "You weren't even there."

"I told you why," he exploded. "Things are crazy busy right now!"

Things were always crazy busy. He always said that.

If you believed in me, you'd help me, I thought. *You'd have my back. You'd help me go to college. You'd at least act like it was important. Like I was important.*

But he didn't care about what I wanted, only about what was most convenient for him.

"Mom would find a way to help me," I muttered. She was the one who'd explored my financial aid options at CC, who had given me hope that such a place was even possible for me.

"I'm not having this same conversation again," Dad said.

"We didn't even have it the first time," I mumbled.

"What?" he boomed. "What was that?"

"Nothing."

"Get your ass on that plane. Saturday. 10 a.m."

I didn't say anything.

"I mean it," he said, and I heard the threat, like something horrible would happen to me if I defied him. He used that dark tone when he was done being nice. I'd seen the switch so many times, seen him yell at Mom. I'd seen him throw things, break things. And while he'd never laid a hand on me, I think maybe that was the threat.

"Do you hear me?" he demanded.

"Yeah," I said.

"Okay, then," he said, and the dark tone faded away. "It's going to be great, Eric. You're going to love Malaysia. You won't believe the house we're living in." Again with the house. "They treat us like kings."

I didn't say anything.

"I love you, kiddo," he said. "I'll see you soon."

"Yeah."

I hung up the phone.

I had just one week left of high school, and he didn't even care enough to let me finish it. This was supposed to be the best moment of my life, but in his eyes, I wasn't good enough to be allowed my full high school experience, to say goodbye to my friends. To maybe ask out Tina Cartwright. To have the summer to blow off steam and take trips to Navajo Lake, to do all those things seniors were supposed to do. He just wanted to pluck me out of my life and sweep me halfway around the world. I'd vanish from Durango, and my friends would move on. Time would move on. It'd be like I'd never even lived here.

Dad kept telling me I could finish school in Malaysia with tutors, get whatever credits I needed there, as if that was the same. As if that was the point.

And that was when I saw the fetch.

Mired in the swamp of my own personal pity party, I looked up and saw a fox gracefully perched on my windowsill. It had bright red fur. Its fluffy red tail wrapped around hidden paws and ended in a snowy white tip. Its mouth was open as though smiling, exposing sharp, sparkling white teeth. The window framed the fox like a painting with the deep blue sky and the sinking sun behind it.

I squawked and fell backward off my bed. When I scrambled to my feet and peeked over the edge of the rumpled covers, the fox was gone.

I went to the window to try to catch another glimpse of the fox. My room was on the second story of our house, overlooking the driveway and the eastern field. I scanned the driveway and the berm that skirted it, rising up to the edge of the house. I scanned the field beyond, all the way to the fence that marked the edge of our land and the beginning of the reservation property of desert dirt and sagebrush that my father had called the Indian Land.

I dashed out of my room and up the long hallway, but by the time I banged out the front screen door, skipped down the stone steps and reached the driveway to get a wider view, there was no sign of the fox.

I hiked up the hill to the side of the house to stand right below my window, looking for some trace of it. It had rained hard a couple days ago and the arid Colorado air had dried the dirt into fragile patterns, tiny pillars of mud turned to dirt. Even a cricket couldn't cross that soil without making a trail, let alone a fox. But there wasn't a single paw mark, not even the slightest indentation.

I stared at that pristine dirt for a long moment. Then I stared at my bedroom window, which was a good fourteen feet above the ground. If I'd run and leapt with all my might, I don't think I could have grabbed that windowsill with my fingertips, and I was nearly six feet tall. Could a fox jump that high? And if it could, would it leave no tracks at all?

I didn't think so. Which meant only one thing. There had been no fox. Somehow, I'd imagined it.

I swallowed, and a cold, eerie feeling crept through me. I could still see the fox in my mind's eye. Soft red fur, intelligent eyes, those white, smiling teeth.

I shivered, then I ran back into my house and shut the door, locked all the windows.

I lay on my bed with my eyes open for hours. I guess I finally fell asleep, because I don't remember anything else until my best friend Gage woke me up the next morning.

CHAPTER 2

I almost didn't answer the phone when it rang. My sleepy brain thought it was my father calling again, but as I came more fully awake I realized it couldn't be. He'd said his piece. I was getting on a plane to Malaysia tomorrow. I was doing what he wanted; he was controlling the situation. No reason to reach out if everything was in hand.

I grappled with the receiver and finally put it to my ear.

"Hello," I mumbled.

"Hey numbnuts," came the voice on the line. "You still sleeping?"

"Hi Gage."

"Dude. Are you ditching?" he asked, sounding excited. Gage had been trying to get me to ditch all year long.

"No m'not." I blinked over at my digital clock radio. It was already 7:30. My alarm hadn't gone off. School started in 45 minutes. If I got in the car right this second and raced all the way, I'd make it. But somehow, I just couldn't make myself feel the urgency. What did it matter anymore? I'd probably be better off staying here and packing. I was going to miss all of next week anyway. All of my finals. All of my friends.

"If you're ditching, you better fucking say so. If you finally grew some balls and didn't tell me, I'm gonna pound you."

I sat up in bed, yawned. "Why are you calling?"

"Canyonlands, dude. This weekend. You're coming. I'm taking my dad's Jeep. I was going to go with Jay, but he pussied out on me. I need someone on belay."

"I can't."

"I'll keep you safe, kitten. Hell, you don't even have to climb if you don't want. Just belay me, drink some beer, sit by a campfire. It'll be wicked. What the hell else you got going on?"

Despite myself, I cracked a smile. Gage could take my mind off a bad situation quicker than anyone else. He veered away from anything sad through sheer force of will. I think he couldn't stand to be unhappy. He was always pushing himself, pushing his boundaries. Strangely, his crude attitude had been the easiest to be around since Mom's death. He'd never once mentioned her, and I was sure he wasn't ever going to.

But he was the only one of my friends who'd come to the funeral. He'd just stood in the back, looking implacable, and then he'd driven me home, making off-color jokes about zombie sex.

We'd been best friends since second grade. We'd played at recess together, made sure we were in the same class every year, played D&D on the weekends, and collected comics. We were the same brand of geek until eighth grade when Gage discovered boxing. I'd stayed pretty much the same skinny, awkward guy whose highlight of the week was the next episode of *Star Trek: The Next Generation*. Gage, on the other hand, grew muscles and became a force of nature.

He worked out most days—footwork, weights, bag work, and sparring. By tenth grade, he'd won the Colorado youth underage something-or-other boxing contest. That year, one of the bullies—who used to pick on us in elementary school—tried that same bullying shit in the boys' locker room with Gage. The guy's name was Mitch Groden, and he thought Gage's boxing title was bullshit. He thought once a geek, always a geek, and Gage could still be pushed around. Gage beat the holy living shit out of him. Just destroyed him. Word got around, and none of the jocks messed with Gage after that.

And, of course, with locker room fame and bulging muscles came girlfriends. Gage was the first of our geeky group to have a girlfriend, and though we didn't know for certain, we were all pretty sure he was the first to get laid, too. Gage would talk about sex all the time—tits and ass, legs wrapped around his head, shit like that—as crude as he could make it and always at the most inappropriate times. But he never named names. I mean, we'd met some of his girlfriends, but he had never bragged on who he'd done it with. I always admired that about him.

Anyway, ever since that turning point in eighth grade, Gage was always game to go harder, faster, more. All the time. He kept pushing his luck with the rules at school, so much that he'd almost been suspended at the beginning of our senior year. But here we were, about to graduate.

"Well? Are you in or what?" Gage tromped on my thoughts.

"I'm moving to Malaysia," I said.

He went silent at that.

"Bullshit," he finally said.

"It's true. My dad bought the ticket."

"Fuck you, you're going to Malaysia."

"Yeah. Fucked me. Going to Malaysia."

"You're a funny guy. So we're definitely ditching today, then."

"No. I'm going. I can make it."

"Hell you can."

"I would if I could ever get off the phone with this asshole I know."

"See you in thirty, dick." Gage hung up.

I got showered, got dressed, and made it into the car with a piece of buttered toast and a Coke. Breakfast of champions.

My car was a 1967 El Camino, painted bright shiny orange. Gage had jokingly called it The Great Pumpkin, and the name had stuck.

The El Camino was my dad's high school car. He'd bought

it new, and about the only thing my dad and I had in common was that we both loved that car. It had come to Colorado with us when we moved from California. The original engine had crapped out three years ago, and my dad picked up a used Corvette engine for a steal. He'd dropped it into The Pumpkin along with a short throw racing shifter. The nicest thing my father had ever done for me was letting me buy The Pumpkin when I'd turned sixteen.

In short, I loved that car. And while it might look like an old pickup from the sixties, it could fucking move.

It was by far the coolest thing about me.

I peeled out of the driveway, throwing gravel. It was easily a fifteen-minute drive to school, but I made it in ten. And I didn't get pulled over by a cop.

Still, I arrived late to Ms. McDunn's English class. She knew—everybody knew—about my mom, but I didn't get any sympathy from her. She marked me late anyway. She made some little speech about how she should send me to the office for being more than twenty minutes late but that she wouldn't, as if that was a compassionate concession. Whatever. It didn't matter. Nothing I did at this school mattered anymore. I was on a plane to Malaysia at 10 a.m. tomorrow.

I sat there, stewing in my thoughts, when I just happened to look up and see Tina Cartwright in the hall, through the propped-open door. She hurried past, head down, the wet glimmer of tears on her cheeks.

I glanced over at Ms. McDunn. She was bent over a stack of books, her back to the class, mumbling something about a passage she wanted to read to us.

First off, I'm not one to break the rules. I'd always believed kids who insisted on breaking the rules all the time only made life harder on themselves. If you lied a lot, grown-ups stopped believing what you told them. They stopped trusting you. If you were a rule-breaker, then when you legitimately asked them for something, they were inclined to tell you no. Sometimes, even when you weren't to blame, they'd blame you anyway because that's what they expected of you. It never made sense to me to do anything but follow the rules. It's why I never ditched classes with Gage.

But today, giving a shit about what the adults wanted...? Well, it didn't seem to matter.

Nothing I did mattered at this school...

Fuck them. And fuck their rules.

I stood up and went to the door. Everyone in the class saw me do it except Ms. McDunn. I gave the class a brief glance. Rory Carpenter gave me two thumbs up. Everyone else just looked at me with stunned expressions.

I walked quickly into the hallway, and a thrill of fear raced through me.

Tina sat on the floor at the end of the hall, her back against the lockers. Her body shuddered as she cried.

I'd been in love with Tina since I'd first seen her in tenth grade. She was student body president. She was also a volleyball and tennis athlete, a straight-A student, and she had the silkiest brown hair. I sat behind her in Calculus and AP History, and I often watched her separate one lock from that cascade of hair and twirl it absently on her finger until it slipped away. She'd do that over and over again. It was the cutest thing ever.

I'd gotten up the nerve to talk to her a couple of times, and we actually had a lot in common. She read fantasy books like me. But she was always busy and, of course, she had a boyfriend. Wade Thompson, quarterback of the football team, if you can believe that. She was like something out of a John Hughes movie.

Suddenly, with only hours left at this school, I decided I was going to tell Tina that I liked her. If I wasn't going to get any of the rest of my end-of-the-year experience, I was going to do just this one thing. I'd been telling myself for years that I'd muster the courage. And even if nothing could come of it, even though she had a boyfriend, I needed to at least tell her. I was out of time.

I went over quietly. She didn't hear me coming until the last second, and she looked up in surprise.

"Eric," she said. She wiped at her eyes. "What are you doing here?"

Before, when I'd talked to her, I'd always been nervous, thinking about what I could say to make her like me. But not this time. If I dorked it, and she ended up hating me, how would it matter? I'd never see her again anyway.

"Is it okay if I sit?" I asked.

She blinked, doing a more thorough attempt to wipe her cheeks. "I...I have a pass." She held it up. "I'm not just...you know."

"Ditching?" I asked.

"Right."

"I'm not the vice principal," I said, sitting down next to her. "I just... You looked upset. Are you okay?"

She swallowed. "You're in Ms. McDunn's class right now?" She nodded at the door, which was only about thirty feet away.

"Yeah."

"And you just left?"

A part of me could hardly believe it either. I just wasn't that kind of guy, and I felt like I was standing outside of myself. It was strange.

"Yeah, I guess," I said.

"Why?"

"Because of you. I saw you crying."

Her lip trembled and she looked upward, blinking fast like she wanted to stop the tears. She couldn't. She brought her hands to cover her face and a little sob wracked her body. "I'm just a mess," she mumbled through her fingers. "I don't know what... I just don't know what to think."

"What happened?" I asked.

She took a deep breath and blew it out through puffed cheeks. She brought her hands down. "I'm just a mess, that's all."

"Tell me."

"You don't want to know."

"I do."

"Really?"

13

"I do."

"Wade broke up with me," she said. She turned her head to look at me, gave me a trembling frown. "I'm sorry, this is kind of weird. Talking with you about my love life in the hallway."

"Weird how?" I asked.

"I mean... I always thought of you as a friend, but we've never really talked, you know?"

"Yeah. I always regretted that," I said, the words tumbling out of me. I felt like I was walking on a pane of glass over a giant drop. I felt exposed, vulnerable, waiting for the glass to crack.

Tina looked surprised. "You did?" she said.

"Yeah. I always liked you. I never said it. Now I wish I had. I wish I'd said it back in tenth grade when I first thought it. Now it's the last week of school and it's too late."

She blinked, like she couldn't believe I'd been so completely honest. Frankly, I couldn't believe it either.

She let out a little breath. "Well... Wow."

"Sorry." I shook my head. "You're upset. I didn't mean to come out here and lay some big confession on you."

"No, it's really sweet, actually." A little smile crossed her face, like the sun peeking between the clouds. "I think you just cheered me up."

"Well that's the best thing I've heard all week," I said.

Her face clouded up again. "Oh God, Eric. I'm so sorry. I didn't even think... I'm so sorry about your mother. I mean, I heard about... We all heard... God, I'm such an idiot. Here I am crying about a boy, and you lost your mother."

I waved it away. "It's okay. I didn't come out here because I was crying. I came out because you were."

She cocked her head, and her little smile appeared again.

I just kept looking at her eyes. She was so pretty.

"I'm sorry about Wade," I said at last, and I realized that, like my Dad, I was just saying the expected thing. I suddenly hated myself for it. Her boyfriend was a dick. He was always making fun of my friends.

"Thank you," she said. She looked down at her knees, then

over at me. "Hey, you like ice cream?"

"Only on Mondays, Tuesdays, Wednesdays, Thursdays, Fridays, Saturdays, and Sundays. The rest of the time, no."

She laughed. "Want to go get ice cream sometime?"

"It'd have to be tonight," I said. "I'm leaving tomorrow."

"What? Why?"

"My dad's making me."

"Oh."

"Yeah."

"Well, how about tonight?" She blushed, and I didn't think I'd ever seen anything more wonderful. Tina Cartwright, blushing while she was asking me out.

"It's a date."

She bit her lip. Then she stood up and smoothed her denim miniskirt. "I really have to get to the kitchen. They need a... It's for student council. But...tonight at Coleman's? 5:30?"

Wow.

"I'll be there." I felt a rush of euphoria unlike anything I'd ever known, and it suddenly seemed incomprehensible that I'd never asked her out before.

She turned on tiptoe in her white Reeboks, walked to the stairs at the end of the hall. She gave me a shy smile before starting down. God, she was perfect.

I sat there for a long moment after she was gone. It felt like a dream. My eyes lost focus and I thought about the many times I'd gazed at Tina and—

Red fur flashed at the top of the steps, like a fox's nose or the tip of an ear. I sat up, snapping alert, but that flash of red was gone so fast I wondered if I'd even seen it.

I lurched to my feet and raced to the steps, but there was only an empty stairwell. No fox. Just like under my window at home—

"Mr. Marks!" Ms. McDunn's voice cracked like a whip. Disoriented, I spun to look at her.

"That's it, mister. To the principal's office, right now." She pointed down the hallway in the opposite direction Tina and the fox had gone.

I went with her without a fight, thinking about the fox. Then I realized: why was I thinking about some stupid fox? Tina asked me out for ice cream!

My smile grew. Ms. McDunn scowled at me fiercely, but I didn't even try to suppress it. I was on Cloud Nine and nothing—not even a trip to the principal's office—was going to bring me down.

I had a date with Tina Cartwright.

CHAPTER 3

As Ms. McDunn took me to the office, it felt like a veil was being lifted from my eyes. I could see so many things I hadn't seen before. I'd never considered myself a fearful kid—I mean no more than any other high school kid—but I suddenly realized I was. I was fearful about almost everything.

Generally, I kept my head down. I steered clear of the jocks, who were always looking to pick on somebody. And when one or a group of them caught me alone, I just took the teasing and shoving. It was the quickest way to make the torment end—eventually they'd get bored, call me a "fag" and move off up the hallway, laughing in their dominance. I never pushed back.

I remembered in tenth grade when Sam Bozeman, newly arrived from Nebraska or Iowa or something, had pushed back when three of the jocks from the football team teased him about his shoes. Sam was skinny and small, but he had a mouth that he couldn't control. He'd called them assholes and punched one of them. The hit wasn't even that hard, but they'd jumped on him like he was an ogre. They'd beat him up pretty bad—and they'd been suspended for a week—but after a week they were right back to prowling the halls like sharks.

Things like that had always terrified me. What had

happened to Sam was my worst nightmare.

I'd always seen my ducking and dodging as smart, as self-preservation. But today, after seeing what could happen when I finally did what I really wanted to do, I hated who I was.

I suddenly saw all my excuses—walking down the lesser-used hallways, smiling and joking with the jocks when they took my hat and didn't give it back, hanging close to Gage when the jocks were around because I knew they wouldn't mess with him—for what they really were. I was afraid of everything.

But now, with only one day left, I could do whatever I wanted. I could talk to a pretty girl, tell her I liked her. I could ditch a class.

Ms. McDunn opened the door to the counselors' offices and pulled me through by my wrist. We went into the waiting room first. The counselors' offices had soft, modern-style blue chairs, and the carpet was a soothing green. Also, the lights always seemed a little dimmer, like they were designed to calm the students.

Framed inspirational posters hung on the walls, each with an eye-catching picture and a bit of bubblegum wisdom, like *Walk the Talk*, *Commitment*, and *Teamwork*.

My gaze lingered on one of the posters. It read: "Make it Happen - There Is No Challenge Too Great for Those Who Have The Will And Heart To Make It Happen." The picture was of a guy rappelling down a rope, hanging from a sandstone cliff hundreds of feet above the ground.

My friends and I always made fun of those posters. But today, the "Make It Happen" poster stood out to me. It didn't seem as cheesy as it usually did.

I shook my head. It probably only drew my attention because Gage had been talking about rock climbing.

Ms. McDunn poked her head into each of the counselors' private offices, but no one was home. My gaze lingered on the guy hanging from the rope.

She kept going through the double doors that connected the counselors' offices to the administrative offices, hauling me along with her.

Unlike the counselors' offices, the admin offices were not designed to make a student feel at ease. Crammed with copy equipment and 1970s metal filing cabinets—some tan, some charcoal gray—no attempt had been made to choose soothing colors or even colors that matched. Cream-colored tiles with dark brown marbling covered the floor, made to confuse the viewer about what was actually dirt and what was part of the design. They just ended up making the floor look dirty no matter what.

"You sit here," Ms. McDunn said, and she pushed me down in a chair by the round table in the room. The table was wedged between the enormous copy machine and a smaller rectangular table hunched beneath a straining set of bookshelves that bowed under rows of binders as thick as my fist.

The rectangular table held the school PA microphone which rose up like the head of the Loch Ness monster, about eight inches tall, with a couple of white plastic buttons on the base. Wedged beneath the table was the control panel—a bunch of buttons, knobs, and switches that, I supposed, allowed the user to make an announcement in any classroom they wanted, or to the entire school.

Ms. McDunn checked the admin offices but apparently nobody was there either. Her lips pressed together in a frustrated line, and she pointed at me. "Wait here until I find Mr. Sims. I'll be right back."

She left in a huff, obviously upset that things hadn't gone to plan: a quick drop-off of the troublemaker in the principal's office, then back to her class.

Yeah. I knew all about things not going to plan.

My gaze fell on the PA system.

I gently pushed my chair back, but it squeaked on the dirty-by-design tile anyway. I got up and seated myself in front of the microphone. The button marked *School-wide Announcement* was already clicked on, glowing red above the toggle.

Before I even knew what I was doing, I pressed the big

square button on the stand. That brief, ear-stabbing feedback that always preceded a school-wide announcement cut through the quiet of the office and, I knew, the quiet of the whole school.

I leaned forward.

"Do it..." I said, and it sounded so lame to me, but I pushed on. I cleared my throat. "Whatever you're wanting to do, do it now. Don't wait. Don't let your parents or the teachers tell you that you can't. Stay up all night. Skip your homework. Skip your entire school day. You have no idea—none of us do—what you could be missing if you don't."

I drew a shaky breath, then kept going.

"You could end up seeing that sunrise you always wanted to see. You could end up winning that contest you were afraid to enter. You could end up on a date with a pretty girl like Tina Cartwright." I paused at this, and I grinned like my face would split.

"What you think matters," I continued. "What you *want* matters. If there's something you want to do, why aren't you doing it? Why aren't any of us? If you have dreams, don't wait for a better time to grab them. The better time never comes. We only get today, right now. Don't..." I paused. "Don't waste it."

I held the button down for another long moment. Static hissed on the line, then I let it go.

I sat back, stunned at myself and stunned I'd actually been able to finish. I'd expected the vice principal, the principal, and the secretary to burst through the door immediately. I'd expected them to smack the PA from my hand before I'd said three words.

I looked up at the clock on the wall and watched the second hand. God, they still weren't here. The second hand completed a full revolution. A minute, a full minute had gone by and—

I glimpsed a flash of red fur through the window that looked out on the hallway.

Spooked, I lurched to my feet so fast the chair went over

backward and clanged loudly on the floor. I wasn't imagining it that time. Not twice in a row. That had looked like a bushy fox tail with a white tip.

I jumped at the window, but as soon I got there, Mr. Sims charged past in the hallway, startling me, and grabbed the door handle to the admin office.

He burst through the door, his face red, his white eyebrows crouched so low that his eyes were just dark shadows beneath. He was a tall man, I mean really tall, like six-foot-six, with white hair and a gray suit. Behind him stood Ms. McDunn. Her face was pale and her mouth hung open.

"What the heck do you think you're doing, young man?" Mr. Sims barked, and he'd barely had time to say it before the secretary burst in, as wide-eyed as Ms. McDunn. I gawked at him for a second, my mind still on the elusive fox.

"Well?" he demanded.

I didn't think Mr. Sims really wanted me to answer, but I did anyway. "It was important," I said simply. How could I pay attention to him? A fox was following me around in a school. How did that even make sense?

Was I going crazy? Was I hallucinating foxes?

"Important?" Mr. Sims demanded, like I'd spoken in Chinese or something. He looked around wildly like he wanted to grab something to hit me with, and his gaze fell on Ms. McDunn.

She gabbled so quickly I could barely understand her. "I brought him down here because he left class without permission, but I didn't find anyone so I went to the cafeteria to look for you. I thought at least one of you would be close by. I mean, someone had to stay with him and I had to get back to my class and how could I have known he'd grab the PA system and—"

"Okay, okay," Mr. Sims cut her off. "Go back to your class." He seemed to be regaining his calm.

Ms. McDunn hesitated, and I saw the fear in her eyes. I felt I should be afraid too, but strangely I wasn't. It was like nothing could touch me.

"Wipe that smile off your face, mister. You're in big trouble. Come here." He grabbed me by the wrist. I could feel his anger in that grip, like he wanted to throw me into his office, but he didn't. He just led me there, sat me down in a chair and closed the door. His office had a big window in the wall that separated it from the waiting room with the copier and the PA system. I could see Ms. McDunn giving her case again to the secretary.

Mr. Sims harangued me about school rules for about fifteen minutes. I heard him but I wasn't really listening. I knew the rules. I'd internalized them years ago. But also...they suddenly didn't seem to apply to me. I just watched Mr. Sims—the wrinkles on his face, the moments when he seemed as bored by what he was saying as I was, and the moments where his eyes lit up with something he was actually passionate about.

I realized I didn't fear Mr. Sims. I felt like I should, but I didn't. I just...watched him. And I nodded when it seemed like he wanted me to nod.

Eventually one of the counselors, a pretty woman with big carrot-colored hair, knocked on the door. Her name was Elaine. The counselors, unlike all the other adults at the school, wanted students to call them by their first names. Elaine had a face that always looked kind no matter what was happening. So many adults want kids to think that they're nice, that they're on our side. They put on a show to get us to buy in. And if we do, it makes things easier for them. And that's why they do it in the first place. To make things easier for themselves. Just like my dad.

But Elaine always seemed genuine. Maybe it was just her training, but I liked her. I never felt like she was putting on a show to get me to do something that made life easier for her.

She cracked open the door and said, "May I talk to you for a second, Frank?"

Mr. Sims hesitated, like he didn't really want to, then he nodded. He left and closed the door behind him, leaving me alone in his office. I saw the two of them standing in the main room, right by the PA desk. I couldn't hear them through the closed door, but it was obvious they were arguing. Mr. Sims kept giving little shakes to his head, and his mouth was clamped in a straight line. Elaine kept talking, making her case, her big brown genuine eyes never leaving his face. Finally, Mr. Sims closed his eyes and waved a hand in a "Fine, I don't care" gesture.

He walked back to his office door in three long strides, opened it, and said, "Go with Ms. Ellsworth." He seemed like he wanted to say more, but he didn't.

I stood up and went with Elaine, who sat me down in her office. She kept me there for an hour, asking questions about me, about my mom, about my dad. I told her everything. I even told her why I'd done what I'd done.

In the end, she told me I could go back to class.

"I'm not getting expelled?" I asked.

She laughed and gave me that warm smile. "No."

"Suspended?"

"I think you've gone through enough this week, don't you?" she asked.

Emotion bubbled up inside me. Sadness. Surprise. Gratitude. They came all at once, and I felt my eyes burn.

"Hey thanks," I said, and I stood up.

"You're going to be all right," she said. "It's going to be okay."

I swallowed, nodded.

I left the offices in a daze. I'd barely gone twenty feet when the bell rang to signal the end of the period, and the empty hallways filled with students. I was halfway down the main hall before I realized how quiet it was. Usually the halls were as noisy as a football game between classes with everyone gabbing, hustling to their next class, slamming locker doors. I looked up. Everyone was staring at me.

Rory Carpenter from Ms. McDunn's class fought his way through the crowd. He was grinning from ear to ear.

"You hijacked the PA? Fuckin' A, dude!" He clapped me on the back. "Balls the size of Texas, man. Live for today. Live for today!"

"Oh," I said. "Yeah. Thanks."

As if Rory's compliment was the crack in the dam, the rest of the students burst out, hooting and hollering. Other people slapped me on the back, jostling me around, and I started grinning. They kept saying "what you want matters" and "don't let your dreams vanish" and "live for today."

Eventually people went to their lockers, started getting ready for their next class, and I was relatively alone. I turned to find Gage standing right next to my locker.

"Hey look, I'm popular," I joked.

"Hijacking the PA? Badass, dude. Cheesy speech, but who gives a fuck."

He held up his hand and I slapped it.

"And you got a date with Tina Cartwright?" he said. "Nice."

"I didn't say that."

"You totally said that."

"No I didn't, I just said, y'know. I said you *could* get a date with someone like Tina. If you, you know... If you just weren't..." I shook my head. "I didn't say that." But for the first time since my conversation with Tina, I felt fear creep back into my heart. Had I just told the whole school that Tina, newly broken up with her boyfriend, was going out with me? Fuck.

Gage was wearing his shark's smile, the one he saved for when he was watching an impending train wreck.

"God, I fucked up, didn't I?" I said. "You think she'll be pissed?"

That smile turned up even more at the corners. "I think you're going to find out." He tipped his chin over my shoulder.

I turned to find Tina standing about ten feet away from me. She hugged a stack of textbooks to her chest, and she didn't look happy.

"Just remember, dude: badass," Gage said softly.

I tried to ignore him and walked up to Tina.

"Why did you do that?" she asked. She was obviously mad. Her shoulders were hunched inward over those books, and her gaze kept flicking to the other students still in the hall. "I'm so embarrassed. Everywhere I go, everyone's talking about how you and I are going out. My girlfriends kept running up to me asking when this all happened. And nothing's happened!"

"I know. I'm sorry," I said. "I didn't think... I mean, I didn't say we were going out."

She looked at me like I was an idiot. "That's exactly what you said. To the whole school!"

"Okay, maybe that's what people thought, but... Is that so bad?"

"When I asked you to have ice cream, I didn't realize you were going to broadcast it all over the school. I wasn't asking you to be my boyfriend!"

"I'm really sorry. I didn't think it was going to come across that way—"

"How did you think it was going to come across?" she asked.

"I was just saying, in general, that if you want something, you should go get it—"

"Hey motherfucker!" A deep voice broke our hushed conversation.

Wade Thompson stalked toward me like he was going to hit me.

And that's exactly what he did.

CHAPTER 4

I slammed into the lockers and almost went down. God, that hurt.

I'd never been hit in the face before. Well, once in sixth grade in a fight with Ernie Williams, but I'd hardly call that a fight. We'd danced around in a field for about five minutes, and when we finally traded blows I punched him in the stomach—barely—and he threw a palm up at my chin. It scraped alongside my cheek and didn't do much else. Then my parents broke it up.

I staggered to the side and managed to dodge Wade's second hit, a wild haymaker that slammed into the locker instead, denting it. Wade didn't seem to feel it.

"Wade!" Tina screamed, but he ignored her.

I almost ran. I honestly don't know why I didn't. Last year, I'd have run. Shit, an hour ago, I'd have run. But I'd opened Pandora's Box this morning. I'd already faced a number of fears, and I felt more invincible each time.

So I stood my ground.

Some things Gage had told me about fighting surfaced in my mind. He'd said the most important thing is to keep your hands up. That way, if someone's poking fists at your face, your arms might get in the way.

I threw my hands up, fists tight, and I'll be damned if my left arm didn't get in the way of Wade's next blow. I mean, I didn't rock it like the Karate Kid. It was more of an awkward clonking of his forearm against mine, but he didn't hit my face.

Wade was swinging for all he was worth, and when he leaned over, putting everything into the punch that got tangled up in my arm, his head came really close to mine.

Gage once said it was way better to take what you could get in a fight, rather than waiting for the perfect punch. Wade's nose was right there, so I jabbed it with my fist. It was just a quick jab, but Gage had said a jab could do wonders to take the fight out of someone.

The result was startling. Wade's head snapped back, and he stumbled away from me into Tina. She steadied him, and his eyes went wide in surprise as he regained his balance. A trickle of red started down from his right nostril.

"Stop it, both of you!" Tina shouted, holding onto Wade's arm and glaring at me with a "what are you doing?" look. Like this was my fault.

My scalp felt like ice cold pins had been stuck into it. My palms were sweaty, my breathing fast, and my head was ringing. My cheek where Wade had hit it felt two times too big.

Some of the fight seemed to have gone out of Wade. For a moment I dared to hope Gage was right, that Wade would be done and go away.

I think he might have, too, if Gage hadn't laughed right at that moment.

Something to understand about Gage. He hates jocks. I mean, he *hates* them with a burning passion. With his natural athleticism, he could have been a jock himself. He certainly had the build, the speed, the strength, but he didn't go out for football, baseball, basketball, any of the big school sports because he couldn't stand being on a team with the jocks. Gage and the jocks passed each other in the hall with barely veiled sneers of hatred. I'd seen one or two of them nod to Gage in respect every now and then. He never nodded back.

So when Wade stumbled back with a bloody nose, Gage's

laugh erupted, mean and mocking, the perfect complement to his shark's smile.

Wade's shocked look turned murderous and he launched himself at me again. I kept my hands up, but he wasn't going for a hit this time. He plowed into me and we both slammed into the lockers so hard I swear something in my spine cracked.

I don't even know what happened next, just that giant fists hit me in the ribs again and again. I tried to grab his fists, but one slipped my grip and he nailed me in the chin, straight up. My jaw clacked loudly. I saw stars and the world went sideways.

I hit the concrete floor, vision blurry. I kept telling myself to keep my hands up, but for a moment I didn't even know where my hands were. A roar filled my ears, and slowly it resolved into a voice.

"...out of the way, Gage!" Wade was saying. I blinked and saw Wade's high top shoes shifting, trying to get around Gage's unlaced tennis shoes. My vision got sharper, and I looked up to see that Gage was standing between me and Wade.

"He's done, fuckwad," Gage said. He had his hands up, almost casually, but he was obviously ready. "You win. Call it good."

"It'll be good when I pulp his face."

"Then go ahead," Gage said, and his voice changed, deepening to a threatening tone. "Take a step. Take a swing. We'll sort it out."

"Fight ain't with you, Gage."

"You're such a chicken shit you'll punch a guy when he's down? Fine. I'll give you a chance to put *me* down, too. If you do, you can just keep punching us both." He beckoned with his raised hands. "Come on."

Wade hesitated.

"Come on!" Gage shouted so furiously Wade flinched, took a step back.

Once again, we'd drawn a crowd. Wade's eyes narrowed.

He pointed at me. "Stay down, dweeb. And stay the fuck away from my girlfriend." He turned, held out his hand to Tina. "Come on, let's go."

To Tina's credit, she hesitated. She actually looked torn. I mean, come on. She'd gone from being mad at me for the PA stunt to afraid Wade was going to kill me to mad at me for punching Wade in the nose to having to choose between the boyfriend who'd just dumped her or the not-at-all-boyfriend who'd just embarrassed her in front of the whole school.

Not an easy choice. I'd have been confused, too.

But when she took that asshole's hand, it still broke my heart. She started walking up the hallway with him. I'd just done all this—ditching class, hijacking the PA, getting the crap beat out of me—for nothing. Just like that, my date with Tina vanished.

Gage watched them go with his shark's smile, then he held out a hand to me. I took it and he lifted me to my feet.

"I'm thinking you don't have a date with Tina anymore," he said. "That's a pisser."

"You think?"

He waved a dismissive hand. "Fuck her. You don't want a girl who dates jocks anyway. Bad taste."

Gage's words were cold comfort. Tina was everything I'd wanted since I'd first laid eyes on her.

"Let's get you to class, Tyson," he said.

"You're an asshole," I said.

He laughed. "Yeah I know." He saw me stagger, then put my arm over his shoulder and helped me toward the stairs.

"What's the hurry?" I asked.

"It's a miracle we haven't seen any teachers yet. We want to be a rumor by the time they show up, unless you want to head back to the office."

We got to the stairs and started up.

"I did hit him once," I said.

"Nice little jab," Gage said. "I was proud to see you make him pay for sticking his face out like that."

"I heard your voice in my head."

"Yeah?"

"The thing about taking what I can get."

He grunted approvingly, then once we reached the first landing, he said, "Okay, enough." He put my hand on the rail. "Walk, motherfucker. I'm not carrying you around like your girlfriend."

"I don't have a girlfriend."

"Maybe next time don't kiss and tell, then."

"I didn't kiss her."

He shook his head. "Should at least kiss 'em before you piss 'em off."

"Well, it's over now anyway," I said.

It's over now....

Except I didn't want it to be over. I'd started something, and—despite my black eye and bloody lip—I felt good, like I'd never felt before. I'd had three firsts today, and it wasn't even lunchtime.

"Hurry up," Gage said. "Bell's going to ring and you'll be late to two classes today."

I stopped on the steps.

"No," I said.

He'd already climbed two more, and he looked down at me. "No what?"

"Let's get out of here."

A grin split his face, and it was his genuine smile, not the shark's grin. "Really?"

"I'm on a roll."

"Fuckin' A. Where we going?"

"Canyonlands," I said.

That rendered him speechless. His eyebrows raised. I just held his gaze as my heart began to race. It would take half a day to drive to Canyonlands. If we left now, we could get there before dark, barely. We'd have to pitch a tent and stay the night. In other words, there was no way we'd get back to the airport by 10 a.m. tomorrow.

"What about your plane ticket?" he asked, reading my thoughts.

"Fuck my dad."

He cocked his head, eyes skeptical. "Bullshit."

"You know what I said on the PA system," I said.

He just watched me.

"Who would I be if I didn't take my own advice?" I asked. "I've never been rock climbing. Now's the time."

"You're not going to chicken out?" Gage asked.

"Try me."

He clapped me on the back. "Well, all right then."

CHAPTER 5

Gage and I spent the rest of the day gathering gear, stuffing it into his Dad's Jeep, and driving to Utah. Gage punched a cassette into the player and we listened to INXS as we raced down the highway. The sun was going down when we navigated Elephant Hill. By the time we found a campsite, pitched our tent and made a campfire, it was dark.

My lip was split, my cheek swollen, and I had a black eye from my fight with Wade, but it wasn't so bad. We were both jazzed to be where nobody else was, and after we ate some sandwiches we'd made at Gage's house, we fell asleep.

The next morning I spent an hour learning about harnesses and climbing ropes, figure eights and belaying. Rock climbing was Gage's new passion. He'd gotten into it his sophomore year, and he said he liked it better than boxing. I'd never gone climbing before, but I soaked his lessons up like a sponge.

Ditching school, ditching my dad, it was like starting life all over again, and there was nothing in my brain except an eagerness to learn something new.

I had no idea what I was doing here in Canyonlands instead of all the places I "should" have been, but at the same time, I didn't want to know. Something was happening, a freedom I'd never felt before, and it filled me with excitement.

When we got to the actual climbing later that morning, it turned out that I was pretty good at it. Even Gage was impressed when I worked my way through a couple of 5.9s. He led, putting protection—or "pro" —in cracks in the rock on the way up. Once he reached the top, he'd set up an anchor and a top rope and we'd climb using that until we were done. After we'd worked that route until we were bored with it, we'd move on to another climb.

By the time the sun was high in the sky, I'd already climbed a couple of routes and I was feeling invincible.

"I'll lead the next one," I said as we stopped in front of the next route.

"The fuck you will. This is a 5.9. We'll start you out on a 5.7."

I looked up at the rock, imagining how I'd do it. "No, I got it. I gotta learn some time."

"So learn on a 5.7," he said. "Leading is way fucking harder than climbing from a top rope."

"No," I said. "This one."

His shark's smile appeared, like he knew he was about to see a train wreck. "Whatever, fuckwad. I'm not hauling your body back when you fall."

"Thanks for the ego boost."

"Don't forget to grab your nuts." He smiled wryly and handed me a fistful of "nuts," pieces of protection that could be inserted into rock cracks and pulled tight to create a fall block. I hooked them onto my harness, and he added some cams. Cams worked under the same principal, except they had a flexible mechanism that made them more versatile. One size of cam could work in varying widths of cracks. Gage said most climbers didn't use them because they were so damned expensive. But Gage had a full rack of equipment. His dad made bucks as a big time lawyer. I'd never known Gage to have money problems.

"Set 'em, then yank on 'em before you clip in. Check for manky rock." He held up a loop of rope. "Rope goes into the bottom of the carabiner. Comes out the top. You put it in backwards, it's harder to pull. Last thing you want is to bind yourself up when you get to a tough spot."

"Got it."

"You get up there, you set up the top rope. There should be two bolts. Use locking Ds, webbing between." He held up a length of the nylon webbing as an example. "Third locking D goes here." He pointed to the middle. "Lock it, loop the rope through there, and rappel down on the double rope. You're good to go."

"Okay."

His eyes glittered above that shark's smile as I clipped the last of the "pro" onto my harness. As I put my hands on the rock and looked up, Gage spoke again.

"What happened to you, man?" His voice was soft this time, not his usual sarcasm.

I craned my neck to look at him. Was Gage being genuine?

His shark's smile was gone. He watched me thoughtfully like he wasn't really watching *me*, but something Important with a capital "I."

I'd never heard Gage talk in this voice before, like he really wanted to know something, like I had an answer and he wanted it. So I paused.

"What changed?" Gage asked. "Is it your dad?"

"I don't know," I said, and I just let the truth come out, good, bad or ugly. "It started with one decision yesterday. Once I walked into that hall to talk to Tina...something broke inside me."

"Broke?"

"Cracked open. Like a box with a lid, but instead of the lid opening, the side broke open. And I can't close it now." I shook my head. "And I don't want to."

"Fuckin' A."

"Yeah."

He checked his watch—the expensive kind with the calculator pad on it. Gage always had the latest gadgets. He was the first to have an Atari 2600 at home, the first to get a Commodore 64—which he said sucked—and the first to get the amazing Apple Macintosh. His shark's smile returned. "I'm just saying... Your plane took off...what...two hours ago? The one you're supposed to be on. Bye bye."

I looked back at the rock, ran a chalk-covered finger along the sandpaper surface. "Yeah, I know." I should have felt something about that, but I didn't. Ever since that box had broken open, I didn't feel anything the way I used to. Not fear or anxiety. Not that sense of trying to live up to what other people thought I should be.

I glanced at the sandstone cliff face towering over me. The only thing I felt was how badly I wanted to get up that cliff. There wasn't anything else.

I cleared my throat.

"On belay?" I asked.

"Belay on," he responded, showing his break hand with the rope in it.

"Climbing."

"Climb on, dude."

I started up.

"First piece of pro is big," Gage added from below. "Place it too low and you fall, it won't do you any good."

"And too high?" I found a niche for my foot, pushed and grabbed a solid, easy handhold—called a "jug"—above me.

"There is no too high," he said, and he laughed.

There is no too high.

I was about twenty feet up when I placed my first piece of protection. My arms were aching, but so far so good. I made it another ten feet and placed another bit of pro.

I kept going, and for those muscle-straining moments, everything seemed perfect. The sky was a crazy dark blue. I could smell the sunbaked rock, the sunblock and sweat on my skin. It was pure. Uncomplicated. There was only one law, only one expectation to live up to: don't fall.

I climbed for the joy of it. I don't know how long I did that, but suddenly I looked up at an overhang right above me.

I understood then why a 5.9 was different than a 5.7. From the ground, this had looked like a bump, but now that I was nose-to-nose with it, it was a freakin' ledge. And there was nowhere to go except upside down and around it.

Panic blossomed in my chest. I looked for a way around the overhang, but it was everywhere. Why the hell did I climb right up to it? Why didn't I go wide around it?

I looked back down, considering backing down and finding a different way. But back climbing was twice as hard because it was blind. Climbing up, your eyes looked straight at your next move. Going down, you had to lean out, search with your toes, which were covered in hard rubber and could barely feel a damned thing. I couldn't see anything, just the rope attached to my harness dangling down and around the corner of an arete to my left. I'd followed the contour of the cliff and now I couldn't even see Gage below me, though I felt a reassuring give to the rope as he continued to slowly let the slack out as I went.

That's when I looked closer at that dangling rope below me. It went down twenty...thirty feet without a single piece of pro.

A cold, wet sensation spread over my scalp as I realized I hadn't placed pro in a long time. I'd been so into the climb I'd forgotten. If I fell, I'd whip for sixty feet before the rope went tight and slammed me into the wall. Or a ledge. It was almost as bad as falling straight to the ground.

My legs started to shake, and I looked up, my gaze darting left and right, looking for a jug to grab, but there was nothing except that deadly overhang. Next, I searched for a place to put pro. If I could clip in here, I could fall and it'd only be a few feet as my body weight pulled the slack out of the line.

But there wasn't anything I could use. Just that sandstone overhang glaring at me. No bolts. No cracks for a cam.

My arms began to burn, biceps trembling, shoulders turning to mud. I'd been clinging to this exact spot for a good minute, and my muscles were going numb as they reached their limits. Gage had called it "melting" off the rock.

Jesus. What the hell was I going to do?

"No..." I said softly. I needed a way out. I needed...

And then I saw it. Up and behind me, a bomber jug stuck out from the edge of the overhang. It just sat there, taunting me, a beautiful hold. It looked like it had been made for a hand, curved upward like the edge of a bathtub. It was about two feet above me and two feet back from the cliff face.

It might as well have been on the moon.

It would take two, maybe three, moves for me to scale the underside of the overhang to reach it, and I couldn't see the moves in between. There was nothing to hang onto under that overhang.

But...

I could jump to it in one insane move. On the ground, that kind of jump would have been no problem. But that was with two feet solidly planted instead of trembling on a half-inch ledge of sandstone. And if I missed my mark, I wouldn't just land easily on my feet. I'd plummet sixty feet before slamming sideways onto solid rock. I could die.

"Jesusfuckshitgoddamnit!"

I didn't have a choice. I couldn't go back. I couldn't shuffle sideways. I couldn't tie in, and I sure as hell couldn't hold on much longer. My legs had started shaking like a jackhammer. It was a miracle they hadn't shaken me off the rock already. I had to go up or I was going to fall.

I took a deep breath through gritted teeth, marshaled all of my strength and tried to get my legs to stop shaking.

I jumped for it.

Everything seemed to slow down. I stretched hard, reaching...

Two of my fingers caught the edge, but they weren't strong enough. When my weight came down, they ripped off the hold. I gave a blood-curdling scream and—

Two slender hands grasped my wrists, jerking me to a stop. I hung there, stupefied, while the hands lifted me just high enough so that my fingers could grip the jug, a good, solid grip. Then they let go.

Instead of falling, my body swung inward, hit the underside of the overhang. I pulled up, hefting my entire weight as my feet scrambled and shoved against the sandstone.

I rolled onto the top of the cliff, breathing like a maniac. The overhang had been the last hurdle, and flat ground stretched out before me. I stayed on my hands and knees for a long moment.

My brain was trippin' balls. It couldn't process what had just happened. I'd missed the handhold. And then, like someone had clicked the "undo" button, I had it in hand again. I sucked in air like a man who'd almost drowned.

That's when I remembered the hands on my wrists. It was like my mind had blanked them out because I couldn't believe that had actually happened. But someone had grabbed me. Someone had saved me. That meant there had to be someone else up here.

I looked up and almost fell off the cliff.

She sat on a rock, legs crossed and hands on her knees like she was posing for a portrait. She had huge green eyes, pale skin with freckles on her shoulders and across her pert nose. She had deep red hair with white tips, tied back in a ponytail, and she wore climbing gear: tight shorts to mid-thigh, a jog bra and a climbing harness. She could have been my age or she could have been thirty; something about her made it impossible to know. Her features were adult and childlike at the same time.

I couldn't speak. Gage and I hadn't seen anyone in this place, but suddenly here was this beautiful girl on top of the cliff.

"Hi Eric," she said, like she knew me.

"Who are you?"

"I'm your fetch," she said. "And we need to establish the ground rules."

CHAPTER 6

"You saved my life," I gasped.

She leaned her head left and right like a swaying tree. "If you want to look at it that way."

"You grabbed me. You just grabbed my wrists! You put my hands back on the hold."

"Sometimes a person needs an extra lift."

I glanced back at the cliff's edge. To grab my wrists as I was falling, she'd have had to be anchored to something up here, or she'd have tumbled right over with me. But there was no anchor.

I spun back to her, blinking. Was I dreaming? Had I died and now I was in some weird afterlife?

"Honestly, I wasn't sure you had it in you," she said. "I saw your fork in the river come and go. That wilting conversation with your dad. I thought you'd been swept downstream like so many. But you proved me wrong. You inspired me. Tina and your cute little speech to the school. Even your fight with Wade. And of course, the gem on top. Leading this climb. That was the moment I fell."

I swallowed down a dry throat. She had just ticked off a list of events a stranger couldn't possibly know. "F-fell?" I stammered.

"Fell for you," she said. "Fell in love with you. In the last couple of days, you made my fetch's heart go pitter-pat. So I'm yours, if you make the choice."

I was still dumbstruck.

"Are you a ghost?" I wanted to reach out and touch her, but I didn't.

"I'm your fetch," she repeated.

I shook my head. "I don't... I don't know what that is."

She smiled, and it was the most beautiful smile I'd ever seen. Her face lit up with an adoring expression that made me believe I was the only thing she cared about—the only thing she would ever focus on. It was intoxicating. I must have stared at her for a full minute.

Then, for some reason, my gaze went to her bright white smile and I couldn't look away. She had pronounced canines. All I could see were those pronounced points in a row of otherwise perfectly human teeth.

I wondered if this was what happened when a person had a near-death experience. Was I hallucinating? Was this an angel? Had the stress of my mom's death finally cracked me?

"You've known me your whole life," she said, and that green gaze held me like a spell.

"I have?"

"But you only first saw me on Thursday," she said. "Fetches stay out of sight until something attracts us."

My mind reeled. I tried to remember back and think of what had happened on Thursday. I'd talked to my father. He'd told me I had to come to Malaysia. I'd fallen asleep. There was nothing else. Nothing else had happened except—

"You're the fox!" I said.

She smiled wider, like she approved. Those sharp canines appeared again, and as crazy as the idea was, I knew I was right.

She raised her chin, giving me a better look at her profile, as though I'd be able to see the fox in it.

"And you showed up now because I'm breaking rules?" I blurted.

"You opened a door, Eric. The death of your mother started it, began to carry you downriver to that fork in the water, that choice every young man gets to make. I watched, waited for you to make yours, but you didn't. You just sat there. Then your father called, and I thought for certain that would force you to choose, but still you sat, nodding along with what he told you to do, even though you hated every word. I thought I'd lost you."

She cocked her head, and a mischievous glimmer came into her eyes. "Then on Friday morning, you did something you'd never done before. Then you did it again, and again, and my heart began to flutter. You're on the cusp of a journey, if you have the courage to take it."

"Journey?"

"This is your last chance. Forks in the river don't last forever. Soon, if you don't choose, you'll get swept along, and then you won't have a choice anymore," she said. "So which will it be? Will you paddle hard for what you want? Or are you going to let the river sweep you along?"

I thought about the climb, that deadly choice to jump. Except it hadn't really been a choice at all. Leap for a chance at getting the hold. Or fall. But somehow, I felt like this was the same kind of choice.

"I don't understand," I said.

"I know. But you will. And I'm here to help you."

"Help me?"

"Fetches bring luck. That's what we do."

"Luck...." My mind raced. "This is for real?"

"Don't I look real to you, Eric?"

She looked like some ultimate MTV fantasy woman.

"No," I said.

She raised an eyebrow.

Hesitantly, I approached her. She stayed sitting on her rock, legs crossed, hands on her knees and that sharp smile pointed at me. I reached out to touch her cheek, expecting her to lean out of reach or even vanish completely.

But my fingers met flesh, smooth and warm as any person's

check. A little jolt shot into me at the contact, like static electricity. I yanked my hand back like I'd been burned.

"You're real!"

"Of course I am," she said.

"Y-you're going to make me lucky?" I asked.

"I'm going to make you legendary."

"So I can go down to the 7-11, buy a lottery ticket, and all the numbers will go my way?"

She rolled her eyes, put a slender hand up to cover a yawn.

"I *can't* win the lottery?" I said.

"I'm not a genie. I don't give wishes."

"I don't understand—"

"Passion!" She hissed, leaning forward. "A fetch is drawn to *passion,* Eric. I am gasoline, but I must have a flame. Give me your passion and I will make such a fire that those around you won't be able to turn away." Her emerald eyes cut into me. "The lottery?" she scoffed. "I'm not here to give you a *smooth* road, an *easy* life. I won't tear down your obstacles, I will make you equal to any challenge. *Security* is the dream of the fearful. The fearful are not inspiring."

My heart beat faster.

"I'm here to make your dreams come true," she said. "But they must be worthy dreams." She made a fist and held it up in front of her chest, clenching so hard it trembled. "Give me the best of yourself, and I will give you everything I am. *Inspire* me, Eric."

"Inspire you," I said numbly.

"Yes..." She drew the word out, hissing through those bright, sharp teeth. "Dance with me, and I will make you invincible. Nothing you try will be out of your reach if you follow your heart."

Her words rushed hot through my blood.

"Do you want to dance with me, Eric?" she asked.

"Yes," I said. I stepped forward and reached for her hand.

She turned her palm toward me, stopping me. "There's just one thing."

"What thing?"

"It will cost you your life."

"W-What?"

"From now until your eighteenth birthday—during these three months of summer—I will make you invincible. They will be the most glorious months of your life. And at the end, you will die."

That hot feeling turned to ice in my veins.

"You..." she said softly. "Will cease to be."

I swallowed. I thought of my mom, of the casket as they lowered her into the ground, of the fact that I'd never see her again.

Then I thought of all the other things that had descended upon me since that moment, the dead-ends every direction I turned. Leaving my friends. Living with a father who didn't want me, only wanted to control me.

I didn't know what was going on. Whether this was real or not. Whether it was true or not. But I knew one thing: I didn't want to go back. I wanted to go forward even if it killed me.

"I'll do it," I heard myself saying.

She smiled again, and I felt her adoration lift me up like the tide lifts a boat.

"Oh Eric," she said, standing, and for the first time I realized she was taller than me. She extended her hand, and as soon as I took it, she pulled me into a hug, wrapped her arms around me and put her head against my neck. "We will dance, you and I."

Then she let go, stepped away while continuing holding my hand, like we were already dancing. Then she stopped and dipped into a curtsey.

"Now," she said, "it is time to return to your friend. But I'll see you soon." She let go of my hand. "There are many choices ahead of you," she said excitedly as she turned and sauntered away. She flickered like a mirage, and a fox stood where she had been. She looked over her shoulder at me, flicked her fluffy tail, and darted away.

CHAPTER 7

I fixed the anchor at the top of the route, ran the rope through it, and rappelled down to Gage at the bottom.

"How did it go?" he asked.

I opened my mouth, but nothing came out. What could I say?

Hey Gage, yeah. It was a great climb. I forgot to place pro and got about thirty feet away from my last anchor. Rookie move, right? And I fell. Except I didn't because a beautiful woman saved me, then told me I was going to be invincible for the summer, and then die. Oh, and then she turned into a fox and ran away.

"Well?" he pressed. "Your first lead, and it's a 5.9, and you got nothing to say?"

"It was...scary."

He laughed and pointed at me. "Fuckin' A, dude."

I kept pretty quiet after that, and Gage seemed fine with it. He was one of those guys who could talk up a storm sometimes, but he also didn't feel compelled to fill empty spaces with conversation. He got the vibe that I wasn't interested in talking, and he just got to work climbing.

We did that same route a few times, and I learned how to work the overhang without having to jump for my life. I was amazed at how many handholds I'd missed—even several that were well-marked with chalk by other climbers—when I'd been deep in the grips of my panic. I'd missed the obvious because I was scared out of my mind. That was a new lesson. Fear wasn't just paralyzing. It could be blinding.

We went on to some other routes, all of which Gage offered to let me lead, but I declined. I'd had enough leading for the day. My mind was filled with thoughts of the fetch.

I still didn't know if my panic-addled brain had conjured that whole encounter or not. It had seemed so real. I mean, it wasn't just a glimpse of some weird thing that I thought maybe I'd seen. It had been a full conversation with rules and everything.

Was I crazy? Or had it actually been real?

I thought about it for the rest of the day, saying nothing. One thing climbing was great for was pushing my thoughts to the back of my mind while I focused on not dying. During the routes, I'd leave my thoughts behind while I pushed my muscles harder than I'd ever done before.

When the sun settled behind the western horizon, smearing orange across the high thin clouds and turning the sky a slate blue, we called it good, coiled the ropes, and went back to camp.

Dinner that night was two cans of Dinty Moore beef stew Gage had swiped from the back of his dad's cupboards. That stew tasted amazing. But I was so hungry, Gage could have thrown dog food in a bowl and I'd have gobbled it down without a complaint.

The next morning dawned cool and blue, sunlight hitting the tops of the cliffs, making the shadowy gray hulks look like they were wearing golden crowns. My arms were sore in the best of ways, like I'd finally used them for what they were meant for.

We climbed a few routes that morning until the sun was high in the sky and my arms were completely worthless. At noon, Gage called it, and we struck camp and drove back, grabbing cheeseburgers and fries on the way.

All morning I had looked for the fetch, but she didn't

appear again. The more time that passed, the less real she seemed. I mean, come on. The most beautiful woman I've ever seen shows up decked out in hot climbing gear and tells me I'm going to be invincible. It sounded like one of my fantasy novels.

But I could still feel that little jolt when I touched her. I could still see her fervently hissing.

Passion!

As we rumbled down Highway 491, I realized I hadn't said more than a dozen words to Gage since my lead climb, and how odd that must seem to him. But it was almost equally odd that he hadn't asked or tried to strike up conversation.

"Hey," I said. "Sorry I've been...quiet."

"You're sorry?" He gave me a smirk.

"You know what I mean. I just... Something happened up there—"

"No way!" He interrupted me, dropping his jaw in mock surprise.

I punched him in his meaty shoulder.

He grinned like he hadn't felt it and held up a fist. "Don't start what you can't finish, dickwad."

"I just..." But I still couldn't find the words.

"I heard you scream, man. I knew you'd got in a jam. But hey, you didn't fall. You worked it out." He looked over at me. "That sound about right?"

"Um... Something like that."

"That's the beauty of climbing. Fuckin' jocks think they're so tough 'cause they pummel each other on the football field, or sink a basket through a goddamned hoop. None of them has looked death in the eye. Not like on a big wall. With climbing, you face your worst fears head on and move past 'em. No other sport does that. So... That full-on freak-out when you almost die for the first time? Happens to every climber."

"Yeah?" I said.

"I got quiet after my first lead, too," he said. "No biggie."

"You just... You've been cool not asking me about it."

"What am I, your shrink?"

I almost asked him if every climber also saw a magical fox lady after their first near-fall, but I didn't.

We rode the rest of the way in silence and he dropped me off at my big empty house before heading back to town.

The Pumpkin was parked right where I'd left it. Everything was right where I'd left it, except the white piece of paper taped to the front storm door. That was new. I pulled it off the glass.

"NOTICE OF DEFAULT" was printed in big red letters at the top of the paper, and cold panic trickled through me. In legalese, it laid out that Mom hadn't paid the mortgage for three months and that they were foreclosing on the house. The notice said I had one month to vacate. I was homeless.

I blinked and stuffed the notice in my pocket, trying not to let my fear paralyze me. How could I feel like this when only moments ago I'd felt on top of the world? Canyonlands had been nearly euphoric, filled with hopeful sunrises, triumph over fear, and magical fetches. But that wasn't real. It was just a stolen moment. In the real world, everything had collapsed around me.

My earlier confidence had vanished, leaving only the crushing feeling that I was buried and had no way out.

Numbly, I went inside, made myself a peanut butter and jelly and poured a glass of milk. I shook the near-empty jug. Food was running low. Mom had always done the shopping, and it occurred to me that I was going to have to get more food soon.

My panic curdled into a sickly feeling in my stomach. Maybe Canyonlands was my last big hurrah. Maybe I should just call my dad, apologize, tell him Mom's death freaked me out and I bailed. Maybe I could even convince him to let me stay on my own through this last week, finish out school, graduate. Maybe he'd agree to that much, even if he wouldn't let me go to college.

I put the milk back, closed the refrigerator door, went into my bedroom and willed the fetch to appear. If she would just show up again, I'd know it was real. I'd have something to hope for....

But she didn't.

The phone rang, and I jumped. I almost answered it out of reflex, but I stopped myself. Instead, I stared at it as it rang six times, then went to the answering machine.

The long beep drew out, and then I heard static on the line, then my dad's voice, deadly quiet.

"I don't know what you're playing at here, Eric. You cost me $700, and they don't refund those tickets...." He paused, and again that static came over the line like he was holding the phone away until he got control of himself. "If you're there, pick up. You pick up right now." He waited. "I mean it," he said in his dark tone, and waited again. Finally, "This is totally unacceptable. When you get this, I expect a call. I mean today, young man. You understand me?" And then he slammed the phone down.

I lay back on my bed, staring at my window. The fetch's window. Eventually, I fell asleep.

The next morning, I got up and went to school like everything was normal. I arrived to find my friends clustered around my locker. They were all D&D, comic-collecting geeks like me, and word had reached them over the weekend about what I'd done on Friday. They congratulated me, marveling that I'd gotten a date with Tina Cartwright, lost a date with Tina Cartwright, and gave Wade Thompson a bloody nose all in one day. They thought I was Superman, and for a moment I felt like it.

I went to first period—Ms. McDunn's room—sat down, then immediately got pulled out of class by the counselor, Elaine. In her office, she informed me that my unexcused absence on Friday afternoon had been noted, but that she'd asked Mr. Sims to give me an official reprimand and nothing more. She told me she knew I was working through a lot, and that she was on my side. Then she sent me back to class.

I walked down the hall, stunned. That was, like, zero punishment for everything I'd done.

A little thrill rushed through me, and the words of the fetch echoed in the back of my mind.

Dance with me, and I will make you invincible.

The thought buoyed my spirits, and I sailed through all of my classes as we prepped for finals, then I went home again to my foreclosed house. The phone rang twice, but I let the answering machine get it. It was my dad both times, yelling that I was going to pay for that ticket out of my own money. On the second call, he slammed the phone down and kept slamming it over and over until the line finally went dead.

I went to the kitchen, poured the last glass of milk from the jug, ate another peanut butter and jelly and watched reruns of *Knight Rider* and *The A-Team*. Eventually, I turned off the TV, went to my bedroom, and slept again.

The next day, school almost felt normal again. I went to class, saw my friends, did schoolwork. On Tuesday, I took my AP English final. And on Wednesday, my AP History final. I didn't think about my dad, and I could almost believe things had gone back to the way they were supposed to be.

But on Wednesday, during lunch, my imaginary bubble popped and the real world caught up with me.

When the bell rang, I went to the cafeteria and grabbed some food from the lunch line—chicken-fried steak, instant potatoes, green grapes, and corn—and sat down next to Gage, who already had a tray of the same stuff. He was entertaining himself by making a miniature catapult out of a spoon, the edge of his tray, and a grape.

"You didn't touch your mashed potatoes," I said.

Without looking at me—or the potatoes—he grabbed my spoon, scooped up the bulk of the potatoes, and slopped them onto my tray.

"You're fucking gross," he said. I loved instant mashed potatoes, and he knew it.

He turned his attention back to his catapult, lined up his shot, and smacked the handle of his spoon. The grape sailed over one table and hit the painted cinderblock wall right next to Jay Portman, one of our friends. He didn't notice.

"Almost," Gage said, and immediately started lining up another shot.

I shook my head and shoveled in a mouthful of instant potatoes. As I did, I glanced up and saw a policeman in the main hall just off the cafeteria. That was a mild curiosity. Policemen didn't usually come to the school, and I idly wondered who was busted.

I glanced back at my tray, then did a double take.

That wasn't just a policeman. That was my Uncle Morty!

I stared at him, stunned speechless. Thank God he wasn't looking in my direction. Uncle Morty was a state trooper who lived in Grand Junction, and while I guessed his jurisdiction was the entire state of Colorado, the only reason for him to be here, four hours from home, was *me*.

He meandered past the cafeteria like he was lost, then turned back.

I dropped below the table just as Morty's gaze swept toward me. I jostled Gage and his catapult, fouling up his shot.

"Hey!" He glared at me under the table. "What are you doing, numbnuts?"

"Don't look at me! I just...I dropped my pen."

He rolled his eyes like he didn't buy that for a second, and he sat up to see who I was hiding from. I couldn't see what he was looking at, crammed beneath the table as I was, but I knew he spotted Uncle Morty almost immediately because his body went really still. His fist clenched. Gage hated cops as much as he hated jocks.

"Don't be a pussy," he said. "You ditched class. You didn't steal a car. They don't arrest you for ditching."

"No, that's my uncle! The only reason he could be here is because my father sent him."

"I thought you told your father you weren't going to Malaysia," Gage said, and his gaze stayed locked on my uncle.

"I didn't tell my dad anything. I haven't answered the phone."

"That's a boner move. You should have told him."

"I'm a minor, you idiot. I can't just tell my dad to kiss off.

They'll send the police after me."

His shark's smile spread across his face. "Looks like they did." His gaze continued to track steadily to the left, watching my uncle move through the cafeteria.

"Don't stare at him! He'll come over here."

"Let him," Gage said. He slid my tray over in front of him and started eating my grapes.

It was no use trying to get Gage to stop. He lived to flaunt authority, and my cowering under the table wasn't going to convince him otherwise.

I crouched there as the seconds crept by. I kept watching Gage's body language for some clue as to what was happening.

After an excruciating minute, Gage said, "He's gone. You can stop licking the floor."

Cautiously, I got up and took my seat, but I wasn't hungry anymore. Uncle Morty could easily have found me just then.

I thought about what the fetch had said about the fork in the river, that if I didn't make my choice I'd get swept along and wouldn't get to choose at all.

If I went back to class, Uncle Morty would be waiting for me, and that would be that. The river would carry me away. My choice would be gone.

I thought of the fetch then, of the promise I'd made, of the way she'd hugged me, like I was the only thing she cared about in the whole world. I remembered how full I'd felt, then and even afterwards, riding back with Gage.

I didn't know what to do. The future the fetch had promised seemed so surreal, so unlikely, as if I could never reach it. I didn't know how to reach it.

But the alternative was my uncle. My dad. Malaysia. Being cut off from everything I knew and everyone I cared about.

I looked around for the cafeteria monitor, Mr. Morrison, a new tenth grade social studies teacher, straight out of college. Every single high school girl had a crush on him, and he was in the corner entertaining three of them right now like he was holding court. They appeared to be asking him question after question, and his back was turned to me.

"Gage," I said.

"Yeah."

"Let's go."

He cocked his head. "Go?" he asked, but then he caught the look on my face. His shark's grin returned. "You want to ditch again?"

"I'm getting a taste for it. Come on. Right now."

"Fuckin' A," he said.

We stood up and took our trays to the huge window into the kitchen, set them on the wide stainless steel counter. Gage seemed to know what I was thinking, and we moved together toward the big glass exit door. Even though Mr. Morrison was preoccupied, there were more than a hundred kids in that cafeteria and at least four cooks in the kitchen. It seemed impossible that no one would notice us leave, but as we approached the door, every single person was looking the other way.

Dance with me, and I will make you invincible.

We slipped out the door quickly and quietly. I felt that rush of euphoria, and for a moment I really did feel invincible.

As soon as we were out of sight of the cafeteria, we jogged around the building to the northern lot where I'd parked The Pumpkin.

Gage was grinning from ear to ear when we got behind the wheel and I fired up the engine.

"Now this is what senior year should be." He thumped the dashboard. Gage loved The Pumpkin. He loved it so much he always suggested taking my car to lunch instead of his dad's Jaguar.

I drove out of the high school parking lot and onto Main Street. At first I didn't know where I was going. I just went south. I drove to the edge of town, drove down a dirt road away from the highway, and pulled off by the side of the Animas River. We hiked down to the water's edge and I plopped down onto the ground. It was right by a fork in the river that went around a small island.

Gage looked around curiously, still standing. "We're gonna

ditch school for a little nature time?"

"No," I said. "I'm ready to tell you what happened in Canyonlands."

"Oh." He looked confused. "I thought you already did."

"There's more. Sit down, Gage," I said.

He looked skeptical, or maybe he just didn't like me giving him orders, but he slowly sat down. He rested his big muscular arms on his knees and watched me with a sarcastic twist to his mouth.

I took a deep breath, then I told him about the fetch. I told him everything. I started with my scary moment at the overhang, then I told him how I'd jumped, and how I'd fallen.

And that she saved me.

I told him what she looked like and what she proposed.

When I was done, he leaned back, holding himself from falling over with his hands cupped on his knees, then he pulled himself upright again. He peered at me like he was trying to see through blinds pulled down over a window.

"That's the most fucked up thing I've ever heard," he finally said. His brow was furrowed like he couldn't decide if I was lying or not.

"Yeah."

"So let me 'summarize,' as Mr. Vidsa would say. This hot chick shows up in climbing shorts, tells you if you go balls-out for the summer you'll live like a rock star then fuckin' die."

"More or less."

"So what did she say to do first?" he asked.

"She didn't tell me what to do. She just said to inspire her."

"Did you kiss her?"

"What? No. She was a freakin' magical woman standing there! I can't even ask out a normal girl."

"But you're supposed to inspire her?"

"Yeah."

"Like how?"

"Like I don't know… Like climbing the cliff, I guess."

"Or asking Tina out or popping Wade in the nose?"

"Maybe. Except I didn't ask Tina out. She asked me out."

He rolled his eyes. "Whatever."

"But you may be right. I think that's what she was getting at. Stuff like that."

"But she's not telling you."

"No. I mean maybe."

"What's maybe?" he drawled.

"She said passion."

"Passion?"

"Passion inspires her."

"Dude," he said. "She totally wanted you to kiss her."

"It wasn't *like* that. She wasn't real, man!" I stumbled as I said that. "No, I mean. She *was* real. At least I think she was. She was just...."

He shrugged. "Okay, man."

"You think I'm going nuts."

"Whatever the fuck, man. Doesn't matter to me. You suddenly grew a pair and I'm on board with that. I'm in."

I shook my head. Gage didn't believe me, and I desperately needed someone to believe me.

"Imagine something with me for a second," I said.

"Imagine?"

"Picture this in your head—"

"Is this going to be one of Ms. Ellsworth's 'creative visualizations'?" he asked, frowning.

"Fuck you," I said. "And...yes."

He rolled his eyes.

"Just do it. Imagine that what I just told you actually happened."

"The foxy chick."

"Yeah."

He closed his eyes with a wry smile. "Okay."

"Seriously. Just imagine that for a second. Imagine it's real and you *know* it's real."

"Okay."

"What would you do?"

"Go balls-out, like she said." He didn't even hesitate, then he opened his eyes and looked at me. "She wants to make you a man, do it. Even if she isn't real, who the fuck cares?"

His words sank in, and I realized he was right. The fetch's words returned to me.

Forks in the river don't last forever. Soon, if you don't choose, you'll get swept along, and then you won't have a choice anymore.

Going with Uncle Morty, letting him put me on a plane...that was me being swept down the river.

But what was the alternative? What was *my* choice? Go climbing in Canyonlands for the rest of my life?

The truth was, I had nowhere to go. All I had was my clothes, my sleeping bag, a box of comics, a stack of D&D books, my boom box, and a one-way ticket to Malaysia. And I had The Pumpkin.

A prickle of fear crept through me. When Dad took me to Malaysia, The Pumpkin would have stay behind.

"Let's go on a road trip," I blurted before I'd even thought it through, and yet the moment I said it, I knew it was right.

"Road trip? Where?"

"Anywhere. We pack up our shit and get the hell out of Dodge."

"Fuck yeah," Gage said. "When? Right after graduation?"

"Now. Today."

"What? I got finals," he said.

"Fuck finals," I said.

He gave me that shark's smile. "That's a bad idea, man."

"If I'm going to die by the end of the summer, what do I care? Look, I'm going," I said, and I felt that reckless thrill of euphoria. "I'm going right now."

For the first time in our relationship, the shoe was on the other foot. It wasn't Gage asking me to throw caution to the wind, to do something I'd regret. It was me asking him. I could see the hesitation in his eyes, and he knew I could see it.

"Fine, fucker," he said.

"I'm getting stuff from the house, then I'm out," I said.

"Where are we going?"

"West," I said.

"That's it? Just west?"

"We'll make it up as we go. And we'll go 'till we hit the Pacific."

"Let's do it."

We ran to The Pumpkin.

CHAPTER 8

We went to Gage's house first. I'd never seen anyone pack so fast. He shoved a bunch of clothes and other random things into an old army green duffel, then grabbed his climbing pack—which had all of his climbing gear—and stacked both by the door.

"Snacks," he said, and raided the cupboards, throwing loaves of bread, boxes of cereal, crackers, tortillas, chips, and other stuff into paper grocery bags. Then he grabbed one of his dad's coolers, turned to the fridge and tossed in chunks of cheese, a half-package of Oscar Meyer bologna, and a dozen other random things.

"Take the milk," I said. He threw that in too. That's when I spotted the case of Dinty Moore beef stew on top of the cupboards. "Oh...." I said, pointing.

"Jackpot," he said. "Grab it."

I was taller than Gage, and standing on tiptoe, I pulled the case down and caught it, carried it to the door.

"Ready?"

"Yeah. No wait!" he said, and he ran to his dad's bedroom with me following. I followed. He opened the sliding closet door and dropped to his knees. There were suits neatly hung on their hangers above and polished dress shoes below. He pushed those aside and grabbed an old shoe box way in the back. It was big, like it was made to carry two pairs of shoes.

He flipped it open, revealing a stack of Hustler porno mags.

"What the fuck, dude?" I said. "Do we really need that?"

He appraised the cover with a smile, then tossed the stack aside and pulled out a black velvet bag. It looked like maybe it was a bag for shoes, and it was pretty full with something.

"Am I going to throw up when you open that bag?" I said, imagining some gross sex toy.

He pushed open the drawstring and I forcefully looked away...then snapped my gaze back to it. He ran his thumb across the edge of an enormous stack of one hundred dollar bills.

"Jesus! How much is that?"

"Thirty-three thousand."

"Thirty-three—! What the fuck? What is your dad doing with thirty three thousand dollars in a bag in his closet?"

"'Cause he's paranoid," Gage said. "End of the world is coming, he says. He's sure the Soviets are going to push the red button."

"But your dad's a lawyer," I said, still flabbergasted. "He's...rational." He'd always seemed like the most reasonable guy to me.

"Nobody's rational, dude. Everybody's fucking crazy. Some people just hide it better than others."

I just stared. I'd never seen that much money in one place at one time.

"And get this," Gage went on. "Everything has to be in threes. It's all about the threes. He's also got a big stash of gold downstairs in a safe. Wanna guess how much? Three pounds, three ounces."

"No shit?"

"Guy's trippin'," Gage said. "But hey..." He cinched the bag, tossed it up and caught it. "Seed money." He winked.

"Your dad's going to kill you."

"Gotta catch me first." He stood up. "Let's go."

We threw all the stuff—except the cash—into the bed of

the truck, but just as we got into the cab, Gage jumped out again. "One more thing." He ran back into the house and emerged a second later with a big paper bag. He threw it onto the seat between us and slammed the door.

I peeked inside. It was full of fireworks.

"What's this for?"

"It's your independence day, man. C'mon."

I laughed and peeled out of the driveway.

It took us fifteen minutes to get out to the mesa. I eased The Pumpkin into my mom's empty spot in the garage and killed the engine. I was feeling the pressure of time. Walking back into my house was like walking into a skeleton of my past. I felt like it was threatening to clutch me with its bony fingers. Now that I'd decided to leave Durango, I just wanted to get out of here.

Not to mention the fact that, as soon as Uncle Morty figured out I wasn't at school, he was going to make a beeline for my house. And while the trip to Gage's house had been fast—barely more than thirty minutes—I was feeling every second tick by. It was like returning to the scene of a crime. At any moment I expected to turn around and find the police in my driveway.

Gage went with me into the downstairs den, and I took the stairs two at a time. He seemed to feel my tension and didn't say a word.

I emptied out my room, giving boxes and bags to Gage and telling him to go throw them in the bed of the truck.

"You gonna take everything you own?" he asked on the third trip, his arms full with two boxes of comic books.

"I'm not coming back."

He watched me for a second and realized I meant it. He got a thoughtful look on his face, then shrugged.

"Then you're going to need a tarp," he said. "It rains and all this shit's ruined."

"It's got a tonneau cover. Behind the seats."

"Yeah?"

"Snaps to the side of the bed. Tight as a drum."

"Wicked." It seemed Gage's opinion of The Pumpkin had gone up another notch, if that was possible. He nodded and left with the boxes.

We got everything loaded in, pulled the tonneau cover from behind the seats and snapped it into place. Gage and I went upstairs one more time and I took a last look around my room.

A cool spring breeze flowed in, fluttering the light blue and white curtains, and I paused as the realization that I was never coming back hit me hard.

I'd grown up with my brother Ryan in this room. We'd played together. We'd fought each other. He'd listened to his heavy metal music and talked about horror movies. I tried to get him excited about the latest fantasy books I was reading. Weis & Hickman's *Dragonlance Chronicles*. Terry Brooks' *Sword of Shannara*. He was never interested, but he did read my comic books every now and then.

For a moment, I could see where Ryan's bed had once been, before he'd moved out. I could see him lying on it, thumbing through *Hit Parader* or *Fangoria*, his guitar leaning against the headboard. I looked back at my own bed, at the wooden sword leaning against the headboard.

"Don't forget that," Gage said.

I'd made the sword with my dad's help after I'd read *The Chronicles of Prydain* by Lloyd Alexander. It was nothing more than a piece of plywood cut in the shape of a sword. Dad had done the cutting and sanding, and I'd painted it black and gold. It was called Dyrnwyn in the books, and when you drew it a flame ran the length of the black blade.

Every kid has bad dreams, but I'd had nightmares worse than most. In the worst one, I'd been chased by Schwarzenegger-sized demons wreathed in flames. I was so scared that I actually sleepwalked—more like sleepran—from the demons, right into my parents' bedroom. It had taken an hour for my mom to calm me down and get me to go back to my own bed.

The next day, Dad and I had created that replica of the sword Dyrnwyn, and I'd kept it by my bed every night. Some people had nightlights to drive away the bad dreams. I had a flaming magical sword. Whenever I'd start to have a nightmare, somewhere in my subconscious I'd remember that Dyrnwyn was by my side, right where I'd need it if I woke up. It kept the nightmares away.

I picked it up. "This kept away my bad dreams when I was a kid," I said absently. "You know, when I held this, I always felt like I could do anything. Like I could face anyone. Like I was a grown-up."

"Perfect," he said. "Take the fucker."

We went back downstairs. I threw the keys up and caught them as I entered the garage—

—and I saw the police car parked on the flat, up on the dirt driveway. My breath caught in my throat.

"Oh shit," I whispered.

Gage, who hadn't emerged into the garage yet, stopped dead in the den.

"What is it?"

"He's here. My uncle."

"Fuck."

Uncle Morty got out of the police cruiser, peered down the slope of the dirt driveway to where it turned into pavement as it entered the garage. I thought about leaping back through the doorway into the den, but he spotted me before I could move.

I was caught.

He took his time walking toward me, not hurried, his hands hooked into his police belt.

"Uncle Morty," I said, trying to sound nonchalant. I flicked a glance at Gage inside the den—

But he was gone.

"Your dad's worried about you, Eric," Uncle Morty said.

With stiff legs, I walked toward the mouth of the garage

and swallowed down a dry throat.

"Your dad and I don't talk much," Uncle Morty continued. "So for him to call me was a big thing."

"Yeah," I said. We met on the pavement just outside the garage door. He looked at The Pumpkin, and I had a momentary gush of relief that I'd put the tonneau cover over all of my stuff. He didn't know I was planning to blow town, but he would have seen that in a second without the cover.

"Why'd you miss your plane?" he asked.

"I don't want to go to Malaysia," I said. I could have come up with a lie. *My car broke down. I had to take a friend to the hospital. I was so violently sick with the stomach flu I couldn't get out of bed.* Something. But the honest truth just popped right out of me.

"Yeah," he said sympathetically. "I didn't want to drive down to Durango today. Didn't really want to do no favors for Hank, either, for that matter. But..." He held his hands outward, palms up. "Sometimes you have to do things you don't want to. It's family."

I swallowed. "Would *you* do it, Uncle Morty?"

"What's that?"

"Give up your friends, your whole life, give up your last week of high school and your graduation? Would you just up and go to Malaysia?"

He pursed his lips, squinted up at the second story windows like he was looking into the sun. "Yeah, that was a bad move on his part, I admit. He could have waited. But your dad always wants to do everything his own way."

"That's what I'm talking about."

"You made your point not getting on that plane, I guess. But your dad's hopping mad now. Those tickets were worth all the gold in Fort Knox, to hear him squawk about it."

I didn't say anything to that. I never asked Dad to buy me that ticket.

"He told me to put you on the next plane, cuff you if I had to," Uncle Morty said.

"Is that what you're going to do?" I asked.

He paused for a second, as though he was thinking that

over. "I guess not."

"I don't want to go to Malaysia."

"And I don't want to do my brother's parenting for him. But we don't always get what we want." He pursed his lips again, those squinty eyes seeming to look anywhere but my face. And yet at the same time, I felt like he was watching me, like he had complete control of this situation and that, no matter where he was looking, his full focus was on me. If I tried to run, I know one of those wiry arms would shoot out and catch me before I could even take a step.

His gaze finally did fall on me. "Tell you what," he said. "What if you got to finish out the week? At school, I mean."

"That..." I stuttered. "That would be great."

"Then we'll put you on a plane this coming Sunday. Even give you a weekend day with your friends after."

"Uncle Morty...."

"Yeah, I know. You don't want to go. But you don't get that choice. You're still a minor and your dad's still your dad." He looked over the house. "We'll stay here. You'll go to school, finish things out. I'll even come to your graduation. How's that?"

I was stunned. I don't know what I'd been expecting. I think I had expected him to put me in cuffs right from the beginning and haul me to the airport, but here he was trying to compromise, trying to make this easier on me. Like a dad should.

But then...it would still end with me getting on a plane, going to Malaysia. And that wasn't me making my own choice. That was the river sweeping me downstream.

As I stood there, conflicted, I noticed movement by Uncle Morty's police car. Gage was hunched over, skulking along the back bumper like he was afraid of being shot by prison tower guards.

In a flash, I realized he was going to do something to the car. I had no idea what, but with Gage it could be anything.

I wanted to yell at him, to wave my arms and tell him to stop...

Then I heard Uncle Morty's words in my head.

You don't get that choice...

But I did have a choice. I could stop Gage and side with Uncle Morty who, despite his kindness, was still going to take me exactly where I didn't want to go.

Or I could support Gage's plan—whatever it was—and jump into the unknown.

Gage gently popped the hood on the police cruiser and I coughed at the same time as the metallic "thump." I thought for sure Uncle Morty would spin around, but he didn't seem to hear it. A cold sweat prickled on my scalp.

"You're being really awesome, Uncle Morty," I said, probably too loudly.

"Well, I understand why you're upset, son. And I'm sorry about your mom." He cocked his head and his stony face softened for a second. "Is that what this is about? You punishing your dad because he wasn't at her funeral?"

Gage fiddled with the engine, then pushed the hood down gently but didn't latch it. He vanished behind the far side of the car.

"The only one I had there was Gage," I said. I tried to think of anything to keep the conversation going, to keep Uncle Morty facing away from his state cruiser. "Don't you think Dad should have been there?"

"I do," Uncle Morty said. "I understand you're angry. So...we'll do this thing our way. All right?" He glanced up at the house.

"Dad's going to be mad."

"Yeah, well. I've never been too concerned with what Hank gets mad about."

I gave a tentative laugh.

Gage appeared again, jogging quickly away from the cruiser along the winding driveway that led down to the main road. He motioned madly to me to follow.

I didn't know what the hell he wanted me to do. I mean, if I ran, Uncle Morty would just grab me. No way I was fast enough to get away from him when he was this close.

That's when the fireworks went off in Uncle Morty's car.

He spun around. "What the devil?" he yelled, as I shouted, "What the hell is that?"

He took off at a run toward his car and I jumped into The Pumpkin. The engine roared to life. I slammed the short throw into reverse and squealed out of the garage. The tires skidded off the concrete and spat gravel like mad as I spun the wheel, backing into the other parking space on the flat. Dust billowed up all around as I slammed the brakes and threw it into first.

For a second, time seemed to slow as I saw Uncle Morty through the windshield and the cloud of dust. He was right in front of me, about a dozen feet from the grill of The Pumpkin, and he was holding up his hand. I couldn't hear him over the roar of the engine and the spitting gravel, but I could practically see a little dialogue bubble over his head saying, "Freeze!"

I jammed my foot onto the accelerator and spun the wheel again. I missed Uncle Morty by a couple of feet as he lunged at the car, and I turned down the winding driveway toward the main road.

Gage waited for me at the end of the driveway. I skidded to a stop, and he dove through the window. We peeled out again, literally leaving Uncle Morty in the dust.

"Oh my god," I said, stunned. "Oh my god, what did we just do?"

Gage was coughing or laughing or both as he tried to flip himself right side up in the cramped cab.

"He's not going to let us get away," I said.

"He's not going anywhere without this." Gage held up a circular plastic thing with rubber wires sprouting from it.

"What the hell is that?"

"Distributor cap."

"What does it do?"

"Nothing without a car attached to it. But then the car won't do anything, either." He laughed.

"It's a fucking police car, moron. He'll call for backup."

"He's welcome to try." He held up the CB receiver, a little

hand-sized box with a button you push to talk...and the curly black cord that should have connected it to the rest of the radio.

We left a plume behind us like a dusty fox's tail as we drove out of my subdivision.

CHAPTER 9

We headed out onto the road, agreeing that going back through town was a bad idea. My uncle was a Colorado state trooper, so we figured the best thing was to get out of Colorado as fast as possible. So we set my wooden sword on the dashboard as a good luck charm and blazed through the backroads to Highway 550 and headed south.

After the initial rush of our escape, we didn't say much. The foreboding of having fled a policeman and vandalized his car began to set in for me. I must have checked the rearview mirror a hundred times in the first ten miles, but no flashing lights appeared.

Once we passed the border into New Mexico, we both relaxed.

"That was pretty badass," Gage finally said, slapping me on the arm.

"I can't believe you did that." I laughed and shook my head. "I thought for sure Uncle Morty was going to turn around and see you."

"It was the only way we were getting out of there. He had you cold."

"Where did you get the fireworks? The bag is right here." I tapped the paper bag on the seat between us.

"On my last trip taking stuff down to the car I got this really strong feeling to grab some and stuff them in my pocket," he said. "So I did."

"A strong feeling?"

He glanced sidelong at me. "You think the fetch was flirting with me?"

I shrugged. "I never had a fetch before. I don't know how they work."

"I think it *was* your fetch. Now she's got the hots for me, not you. And she was nibbling my ear, telling me to grab fireworks," he said.

"This whole thing seems kind of like a dream, doesn't it?" I asked. "Like it's not really happening."

"Best time of my life so far," he said.

"What if it's true?"

"What if what's true?"

"That I'm invincible. That as long as I'm following my heart—as long as I'm inspiring her—I can't get hurt."

He chuckled. "Sure, dude."

"You don't believe in the fetch."

He grinned his shark's grin. "Sure I do. I mean look what you've done so far."

His eyes glowed when he looked at me, like he was watching an Olympic gymnast do backflips or something.

I wanted to explain that the fetch had been a flesh-and-blood person, that this wasn't just some wild rebellion, but I didn't know how to make him believe me.

And really, did it matter? Gage wanted to be on this journey, and I wanted him here.

I drove west, as I'd said we would. We passed Farmington and headed into Arizona. About three hours into the trip, and about twenty miles outside of a town called Kayenta, Gage said, "Hey, you ever been to Zion National Park?"

I hadn't even heard of it. "Zion?"

"Killer climbing spot. Big walls," he said.

In the aftermath of escaping Uncle Morty, I hadn't given much thought to destination, but it did seem like time to make a choice. I envisioned us just driving until we hit the Pacific without going anywhere else first. That'd take about two days. We had a whole summer and $33,000. We could go anywhere, do anything we wanted.

"Are we close?" I asked.

"Utah."

"How far?"

"The fuck do you care? Are we late for something?"

I laughed. "Let's do it. There's a map under the seat."

He pulled out the oversized Rand McNally Road Atlas, thumbed it open. He measured the distance with his fingers and did the calculations.

We stopped in Kayenta for gas and switched drivers, then headed toward our new destination which, it turned out, was about three hours away.

As Gage hung a right onto Highway 98, I imagined me doing a monster climb up some giant cliff face, and I wondered if that would inspire the fetch. I wondered when she'd show up again.

"So I'm supposed to be invincible," I said.

His shark's smile appeared. "Yeah. So?"

"So I've got an idea. Keep driving."

"What are going to do?"

I rolled down the window and the air rushed in. At 70 miles per hour, the blast pushed me into my seat. Fighting it, I pulled myself up on the door frame, climbed out and sat on the door.

"Dude!" Gage said.

"Keep it steady," I shouted through the wind. The wind felt like it was trying to shove me onto the pavement that raced beneath us.

"You're fuckin' crazy!" he shouted.

I slapped one hand onto the smooth metal of the roof of the cab, testing my balance, then pushed slowly with my feet. I fought the wind, squinting as it shoved at me, tried to push me off.

I extended my body across the top of the cab, lying on my belly. The road raced at the front of the hood, and I leaned into the wind as I slowly stood up.

I twitched, every muscle in my legs, torso, and arms flexing, adjusting and readjusting as I faced the highway. A couple of times I almost lost my balance, but I caught it quickly.

Gage kept the car as steady as he could, but it still wobbled a little as he stayed with the mostly-straight road. Every jerk almost took me off my perch, but I surfed through it.

Then the wind changed. For just a moment it was less fierce, and I fell forward. I immediately jerked myself backward, but then the wind came back full force and hit me. I flew off the cab.

"Shit!" I yelled.

I fell on my back, spread-eagled, on top of the tonneau cover. It collapsed like a deflated parachute. Snaps broke away from the tailgate as I smashed down onto whatever was beneath me. Gage slammed on the brakes and swerved to the right. We squealed to a stop by the side of the road and he leapt out of the cab.

He spotted me and let out a giant breath.

"I thought you were dead," he shouted. "I just caught movement as you fell. I didn't see you go into the bed, and I totally thought you were a smear on the pavement."

He held out his hand. I took it and he pulled me off the top of the deflated tonneau cover.

I just stood there, stunned. That was the craziest thing I'd ever done, even more than leading the climb in Canyonlands or running from Uncle Morty. I didn't know the odds of survival for someone surfing the top of a tiny El Camino going 70 miles per hour, but they couldn't be good.

And I hadn't died.

The hot wind blew over my skin, cooling the sweat on my skin and, just for a second out of the corner of my eye, I thought I saw a flash of something red and furry on the sandy expanse behind The Pumpkin. I spun quickly, scouring the desert with my gaze.

But I didn't see a fox.

"You're fucking nuts, man," Gage said.

"I know," I said, barely able to catch my breath. "Have you ever seen anyone do that?"

"On TV maybe." He paused. "You fucked up your cover, though," he added, flapping the naugahyde by the tailgate. While the buttons on the sides of the bed had just unsnapped, several had ripped free at the back.

But I barely heard him. I stepped off the hot blacktop and into the desert. A barbed wire fence separated me from the dry land beyond, and I just stared at it in a daze, watching the flat horizon shimmer in the heat.

"What if I *am* invincible?" I whispered.

He didn't say anything.

I glanced over my shoulder at him. I could see he still didn't believe in the fetch, but I could also see that he believed in pushing our limits as far as I wanted to go. He'd proven that when he'd vandalized a cop car.

But *my* belief in the fetch continued to grow. The more I thought about it, the more today's string of incidents seemed ridiculously unlikely. Any one of them could have been random luck: my uncle not finding me in the cafeteria when he'd clearly been looking, nobody in the cafeteria seeing Gage and me slip out, Gage's seemingly random idea to grab fireworks and stuff them in his pocket, him just luckily being out of sight when Uncle Morty spotted me, our ridiculous getaway.... And now this.

Any one of those things, just one—even standing on top of the cab—I could have dismissed as sheer luck. But all of them together?

It was impossible. It was magic.

I swallowed. I had a fetch.

I half expected her to appear, wink at me, and say, "I told you so."

Passion...

"Let's climb," I said. "Let's climb the hell out of Zion."

Gage clapped me on the back. "Fuckin' A." He tossed me the keys. "You drive. I need to drink a bottle of Pepto Bismol."

I laughed. Together, we snapped all the buttons on the tonneau cover that were still good, then I jumped behind the wheel. We roared off the shoulder and sped down the highway.

We reached the campground at Zion as the sun was falling. The attendant at the gate took our money, gave us a map of the park, and directed us to the campground.

We chose the best spot—right next to a stream that wound through red clay. We dropped our stuff in the dirt, then went to look at the river. The riverbank was tall, as though the current had been eating away at it for centuries, and a few trees hung over the gurgling water. There was absolutely nobody else in the campground.

"Too early in the season?" Gage asked, looking at all the empty camping spots.

"Or we're just lucky," I said.

Gage and I went to the edge of the riverbank, gazed past the river at the rising cliffs in the distance. I felt like a king looking over some red earth fantasy land. And we were going to explore it all. A thrill went through me at the thought that I might see my fetch again, maybe as I crested the rise of another climb.

"I'm going to inspire you," I murmured.

Gage chuckled. "C'mon lover boy. Let's make a place to sleep."

We put up Gage's dad's tent, a baby-blue Coleman that looked like some miniature circus tent. The fabric was smooth and thin. My dad's tent was army green canvas, and huge. All rolled up, it looked like someone was trying to get rid of a body. Gage had pulled this tent out of a sack the size of a small backpack.

Once it was set up, we rolled out our sleeping bags and hunkered down by flashlight to go over the map of the park.

"Angel's Landing," Gage said, tapping at it on the map. "I've heard of that. And a guy I was climbing with said he did a climb called Flapjack Crack out here. We should hit that too."

"Let's hit them all."

The next morning, we got up with the sun, stuck slices of cheese and bologna into tortillas, wolfed them down, then hit the climbs.

We climbed all day, hitting at least half a dozen different routes. I kept hoping to see my fetch, but she never showed. We went until our arms were pumped and worthless, then we came back to the campsite and cooked up Dinty Moore beef stew in an old pot Gage had thought to swipe from his dad's house.

We woke up the next morning and did it all over again. I went to bed aching, but I took the pain in my muscles as a badge of honor. Gage never complained about any aches and pains, and I resolved that I wouldn't complain until he did.

Those first two days, despite my pains, I came to revel in being out in the sun, in the spring weather, and being on the rock. God, the rock.

On the morning of the third day, I woke to find my arms curled up—my hands practically touching my shoulders. I tried to uncurl them, and pain shot through my muscles down to the bone.

"Fuck me," I whispered.

Gage blinked awake. "S'going on?" he asked, peering through the dim tent. The sun hadn't quite risen yet, and it was still pretty dark.

"I can't uncurl my arms," I said.

He rose up on one elbow. "What?" He blinked some more and looked at my arms, which bent at the elbow like I was carrying a box. Except with no box. "You can't straighten them?"

I grunted, tried again, but it was like the muscles wouldn't engage. "No." My heart started beating faster. Had I screwed up my arms? What the hell was wrong with them?

He started laughing. "Man, that's hardcore. Bet you're

wishing you had come to work out with me this past year, huh?"

"What the hell do I do? I can't move my fucking arms!"

"Don't be a crybaby. Hang on." He got out of his sleeping bag and knelt next to me. He took hold of my bicep and my wrist.

"What the fuck are you doing?"

"I'm going to push them apart."

"No way. It fucking hurts!"

"Sore muscles, man. Gotta stretch 'em out."

"This is sore muscles?"

"You been going balls-out for two days with your noodle arms. What did you think was going to happen?" He started to push.

"Ouchjesusfuck!" I squawked, but I grit my teeth until the arm was straight.

He went slowly, and once the arm was straight, the pain eased. It was much easier to hold the arm straight than it had been to straighten it. He did the same with the other arm, slow and sure. It wasn't as bad, maybe because this time I knew my ligaments weren't going to snap in half.

I spent the next half hour working my arms slowly up and down until they felt somewhat normal. We each had three slices of Wonder bread slathered with peanut butter and Country Crock, then headed out to the rock again.

After the first climb, my arms started to feel normal, and for the rest of the day they didn't bother me at all.

We took The Pumpkin everywhere it would go in the park, climbing everything we found. When we couldn't drive somewhere, we'd hike in and spend the day.

We hit Angel's Landing, rocked Lucifer's Ladder, Days of No Future, and South East Buttress. We hit the Touchstone Wall, the Organ Grinder, Tooele Tower and Lovelace. I pushed through the aches and pains. After the first week, I still went to bed sore every night and woke up stiff, but my arms never locked up again. The next challenge was ripped fingers. The rock scraped up my fingers until some of them bled, but I taped them up and kept going. Also, the climbing shoes I borrowed from Gage were so tight they were torture, but soon I just got used to my feet hurting. Gage told me climbing shoes were supposed to be that way. It became a ritual for Gage and me to sit by the river and soak our feet after the day was done.

Soon my fingers stopped ripping, callouses built up, and I stopped using the tape. I also started seeing definition in my forearms, biceps, and legs.

We lost track of the days. We had to drive into the small town nearby a couple of times to stock up on food and to resole our climbing shoes. But aside from that, we woke up, we climbed, we ate, and we crashed. Then we did it all over again the next day. We got into a rhythm. It was like we began to breathe with the valley, in and out, in and out. I'd never done anything that had felt more natural.

Somewhere in the fourth week, we were camped out beneath our climb of the day. It didn't even have a name. We'd found the route on our own after hiking around for a while. We were both lying on our backs beneath the wall, the line of shadow slowly moving up the rock as the sun went down. We ate tortillas stuffed with beans, scrambled eggs, and cheese.

Gage set his burrito on a patch of bare rock and put his legs and arms up in the air like a beetle on its back. He cocked his head to one side as he moved his hands and feet like he was on the rock.

"What are you doing?" I asked.

"Working out that problem." There had been a crack that had denied him all day. "Gotta be a different way to do it." He glanced at me with a smug smile. "I'm using some of your creative visualization."

I took a deep breath of the pristine air. Nothing else smelled like Zion air. It was like...inhaling nature: pine sap with sagebrush, and that clean smell of warm sandstone.

"I love this," I said. "God, I love this. I want to do this forever."

"Go pro," he said, still twitching his hands and feet.

"There are pro rock climbers?"

"Sure." He picked up his burrito and took a bite.

"I wonder how good I'd have to get to do that."

"You're pretty good now," he said around a mouthful.

That made me look over at him. "What?"

He stopped his bug-on-its-back impersonation, propped up on his elbow and swallowed his bite. "Dude, you did your first climb a month ago. Now you're flashing 5.9s and starting to lead 5.10s?"

I didn't say anything.

"You know how long it took me to lead a 5.10?" he said and took a savage bite from his burrito. "A year," he said, and a bean flew out of his mouth. "You suck."

I blinked, then said, "Well, I had a good teacher."

He went back to working out his problem, legs and arms up in the air. "Fucking freak is what you are."

I looked up at the rock and thought about this insane month. I really could just live here forever, climbing, eating, and sleeping. Zion was perfect. Why would I go anywhere else?

But Canyonlands had been perfect too. I hadn't been as crazy about climbing as I was now, but I'd felt that same feeling there. I suddenly wondered how many perfect places there were in the world.

I also wondered where my fetch was. I'd been dreaming about her where I'd turn and catch a glimpse of her, that dark red hair, those huge green eyes, the freckles across her nose.

Maybe I wasn't seeing her anymore because I didn't need to. The euphoria I felt here in Zion was exactly what I'd felt when I'd first met her, exactly what I'd felt every time I did something crazy. Maybe she hadn't shown up because I was already inspiring her, just by doing this. Maybe I could spend the whole summer in Zion, and my last act would be a swan dive off the top of a cliff the day before my eighteenth birthday.

As soon as I thought that, I felt a sick pit in my stomach. And I saw...what I was going to do next.

"I'm going for a walk." I stood up.

"Knock yourself out," Gage said, still working out the

problem.

I followed the edge of the wall until it split into a ravine. I wended my way up between the towering walls of sandstone. I scrambled over the rocks, getting higher and higher until the two walls started to come together. At that point, it was only about ten feet to the top, so I pushed my feet against one wall and my back against the other and crab-walked up until I got to the top. At that point, I stemmed up the rest of the way, pushing hands and feet against the opposing rock faces and shuffling upward until I got a grip on the top. I pushed with my legs and hit the northern cliff with my belly, did a quick push up and was on top.

Most cliffs were like this, where you could actually get to the top fairly easily if you didn't take the rated routes. I'd learned that climbing wasn't just about getting to the top. It was working a satisfying route—something that challenged you.

But I wasn't looking for a challenge right now.

I walked to the edge of the cliff overlooking the panorama of Zion. The sun had gone down and the moon peeked over the far horizon. The green of the valley, the red of the sands, and the twisting blue of the stream all looked like different shades of gray in the newborn moonlight. I couldn't see Gage, but I knew where he was around the bend of the rock to my left. I'd seen this view a dozen times today, but it all looked brand new now. God, I loved this part.

I considered my last thought before I'd decided to head up here: the day before my eighteenth birthday, leaping off this cliff.

I stepped back a few paces, and my heart beat faster. I'd pushed the limits. I'd done things I would have considered insane a month ago, but had I really tested my invincibility? I mean, a fall into the bed of The Pumpkin was nuts. Leading 5.10s in my first month of climbing was, as Gage said, pretty damned good. But both were possible.

What would the fetch do to save me from jumping off a cliff? Everything else I'd done was still something a human could do, even if most wouldn't. No human could survive a two hundred foot fall.

I swallowed, crouched, and prepared to run.

"You sure know how to get a fetch's attention," a voice purred from behind me.

I had been about to put on a burst of speed. I stopped to crane my neck, lost my balance, and fell over.

She stood in the moonlight, this time wearing a green mini-skirt, a white crop top, and a jean jacket. Big round earrings punctuated her ears. She looked like she was ready for a night on the town.

Once again I was stunned. "God, you're actually here," I breathed, then I got to my feet.

"Were you going to throw yourself over the cliff?" she asked.

"I wanted to inspire you."

"Oh, but you have, Eric. I've never felt so alive, watching you these last days."

"Then where have you been?"

"I've been here the whole time. I liked your stunt on top of the car, by the way. Original. But your time here in Zion." She kissed her fingers and splayed them. "Gorgeous."

"I kept looking for you. I dreamed about you."

"I'm here now." She held out her arms. "Would you like to dance?"

"Yes." I closed the distance, put my hand in hers and my other hand on her waist. Slowly, we began to move across the flat sandstone, and I thought I could actually hear music. It sounded like some distant rock and roll song. I couldn't hear the lyrics, but I would have sworn it was U2.

I felt euphoric, like there was nowhere else in the world I'd rather be than here.

She put her head against mine, then bent her head down. Her lips came close to my ear. "Tell me you weren't going to jump off that cliff," she said.

"I was," I said.

She leaned her head back and looked at me skeptically.

"Suicide is not inspiring, Eric. Is that what you thought I was? Some demon pushing you to suicide?"

"Well, no. But every time I did something dangerous, everything turned out so lucky."

"Of course."

"I just thought if I did something really dangerous, you'd show up."

"I like it when you push your limits, but did you really think I'd save you if you hurled yourself over a cliff?"

"Uh, you saved me in Canyonlands."

"That..." She licked her lip like she'd tasted chocolate pie. "That was delicious. You wanted that ledge so badly, and you bet your whole life on it."

"Yeah."

"What did you want so badly that you were going to hurl yourself over this cliff?"

"To dance with you," I said.

She laughed. "Silver-tongued devil," she murmured and pulled me into a hug. She put her head against mine again and we swayed to that distant music. "I'm going to warn you, Eric. And I'll only warn you once. I'm here for you, to help you become the most spectacular you that there is. When you run, I will be the wind at your back. When you jump, I will be the springs under your feet." She shook her head. "But a fetch appears when and where she wishes. Hurling yourself to your death to force me to appear... That isn't inspiring."

"I...I'm sorry."

"Well, I forgive you." I could feel her grin against my cheek, and she nuzzled my neck playfully. "Do you still want to dance with me?"

"More than ever."

"Then dance, Eric. And I will be with you. I am that flame in your heart, that rush in your veins. I'm always here." She curled up my arm, wrapping herself in it. She playfully bumped my hip with hers, then rolled out in a graceful spin, giving a little flourish with her free hand. As she rolled out, she became more and more transparent, and when she reached the end of the spin, her hand slipped from mine and she vanished.

In her place stood the red fox. She flicked her tail and raced away, jumping down the chimney I'd climbed to get up here. I ran after her, but by the time I got to the edge, she was gone.

"Dance..." Her voice came on the breeze, then it faded. The distant music went with it.

"Man..." I whispered.

I sat down on the rock and looked at the moon for a long time. Finally, I got up and made my way back to camp.

Gage was sitting by a newly made fire, poking at it with a stick and making the flames dance.

"It's time to go," I said softly.

"Oh?"

"Out of Zion."

"Oh." He thought about that for a second, then nodded. "Schweet."

"What's another great climbing spot?" I asked.

"Joshua Tree," he said immediately.

The music returned, the same song that had floated around the fetch and me while we'd danced. I pointed my finger at him, and my heart started hammering excitedly. "U2!" I said. "Joshua Tree is a climbing spot?"

"One of the best," he said. "I've always wanted to go there."

"Because it's a U2 album."

"Fuck you. 'Cause it's a bomber climbing spot, dickwad."

"You're full of shit. You want to go because of U2."

"Whatever, man."

I laughed and sat down next to him. "Joshua Tree it is," I said. "We'll get out of here first thing tomorrow."

And I had just the cassette for the drive.

CHAPTER 10

We lit out of Zion the next morning going 80 miles an hour. Though twelve hours ago I would have gladly stayed for the rest of my life, it felt amazing to get back on the road. The blacktop rushing beneath us, the yellow centerline flashing like dots. The horizon was open and full of possibility. All of it coursed through me. Gage felt it too. We cranked up the stereo and sang along at the top of our lungs to "Where the Streets Have No Name."

I couldn't stop thinking about the fetch. Just calling her to mind—her alluring smile, her inciting words and daring green gaze—dazzled me. I'd translated what she'd said at Canyonlands into a death wish. But now I understood what she meant about inspiring her. Her final word echoed in my mind.

Dance...

This was about following dreams, about hearing the music in my own soul and dancing to it, whatever that may be, no matter how crazy it might seem. My inhibitions were going to take a back seat this summer. Gage and I would pursue only what we loved. I thought about what I'd learned in Zion, how my heart felt on the rock.

I turned the blasting music down and said, "This road trip

is about climbing."

Gage looked at me. "Fuck yeah, it is."

"No, I mean that's what we're going to do. We're going to drive, and then we're going to climb. Everywhere we go. We'll hit Joshua Tree first."

"And after that?"

"We don't think about after that," I murmured. "We just dance with what's in front of us, then when it's time to move on, we move on."

"When the fetch inspires us to go, we go," Gage said.

"That's right."

He grinned and cranked up the music. We both started singing again.

It was only about eight hours to Joshua Tree, but we decided to take a small detour to see Las Vegas. Gage's idea.

We stopped for breakfast at a casino, and it took me all of two seconds after walking inside to feel queasy. The whole glittering, blinking, flashing place smelled like stale smoke. It was so bad I expected to see a haze drifting everywhere, but strangely the air *looked* clean. It just stank of smoke and burned my eyes.

"I think this place is the anti-Zion," I said. I couldn't get the taste of smoke out of my mouth.

"I wonder if they'll let us gamble," Gage said.

Turned out the answer was no. The moment we tried, we got chased out. Gage insisted on trying two more casinos, but no dice. Nobody bothered us if we walked down the main aisles, but the moment we sat at a table or stopped in front of a slot machine, security materialized. When we couldn't produce ID that said we were 21, they asked where our parents were. When we couldn't tell them that, they booted us.

Gage said he wanted to see all the lights in the dark, so we stayed until nightfall and walked the strip.

I was astonished at the spectacle. I marveled at how much money it must take to light all this up in the middle of the desert, night after night. It was surreal. We passed an ad for a strip club, and Gage pointed up at it.

"Yeah?" he said.

"No."

"Fucker," he said. "You don't want to go?"

I didn't know what to say. Don't get me wrong. I wanted to see naked women just as much as the next guy. And I didn't have any problem with strip clubs, but...

"It's not...real," I said.

"What?"

"It's just a fantasy."

"What's wrong with a fantasy?" he asked.

"Nothing. I just... I don't know."

He rolled his eyes. "Don't get all deep on me. I was just saying, 'Look! Boobies!'"

I laughed, but my heart was heavy. Las Vegas had completely discombobulated me with its over-the-top glitz. It was hard to hear what my heart wanted when my eyes were burning from smoke, dazzled by bright lights, and drawn to half-naked women on billboards. I felt pulled in a hundred different directions, but never all the way.

"It's a distraction," I finally said, trying to understand what I was feeling. "What we did at school, what we did with Uncle Morty, at Zion, that's real. We're risking real things to follow our hearts. It's like we're going somewhere, and I want to get there. But this...this just seems like...I don't know. It seems like a pit, like we could fall in it for the whole summer and never get out, never get closer to...what we're looking for."

Gage was silent for a moment. "Still..." He pointed. "Boobies."

We didn't stop at the strip club. In fact, once I'd made my statement, Gage was as eager as I was to get back on the road. We headed back to The Pumpkin and sped out of Las Vegas.

We hit the Joshua Tree National Monument next. The place was surreal, with pale sands, spiky yucca plants, and those oddly shaped Joshua trees everywhere. We turned down the blaring U2 cassette to take in the bizarre landscape. It felt like an alien planet with an army of Joshua trees slowly closing in on us. I'd never been anywhere like this before.

"Good call," I said to Gage as we parked and got out of the car. Just like with Zion, there was no one around.

"Think your fetch is clearing these places out before we get here?" Gage asked, seeming to read my mind.

"Who can say?"

"Don't get me wrong. I'm down with no crowds. Getting the whole park to ourselves is badass."

We picked a camping spot right next to a tall cluster of rocks with an ear-like flake of rock sticking out, and pulled out our stuff. By the time the sun went down, we'd set up the tent, made a fire in the steel ring by the campsite, and cooked up some Dinty Moore beef stew. I didn't think it would have been possible, but I was getting sick of Dinty Moore beef stew.

Joshua Tree went much like Zion. We climbed all day, shoved food in our mouths when we were off the rock for a moment, and we slept.

My skills increased. After three days working the rock, I noticed that my relationship with Gage had begun to shift. I didn't feel like the tagalong trying to keep up with him anymore. He'd gone from mentor to climbing partner.

He had tremendous strength, more than I did. He could muscle himself up and over things with surprising ease, but I was getting stronger every day, and my longer reach gave me an advantage that, at some places on the rock, he couldn't match. I now led as often as he did, and we mostly worked on 5.10s. Every now and then we'd tackle a 5.11, if one of us felt we could lead it.

We spent three weeks in Joshua Tree, climbing every single thing, talking across the campfire at night, or just enjoying the gorgeous silence of nature.

One night late in the third week, we were sitting around the campfire. Gage was stretched out on his side, propped up on one elbow, lazily throwing sticks into the flames with his free hand.

"You work harder than anyone I've ever seen," Gage said suddenly, out of nowhere.

I glanced up at him. "What?"

"On the rock. You push yourself like..." He trailed off, shook his head. "I don't even know."

"Well...thanks."

"You know how hard it is for someone to get to working on 5.11s?" he asked. "You know how long that usually takes?"

"Um, no."

"Years. Not weeks."

"I'm not better than you," I said.

"Fuckin' A you're not. But I've been doing this for two years. You're way better than I was after two weeks. I've never seen anyone get so good so fast. And especially you."

"What does that mean?"

"It means I've never seen you push this hard at anything. Not your grades in school. Not in any kind of sport. Nothing. Why now?"

"I don't know. The fetch, I guess."

"Uh huh," he said, and I was reminded that Gage probably didn't believe in the fetch.

I hadn't thought about why I tried so hard at this. I could come up with a dozen reasons, but none of them seemed right. From the moment the fetch gave me the chance to be something more than ordinary me—from the moment I believed in her—I'd wanted to prove I was worthy of her trust, worthy of her magic. That I was enough.

"I feel like I'm trying to reach something," I said. "That if I just make that next move, get closer to the top, I'll reach it, you know? I'll be the person the fetch wants me to be. And every time I get to the top of a climb, I feel it, but only for a second. It's this great sense of satisfaction, like I actually *have* it for a second." I looked up at the stars overhead, past the cinders floating up from the fire. "I'm in love with the rock and the sky and my own body and my muscles and everything in the world. I feel..." I looked back at Gage. "*Full.* For a quick moment, I'm that person the fetch could love. I'm invincible."

"Yeah?"

"And then it's gone," I said. "The *something* I was chasing moves. Moves to the next route, I guess."

He watched me. "You crave the fetch's approval."

I thought about that. "I guess."

"Not anyone else's?"

"Like someone who's not a figment of my imagination? Is that what you're saying?"

He shrugged.

"Like *your* approval?" I said, smiling wryly.

"Fuck you."

"Then who?"

"Like your dad," he said.

"No," I said immediately. Vehemently.

"Okay."

I looked into the flames, and my quiet mood turned tumultuous. No way did I fucking care what my dad thought. He didn't care about what I wanted, and I didn't care about him.

Gage rolled onto his back, looking up at the stars. "Well, you're a fucking beast," he said. He didn't say anything else, and after a moment, I heard him snoring softly.

My brain felt scrambled, and I felt angry at Gage. I lay there wondering if he was right about me trying to prove something to my dad with all these crazy chances and becoming a good climber. It couldn't possibly be true. I hadn't thought of my father this whole trip.

But what Gage said seemed to stick in my mind like a sliver. It bothered me, and I kept trying to dig it out until I finally fell asleep.

The days at Joshua Tree got steadily hotter, and the traffic at the park increased. We kept climbing, and we both kept getting better, but one night, as we ate soft-shell tacos with ground beef and cheese—we'd bought a frying pan last week when we'd driven into Yucca Valley to get more food—I realized I was done with Joshua Tree.

"I'm done with Joshua Tree," I said aloud.

Gage looked up, his mouth stuffed full. "Yeah?" he managed to say around the food. He chomped vigorously, then swallowed. "Where does the fetch say we go next?"

"Nowhere. But *I* say we go to L.A."

His brow wrinkled. "L.A.? I thought this road trip was going to be all about climbing. What the hell can we climb in L.A.?"

"I've got something to do. I have to visit my brother."

"Dude, your brother's a wastoid. Didn't he go to L.A. to join Mötley Crüe?"

"More or less."

He made a face. "You know, Ryan isn't even a headbanger name. He's not going to become rock star with a name like Ryan. Gotta be Mick or Nick or Fang or something. So is he part of the Crüe yet?"

I chuckled. "No."

"Why we visiting him, then?" Gage shoved another big bite into his mouth.

"He didn't come to Mom's funeral."

Gage paused for a second. "Yeah. I spotted that."

"I'm going to find out why."

He looked dubious. "That doesn't sound like much fun. I thought this road trip was supposed to be fun."

"Yeah, but he's going to remember Mom, even if I have to drive to L.A. to make him."

"I get it now," Gage said. "Fetch said to do all the things you wanted to do."

"*Want* isn't the word. I think I *need* to do it."

"Fuckin' A." Gage said.

I lay back on the ground, looking up at the incredible stars, soaking up everything I could of our last night in Joshua Tree.

CHAPTER 11

We weren't even thirty minutes out of Joshua Tree when Gage got pulled over for speeding. The cop got out of his car and strode toward us. His mirror sunglasses made him seem like a stereotype from some bad movie. I didn't think cops actually wore those. I remember Uncle Morty laughing at the portrayal of cops in mirrored sunglasses. He'd always worn a completely normal pair when he drove, and he said he always took them off when he pulled someone over.

The cop informed Gage he was going 78 in a 65 mile-an-hour zone, and could he please see Gage's license and registration. As the cop was writing out the ticket, I felt betrayed. We hadn't run afoul of anything like this since we'd begun the journey. Wasn't my fetch supposed to be protecting us? Wasn't she supposed to make us invincible?

The cop tore off the ticket and handed it to Gage.

"Keep it under the limit, son," he said. Gage didn't say anything. He just waited until the cop started back toward his car.

Gage fired up the engine and pulled out before the cop. His knuckles were white on the steering wheel, but I was happy to see that he didn't peel out or race away.

"The hell happened to your fetch?" he said. "A speeding

ticket? Really? She'll let us tear out of your driveway with a state trooper just standing with his dick in his hand, but we can get a fucking speeding ticket? Where's our invincibility now?"

I shrugged. "Maybe she thinks Los Angeles sucks."

"You suck," he said.

"You're the one with the ticket."

"Fucker."

"Who can predict the ways of the fetch?" I said, trying to play off my own annoyance by poking fun.

"I thought you were the one saying."

"I don't make the rules," I said, shrugging and turning my palms upward helplessly. "I just dance."

"I think you're full of shit."

I just grinned at him, trying on that shark smile he liked so much.

It was only a few hours to get to L.A. from Joshua Tree, but we meandered after getting pulled over, turning it into half a day's journey. Gage and I spent the time with the windows down, letting the hot air blast us while drinking Cokes from big fountain-drink cups we'd gotten at 7-11.

As we neared L.A., the traffic built and we could see the haze of smog over the sprawling metropolis. The deeper we got into the smog and traffic and people, the more claustrophobic I felt. This place was exactly where I didn't want to be, and I knew Gage felt the same. We both swore we would never live in big cities.

"So where are we going, exactly?" Gage asked, thumbing through the Rand McNally road atlas to find the blown-up map of L.A.

A motorcycle whizzed past his door going 20 miles-an-hour faster than us, squeezing between the cars. "Jesus!" He yanked his arm in from the window. "They're allowed to do that?"

"Do I look like a traffic cop?" I asked.

"Damn. Now I kinda want a motorcycle." He grinned.

"UCLA," I said, answering his previous question. "We're going to UCLA."

"No way does Ryan go to UCLA," Gage said.

"He's a janitor there. His friend's dad hooked him up with the job."

"Wait, he's a janitor? Not a rock star?" Gage chuckled. "Burn."

"Don't rip on my brother."

"I thought you were here to rip on your brother."

"Me, yes. You don't."

"Whatever, man."

We reached the UCLA campus and parked. Oddly, once we got on campus, the noise, the traffic, and the smog seemed to vanish.

"This is beautiful," I said.

"It's a college campus. They're all beautiful," Gage said. "Big stone buildings. Trees. Grass. What I want to know is where all the girls in bikinis are."

I looked over at him.

He pointed at a couple of girls walking toward us. "These girls have clothes on. I thought everyone in L.A. walked around in bikinis."

"Shut up, Gage."

I fell into a funk after my initial wonder at the campus. I longed for this kind of experience. This collegiate atmosphere, the students strolling across the green for summer sessions— focused on their studies—it suddenly hit home how none of it was in the cards for me. I felt an ache, and suddenly I was back in my house, clenching that useless acceptance letter to The Colorado College.

"Come on," I said to Gage, and started walking.

"There *are* quite a few mini-skirts, though," he said, turning and looking around appreciatively as he walked.

We wandered around for about an hour—admiring both the architecture and the mini-skirts—before we got down to business and searched for the admin building. A nice receptionist directed us to the math building, where we found my brother Ryan pushing a wide dust mop across the polished tile floor. His wavy dark hair, which he usually wore loose down to his waist, was tied back in a relatively neat—for him—ponytail. He had on a blue collared shirt with his name on a little patch over his left breast, and he was jamming to a Walkman clipped to his belt, oblivious to our approach. He was in a different world than everyone else around him, which was typical Ryan.

Gage and I walked right up to him and he didn't see us until his broom hit my feet.

He looked up. "Oh, sorry dude," he said, and slid the mop around to the side of us. He was already past us when he stopped, then spun back.

"Dude!" he exclaimed.

"Hey Ryan."

"What the hell are you doing here, dude?"

"I go here now, didn't you know?" I said.

"You do not," he said dubiously, turning his head to the side while his eyes stayed on me.

"No, you spazz. I came to see you."

"Oh," he said, and I think he started to think about all of the reasons I might come visit him. Probably none of them were good. "Yeah?" he said hesitantly.

"We need to talk about Mom," I said.

"Ah hell." He looked up the long hallway nervously like he wished he were closer to the doors so he could bolt.

"Ryan, you weren't even at her funeral."

"Yeah, no, I know. Look, I know you're probably mad or whatever, but it's not..." Again, he looked up the hallway. "I can't really talk right now. I gotta finish all the stuff on this floor, and I only have an hour left to my shift. So I gotta get this done."

"I'm not leaving, Ryan. I drove all the way out here."

He looked at Gage, then at me like he couldn't figure the pair of us out, why we'd come all this way just for him. Gage crossed his muscular arms and frowned. Ryan and Gage had never gotten along. Ryan thought Gage was wound too tight, and Gage thought my brother was a weirdo.

"Hey, I tell you what." Ryan shoved his hand into his pocket and came up with a bunch of keys. He fumbled with them for a second, then slipped one off the ring. "Go to my apartment. It's in Culver City. 105 Venice Boulevard. Third floor. Apartment 3C. I'll be off in an hour, and I'll meet you there, okay?"

I hesitated.

"Seriously, man. I'm not supposed to be talking on the job, and I got two strikes already. My boss is right around the corner." He pointed. "If he sees me talking to you, he's going to freak. Just do me this favor. Go to my apartment. Raid the fridge. Grab a beer. We can talk about Mom when I get home if you want."

I took the key, and Gage rolled his eyes. I knew he didn't want to stay in L.A. any longer than necessary.

But we left Ryan to his work and Gage took his turn at the wheel, drove us through L.A. to Ryan's apartment. It was a beige concrete complex with a red tile roof and over thirty units. The thing was four stories tall with no elevator.

We jogged up the steps, found 3C, and went inside. His apartment had brown carpet, beige walls to match the outside of the building, and almost no furniture. There was a ratty couch that looked like he'd gotten it off the street, a plastic yellow school chair, and a white patio furniture table with rust spots.

"Choice," Gage said sarcastically.

"Hey, he's my brother."

"How many times you going to use that line?"

I didn't answer, just moved further into the apartment. A sliding glass door led out to the balcony, and I could see a few palm trees outside, their fronds just a little higher than the balcony. To the right of that was the kitchen. It had blue and white linoleum tiles and formica counters.

Gage went to the sliding glass door, unlocked it, and opened it to the humid air. He stepped out and stayed for all of twenty seconds before coming back in and saying, "That view isn't nearly enough to make this trip worth it." He went to the fridge. "At least we scored some free beer out of the deal—" He stopped talking, frowned, then reached in and brought out a six pack of Heineken with only one bottle left.

"Fuckin' poser," he said, holding up the nearly-empty six-pack. "'Have a beer, dudes. On me. Eat whatever you want, too.' He's got one beer. And half a brown lime and a jar of mayo. Want some mayo?" He rummaged around inside the fridge. "Wait! He's got soy sauce and ketchup packets, too."

"All right, let's just wait for him," I said.

He opened the beer, went over and sat down on the carpet. I looked down at him curiously.

He nodded at the ratty couch and took a swig of the beer. "I'm not sitting on that thing."

I sat cross-legged on the ground next to him, and he passed the bottle to me. It was cold and it tasted awesome.

"Silver lining," I said, raising the bottle. We drank the beer, then reminisced for close to an hour, talking about the Joshua Tree climbs, and Zion too.

Gage grunted. "So once we're done with the Mom talk with your headbanger brother, we're leaving, right?"

"You don't want to stay the night?"

"Eat me."

I laughed. "No trip to Disneyland?"

"Joshua Tree *was* Disneyland."

"You're chomping at the bit. Do you have our next destination in mind?"

"Yosemite. The only obvious choice."

"What's in Yosemite?"

"What's in...?" Gage stuttered. He shook his head. "And you call yourself a climber."

"As of last month. Don't be a dick."

"It's got Half Dome. It's got El Cap. It's big time."

"Yeah?"

"Big time pro time."

"Half Dome's the one in all those black and white posters?" I snapped my fingers. "Ansel Adams. The Ansel Adams posters. It's, like, sliced down the middle?"

"Like half of a dome, fuck nuts."

"And what's El Cap?"

"El Capitan. It's only the hardest climb in the whole world. It's all 5.13s and 5.14s."

"Get out."

"Multi-pitch."

"Jesus. Could we even attempt that?"

"Fuck no."

"What about Half Dome?"

"Maybe. It's all over the place, from what I read. 5.8s up to 5.12s."

"That sounds more our speed."

"It's also tall as fuck. Two-day climb."

"Two days? How do you do that?"

"Portaledges."

"What's that?"

"A tent that hangs from an anchor," he said. "You spend the night on the rock, hang there like a spider." He made a motion with his hand, fingers splayed and hovering in the air.

My heart beat faster. "Righteous."

"We'll have to get some portaledges when we get there."

"They have a store where you can get climbing equipment in Yosemite?"

"They got everything, man. It's like the mecca of climbing."

"Done. That's where we're—"

The door handle rattled and the door opened. Ryan came in, holding another six-pack of Heineken under his arm. His hair was down now, a true heavy metal mane, and he flung it back, then closed the door. "Hey thanks for waiting. I really am on thin ice at work."

"Sure," I said.

"You got my key?" he asked.

I tossed it to him, and he caught it with his free hand, fumbled, then caught it again before it hit the floor.

Gage rolled his eyes. "All right," he said. "You girls have your heart-to-heart. I'll wait outside." He lifted two beers from Ryan's six-pack as he headed out the door.

Then it was just Ryan and me. He popped the cap off one of the beers, put the rest in the fridge. He was about to raise it to his lips when I held out my hand.

He gave a little frown, watching his six-pack dwindle before his eyes, then reluctantly handed the beer to me.

"Hey...I meant to come to Mom's funeral," he said, pulling another beer from the fridge and opening it. "I mean, I wanted to be there."

"Then why weren't you?"

"There was a... I had a thing."

"A thing?"

"I couldn't get out of my job."

I let out a sigh. "That's exactly what Dad said."

"They'd have fired me."

"Bullshit. They give people time off for funerals, Ryan. Every job does that. You could have made it if you'd wanted."

His eyes glistened, and he looked down. "Look, I couldn't..."

"You couldn't what? I was there alone. You know who showed up? About twenty of Mom's friends. But not her husband or her oldest son. Even Gage was there, but not you. What the hell, man?"

"I'm sorry."

"Don't fucking apologize to me. Apologize to her."

"I just didn't want to..." He trailed off.

"You think this is about what *you* wanted?"

"I didn't want her to be dead!" he shouted, and he looked up at me. "She can't be dead because she...she can't."

I leaned back, stunned.

"She taught us how to... She taught us everything, man!" Ryan said. "She was always following her dreams, even when... You know, even when they didn't work out. She's the reason I'm out here trying to make it. I just... I couldn't... I felt like if I went there, then it was real, you know?" he said. "And I couldn't see her like that." He went and fell onto his ratty couch, took a long chug of the beer. "I don't want her to be dead."

"You think I do?"

"Yeah well, if I'm out here and the funeral's in Colorado, I could still...imagine she was there, you know. At least for a little while. Imagine she's just late for our weekly call."

I thought about my reaction to Mom's death. Maybe it wasn't all that different from Ryan's. I'd seen my whole world coming apart, and what did I do? I'd thought of graduation, of summer, of Tina Cartwright in a bathing suit, anything to take my mind away from the horrible truth.

"Hey," Ryan said. He raised his bottle. "To Mom."

"To Mom," I said softly, clacking my bottle against his.

We drank in silence for a time, then I said, "I didn't just come here to be pissed at you, man. I have something for you. Something Mom would want you to have."

I pulled a keychain with no keys on it from my pocket. It wasn't for the Pumpkin—Gage had the Pumpkin's key—but it was something I'd been carrying for Ryan since Durango. The keychain was a Gibson guitar painted like the Union Jack with the words "Hard Rock Cafe" emblazoned on it. I tossed it to him. He caught it and looked confused.

"She bought it for you," I said. "Saw it in a little gift shop in Denver."

He swallowed, then said, "When?"

"Last year, right after you left. She was going to mail it to you, but she said every time she looked at it, it made her think of you. So she just kept not sending it, ended up using it herself. Anyway, they gave it to me after...you know. But you should have it."

He stared at it in his hand.

"I didn't think about you," he said after a moment. "About how you were all alone out there." He closed his fingers over the keychain. "I'm just... I'm sorry, man."

"Don't worry about it."

A knock sounded on the door. Ryan and I looked at one another, and I shrugged.

"You don't have to knock, Gage," I said. "We're done. Just come in."

The door opened, but it wasn't Gage on the other side.

It was Uncle Morty.

CHAPTER 12

"Holy shit!" I leapt to my feet.

"That's about sums it up," Uncle Morty said, entering the room and closing the door behind him.

I glanced at the door handle as he locked it. He held my gaze as he deliberately reached up and threw the deadbolt, then twirled the handcuffs in his left hand.

"How the hell...?" I said, stupefied.

"What are you doing here, Uncle Morty?" Ryan said, flabbergasted. He also stood up.

"Chasing this flight risk." He gestured at me. "He was supposed to be on a plane over a month ago." He didn't seem amused. But then, Uncle Morty never did. He also didn't seem angry, though the ramifications of him being in California rushed through my head.

"I'm not going to Malaysia," I said.

Uncle Morty shook his head and leaned back against the only door into or out of the apartment. "Well, that's where you're wrong. I told you before. You're a minor, and that's not your choice to make."

"How the... How the hell did you find me?" I stammered.

"'Cause I've been a cop longer than you've been a fugitive, son. You get a speeding ticket, it shows up in the system. Tell your friend not to speed in the desert, you don't want to get caught. I was actually having a hard time finding you before that."

"That was, like, six hours ago!"

Uncle Morty just watched me.

"I figured there weren't too many places you could go in L.A., and one of them was definitely going to be your brother's apartment." He paused. "So, here's what we're going to do. The three of us are going to have some good Chinese takeout and settle in. A little family meal. My treat. I hear L.A. is supposed to have good Chinese food."

"Yum," Ryan said. I glared at him.

"Then tomorrow you and I are going to LAX," Uncle Morty gestured to me. "Put you on a plane."

"No," I said. My heart beat faster.

"This plays out two ways, son. You calm down, and we have a nice time. Reminisce and all. Or you try to get past me, and I use these." He spun the cuffs on his finger again.

"Why are you running from him?" Ryan asked.

"I'm not going to Malaysia just because Dad wants me to," I said. "No fucking way."

"Well, what else are you going to do?" Ryan asked.

"Shut up, Ryan," I said.

"Which will it be?" Uncle Morty asked.

I wanted to make a break for the door, but Uncle Morty was right in front of it. And he was ready. He looked like he expected me to try it.

My shoulders slumped and the wind went out of me.

Uncle Morty read my body language like he was reading a book. He spun the cuffs on his fingers, then slipped them into his pocket. "Good choice, son." He glanced at our beers, then said, "Got another one of those, Ryan?"

"In the fridge," Ryan said.

Uncle Morty went into the kitchen, slow and relaxed, but his gaze never left me as he opened the fridge and grabbed a beer. I seriously thought about bolting for the door, but I knew I'd never make it. Not with the lock and deadbolt set. It would take two twists, then a third for the handle. That was plenty of time for Uncle Morty to stop me.

I swallowed.

Uncle Morty came out of the kitchen, took a swig of the beer, and I wilted. He was even closer to the door now. If I'd ever had a chance, I'd missed it.

Then I saw movement behind Uncle Morty, out on the balcony near the bottom of the rail. At first I thought it was a bird, but it was long and thin. I thought maybe it was a strange leaf or something—

And then I realized it was a rope. A hand rose into view, looping the rope around the metal bar, then pulling it through.

Like a top rope on a climb.

My heart started hammering. I made myself look at Uncle Morty—who was facing away from the whole thing—so he wouldn't notice me staring at the balcony.

"So what's a good Chinese restaurant around here?" Uncle Morty asked.

"Jade Palace," Ryan said immediately, like he ate there all the time, excited only at the prospect of a free meal, not that Uncle Morty wanted to ship me off to Malaysia—in cuffs if need be.

I looked down at my beer, then raised it to my lips, chugging it while trying not to seem like I was. I finished it and lowered it to my lap.

"Why don't you get your menu and make the order," Uncle Morty told Ryan. "Like I said, my treat."

"Fine," I said, trying to sound defeated-but-game-for-a-family-dinner. "But get some more beer too, okay? I'm taking the last one." I held up my empty bottle. "If I have to go to Malaysia, I'm going with a hangover."

Uncle Morty actually smiled at that.

I stood up, and his face returned to that stony expression. He went back to the locked door and leaned against it.

Which is exactly what I'd hoped he'd do.

I went past him, trying to keep my stride normal, but when I reached the kitchen, I put on a burst of speed.

I ran through the open sliding glass doorway and vaulted over the rail, hanging on tight with my hands. My feet hit the deck on the other side and I grabbed a fistful of the rope.

"Son," Uncle Morty said as he walked toward me, not seeming in a rush. "You're just going to hurt yourself—" He cut himself off.

That must have been when he saw the rope.

He lunged toward the balcony just as I pushed away. I rappelled down with my bare hands, kicking the second floor balcony and pushing out again, lowering as I went.

The rope burned fiercely, but my callouses helped. I kept going.

Uncle Morty reached the edge of the balcony and stared in shock as I landed on the ground.

"The rope!" Gage shouted. I glanced over my shoulder to find him behind the wheel of The Pumpkin, engine revving.

Uncle Morty stood there paralyzed, stunned that I'd just jumped off a balcony and maybe wondering whether he should jump after me.

I took the choice away from him.

Gage had looped the rope around the bar on Ryan's balcony, then pulled it so it was equal length to the ground, creating a double rope just like on a climbing route. In doing so, he'd also created an easy release. I yanked hard on one side of the double rope, and the slack side slithered up and around the bar before Uncle Morty realized what I was doing. He made a grab for it, too late.

I ran to The Pumpkin, gathering the rope as I went, then leapt through the open passenger door.

Gage peeled out. The door slammed, and we booked it.

CHAPTER 13

The sun was setting as we drove toward the freeway. Gage turned the lights on and stayed prudently under the speed limit to avoid drawing the attention of any actual L.A. cops.

I turned to Gage. "Dude!" I said. "The rope? That was genius."

"Nice rappel," he said. "How are your hands?"

"Uncle Morty's going to be right behind us. We've got maybe a couple minutes' head start."

"I don't think so," Gage said.

"What? No!" I looked between us. A circular distributor cap, rubber wires sticking out of it, sat on the bench seat. "Gage!"

"Guy needs to put a lock on his hood. Damn vandals."

Uncle Morty was going to shit himself.

We hit the 405 and headed north. With every second that passed, I expected to hear sirens. I didn't know what kind of pull a Colorado state trooper would have in L.A., but it was probably enough to get an APB out on us, assuming Uncle Morty wanted to take it that far.

But then the 405 turned into I-5, and both Gage and I started to breathe easier. Soon we were out of L.A., and no one had pulled us over.

"So, Yosemite, huh?" I said.

"Unless you have another plan," he said.

"How far?" I asked.

"About five hours. Please tell me you didn't tell your dweeb brother where we were going," Gage said. "He'd give us up in a second."

"I didn't tell him squat. Not about Yosemite, anyway, or even Joshua Tree or Zion. We didn't talk climbing at all."

Gage grinned. "Righteous."

We talked for a while, letting the adrenaline settle, then decided we didn't want to drive into Yosemite at midnight, so we stopped at a hotel just outside of Bakersfield. With all the day's events, we crashed hard and didn't wake up until noon. We killed a little more time in the hotel, eating potato chips and drinking Cokes and talking about the climbs at Joshua Tree. Finally, around one o'clock, we got back on the road.

The hours went by as my thoughts gradually settled down, and I listened to the hum of The Pumpkin's engine. I just loved the open road. I shook Gage awake when we reached the park entrance.

As we drove into Yosemite National Park, I was thunderstruck. Zion and Joshua Tree were desert climates—sandstone and metamorphic rock—but this was like some lush faerie land with towering granite castles all around.

"God," I murmured.

"That's El Cap right there," Gage said.

I strained, trying to keep one eye on the road and one on the cliff that just seemed to go up and up forever.

We kept driving, turned another corner, and Half Dome came into view. It was just like every picture I'd ever seen, monstrously tall and...majestic. My heart beat faster. The idea of climbing that thing seemed impossible.

"Welcome to granite," Gage said. "Crack climbing at its best. Big time walls."

I leaned over the steering wheel, gazing up.

"You up for it?" he asked.

"Gotta inspire the fetch, don't we?" I replied.

"Fuckin' A, dude."

As we drove into Yosemite Valley, we saw cars coming out, other cars behind us. We definitely weren't going to have *this* place all to ourselves.

We passed a complex called Curry Village that had a restaurant, and Gage hung out the window. "God, I can smell the pizza," he said.

We'd been living off tortillas, beans, lunchmeat, and Dinty Moore for two months now. The one thing I'd been looking forward to about L.A. was getting a good meal, and we hadn't had time.

The sun was going down already. It couldn't have been past four o'clock, but the valley was so socked in between these gorgeous mountains that it felt like twilight.

I pulled into the parking lot and stopped the car. There were already quite a few people going into the Curry Village Pizza Patio. The restaurant had a big red wooden deck that held about twenty tables with umbrellas that had been folded down. I was just as intoxicated by the smell as Gage. "You go get us a table," I said. "I'll find a campsite."

"You're the man." He hopped out of The Pumpkin, slammed the door. "I'm getting a bucket of fries." He leaned down and winked. "I'll try to save you one or two."

I just smiled and drove on.

When I reached the campground desk, I discovered that Curry Village gets booked up months in advance. All the regular campsites were long gone. However, there had just been a last-minute cancellation. There was one tent cabin available.

I paid the attendant and she told me I was in cabin #27, then I hauled our stuff out there. The tent cabin was a wooden frame structure with tan canvas stretched over it. I opened the spring door and looked inside. There were two cots with mattresses and a wooden plank floor painted army green. I dropped our packs and fell onto one of the beds.

I moaned and closed my eyes. I'd gotten a taste of having a real bed last night in the hotel, and it was glorious. My thoughts drifted, and I took a moment to just relax. I flashed back to our narrow escape from Uncle Morty in L.A. That had been close. I thought about UCLA, about how I so wanted to go to CC.

Then I was talking to the campground attendant again, paying for this tent. She smiled and suddenly she was the fetch, her red hair twining down to her shoulders, and she winked at me.

I jolted awake and sat upright. It was dark inside the tent cabin.

"Fuck!"

I'd fallen asleep and Gage had no idea where I was. He'd have no way to find me. I rummaged through my pack until I found my little portable clock. I blinked wearily, trying to believe what it was showing me. Its glow-in-the-dark numbers told me it was 9:00 p.m.

"Dammit!" I shouted. "Fuckshitpissergoddamn it!"

I shook my head to clear it and headed back outside. It was dark now, but the walk to Curry Village was short and the paths were well-marked.

I arrived at the restaurant just as they were closing up.

Gage was nowhere to be found. There was no one around, in fact. The only person left was a tall skinny guy wearing a tie-dye T-shirt, jeans, and grimy tennis shoes. He had curly blond hair tied into a snarled ponytail at the back of his head and a short apron tied around his waist. That apron had once been white but was now covered with charcoal smears, spaghetti sauce, and other stuff I couldn't identify. I asked him if he'd seen Gage.

"I don't think so, man," the guy said. His eyelids hung half shut. He looked exhausted. Or wasted.

"He's about five-nine," I said. "Pretty ripped. Brown hair."

"Dude, you just described every climber who comes here to take a shot at the Dome. I can't help you. I gotta sleep."

I sighed as he pulled the rolling gate down to the counter and locked it. He ambled across the wooden deck, then stopped as he got to the steps and snapped his fingers.

"Actually, man... Come to think of it, I saw Winsley talking to some climber dude. *He* had brown hair."

I perked up again. "About this tall?" I held my hand up.

"I don't know man. He was sitting down." The guy shrugged. "But he was ripped like you say."

"Who's Winsley?"

"You don't know Winsley?" the guy asked.

"I just got here tonight," I said.

"Oh. She's a waitress. You'd know her if you saw her."

"I would? Why?"

"Cause she's fuckin' hot, dude. And she's a climber, too, so they probably hit it off."

"A climber? Really?"

"Totally. Most dudes come out here thinking they're all that, but Winsley smokes 'em. She's pretty badass."

I was beginning to think tie-dye guy had a crush on Winsley. But maybe that was a lucky break for me. After all, he'd noticed the guy she was with.

"Where is she now?"

"What, I'm gonna tell you where she sleeps? I don't know you." He shook his head. "For all I know, you could be Mr. Creepy Ex-boyfriend. But hey, if that *was* your friend, he's probably not hurtin', you know what I'm saying? Look for him in the morning. Curry Village ain't a big place."

And with that, tie-dye guy walked off into the darkness.

Well, leave it to Gage to gravitate to the hottest girl in the valley and then go home with her. Dejected, I made my way back to cabin #27, shoveled down a distinctly uninspired meal of tortillas, butter, and water. Once I'd eaten, I fell onto the bed and crashed hard again.

I was vaguely aware, many hours later, when the canvas walls of the tent started to glow with sunlight. The bed was so comfortable compared to the rock I'd been sleeping on that I didn't ever want to leave. The newly-risen sun warmed the tent, and it was awesome. I ignored the light and drifted back to sleep.

A thumping shocked me back awake.

Disoriented, it took me a second to remember where I was, then another to remember where the tent cabin's door was. I got pointed in the right direction and staggered to it, pulled it open.

Gage stood there with a girl. She wore a purple and green jog bra over loose and ripped jeans with a hole in the right knee. The laces of her hiking boots were loose, as if she wore them like slippers. Her long brown hair was tied back in a messy ponytail that somehow looked perfect, and she had a big pack slung over one shoulder. I could see a coil of rope peeking out the top. Climbing equipment. Winsley.

Tie-dye guy had been right. Fuck me, she was hot.

I looked at Gage, then at the girl, then back at Gage.

Gage got that shark's smile, and he glanced at the girl. "Winsley, this is my friend Captain Underwear. Captain Underwear, this is Winsley."

I looked down and realized I'd opened the door wearing only my tighty whities.

"Fuck!" I leapt back into the cabin, letting the door slam. "Hang on!"

I heard them both laughing as I jammed my feet into my rumpled jeans. I should have sat down first, but I didn't, so of course in my haste my feet got tangled up in the pantlegs. I fell over, cursing.

Their laughter erupted louder.

I finally managed to get the jeans on, pulled on a relatively clean T-shirt, and I opened the door again.

"S-Sorry," I said, looking at Winsley. She held my gaze for a second, then looked away.

"That's okay," Gage brushed past me into the tent cabin. "I already told her you're a dweeb."

My face felt hot, and I knew I had to be blushing. Mortified, I held the door open for Winsley, and she followed Gage into the cabin. She looked around for a second, her blue gaze darting to my rumpled bed, the strewn contents of my pack, and then to the made bed on the other side of the cabin. She went and sat down on it as Gage knelt next to his pack and rummaged around.

"It's almost nine," Gage said as he pulled his harness and some quickdraws from his pack. "Time to hit the rock."

"Uh, yeah," I said, trying to look anywhere but at Winsley when that's the only place I wanted to look.

I'd never seen a girl rock climber before. Her hands were calloused, strong, with the nails cut short, and her blue-eyed gaze seemed to cut through the darkness. And oh-my-God, what a body. I'd seen girl athletes before, but they were usually long and lean. Winsley had curves and muscles together, with a definition to her arms and shoulders that made me think I'd never before seen the best of what a girl's body could be.

God, I thought to myself. *Get it together. It's like you've never seen a girl before!*

"Winsley knows the best routes," Gage said. "Quiet ones where we can avoid the fucking masses and just climb."

"Oh," I said. "Okay. Well, have fun."

Gage stopped what he was doing and looked up. "Fuck you with your 'have fun.' You're coming with us."

I glanced at Winsley, then back at Gage. "Oh. Okay."

Gage rolled his eyes, then went back to rummaging in his pack. "You'll have to forgive numbnuts here. He never made it past the adolescent tit-worship stage. Boobs get in the way of him forming a coherent sentence."

My eyes went wide, and I shot a horrified glance at Winsley. She looked down at her hands, an amused smile on her face.

I glared back at Gage, who had his back to me. If my face was red before, it had to be purple now. I'd never wanted to hit him more than I did right then.

I swallowed and tried to salvage some composure.

"You'll have to forgive Gage," I said. "He never got past the adolescent *asshole* stage."

Gage grinned over his shoulder, pointing and nodding at me as if agreeing.

Still mortified, I gathered my climbing gear, grabbed a granola bar and some beef jerky, and didn't say a thing. We headed out, and Winsley led the way, taking the marked trails with confidence, then breaking off the path onto a little beaten trail I'd have walked right past.

She ranged ahead of us, sometimes about five feet away and sometimes about thirty. At one point when she was far enough ahead that I thought she was out of earshot, I tugged on Gage's pack.

He looked over his shoulder.

"What the fuck, man?" I whispered harshly.

He looked confused and stopped.

"No, keep walking, you idiot." I pushed him up the trail to get him walking again. "I just meant..." I tipped my chin at Winsley. "You couldn't leave me a scrap of dignity in front of the most beautiful girl in the world?"

He glanced at her and grinned. "Pretty hot, right?"

I rolled my eyes and mouthed, "Oh my God!"

"Met her last night at the pizza place. I waited for you, but you never showed."

"I...fell asleep."

"I thought you'd gone night climbing without me. I was going to kick your ass. Glad I was wrong. Anyway, I ate all the fries."

I laughed. "And Winsley just fell into your lap?"

"She was talking about climbing in Zion, describing it to some guy who was bragging on himself. I overheard and I corrected her."

"You what?"

"Yeah, she was talking about Tourist Crack when she really meant Flapjack Crack. Should'a seen the sneer she gave me. I thought she was going to pour a drink on my head."

"Did she?"

"Naw. She came over to my table and told me I was full of shit. I told her I definitely was, but that I was right about Flapjack. I said I never forget a 5.10 if I'm leading it."

"*I* led that climb."

"So fuck you for not being there. You want to brag to hot chicks, don't leave your friend high and dry."

I couldn't argue with that.

"Anyway, when she realized I wasn't *completely* full of shit, we talked shop. Girl's got some balls. She's climbed more than you and me combined. Up in Montana. Utah. Colorado, too. She's the real deal."

"Did you..." I nodded at her, then at him.

He grinned. "You know me." He rotated his hips in an exaggerated circle that ended with three pelvic thrusts. "I never kiss and tell."

"You're a fuckwad."

Winsley turned around at that moment, almost as though she knew what we were talking about. She cocked her hips, put her hands on them and called back, "You coming or not?"

Gage winked at me and hiked to catch up with her.

We finally reached the place Winsley wanted to climb and, true to Gage's promise, there was no one else around. Winsley dropped her pack, pulled out the pro she wanted, hooked them into her belt, then turned. She looked at me first, then at Gage.

"You boys warmed up? Ready to play?" she asked.

Gage grinned. "Whenever. You leading?"

"My route. My lead," she said.

He bowed low. "After you." He looped the rope through his figure 8, clipped it into his locking D-ring, and tugged on his break hand. She set her foot and hooked her fingers into her first hold.

"On belay?" she asked over her shoulder.

"Belay is on," he replied.

"Climbing."

"Climb on, dude."

Winsley started up slowly and smoothly, like she'd done this her whole life. I'd watched Gage a hundred times, always impressed by how he could muscle his way up and over things when he needed to. The guy had no end of upper body strength, it seemed, pulling off moves that required amazing amounts of grunt and effort. I was always striving to keep up with him, but I just wasn't that strong.

Watching Winsley was completely different. It was like she was doing some kind of modern dance. I saw her do a grunt move just once, working an off-width crack—a crack useless for pro—with a hand jam. She just crammed her fist in the crack and clenched it to hold her weight. But the rest of the time, she worked her legs, catching a tiny ledge with her climbing shoe, then swinging into it, working her thigh muscles and sparing her arms.

Don't get me wrong. The girl had impressive upper body strength. That hand jam was righteous, but most of the time she kept her arms straight, clinging to micro-ledges with her fingertips and using her arms like pendulums while her legs did the work. It was beautiful.

My mouth was open by the time she reached the top. She climbed over, out of sight, then her head appeared at the edge. She grinned down at us.

"It goes, boys. It goes." She laughed. Once she secured the top rope, she clipped in and rappelled down to us, smoothly dropping, stopping, collecting her pro, then dropping to the next site.

When she reached the bottom, she unclipped and winked at us. "I think you'll like this one."

"That was amazing," I said.

She stuck her tongue out and bit it gently. "Let's see how you do."

"I'm next," Gage said. He grabbed the end of the rope and tied in.

"On belay?" he asked.

I stepped up to belay, worked the rope through my figure 8. "Belay is on," I said.

"Climbing."

"Climb on, dude."

Gage started up. It was fascinating to see how he worked the same problems Winsley had in completely different ways, relying on his tremendous arm strength instead of his legs. All this time, I'd tried to emulate Gage, but now I wondered what it would be like if I tried Winsley's brand of climbing. I could probably never compete with Gage's arm strength, not if I had a million years to work out. But if I combined Winsley's arm-saving techniques... Well, the thought had possibilities—

"So Gage says you've got a death wish." Winsley interrupted my train of thought. "Intrepid swashbuckler type."

"H-He did?" I stammered.

"Wouldn't stop talking about you. I finally had to kiss him just to shut him up."

"Is...uh, is that why you kissed him?"

She watched me for a second, amused, then she gave a crooked smile, like she could see right through me. "Is that why you keep that wooden sword by your bed in the tent cabin? Remind you to be brave?"

"Um...I don't know," I said, uncomfortable at just how close she was hitting the mark. What had Gage been telling her? Why did he have to bring the sword into it?

"You don't seem like the daredevil he describes," she said.

"Daredevil? Well, um—"

"Surfing on top of your car going down the highway?" she said.

"Oh, that."

"Jumping for that ledge in Canyonlands? Pretty flash. Did you really do that?"

"Well, uh, that was... I was scared and...you know." I suddenly wondered if Gage had told her about the fetch, too. I really didn't like the idea of that.

"Are you always this shy? Or is Gage right about what he said in the tent? Would you talk to me if I didn't have boobs?"

"What?" I blurted. "No! I mean yes. I mean, I'm talking to you right now." My face felt uncomfortably hot again.

She laughed. "Okay, Thunderstruck. I'll leave you alone. Besides, I think Gage is done."

I looked up. Gage had reached the top. I'd been unconsciously feeding slack as he went, but taking my eyes off him for so long was totally crap behavior for a belayer. I hastily made the rope taut just as he backed off the wall, and I eased him back down.

"Your turn, dickwad," Gage said when he reached the bottom. He glanced at Winsley as he untied from the rope.

"That's a nice little 5.10. Is it a B or C?"

"C," Winsley said. "It's called Moonpath."

"I like it."

I roped in. Gage started to set up the belay, but Winsley took the rope from him.

"What is this, the boys' belay club?" She set up the brake through her own figure-8 and bumped Gage with her hip. "Out of the way, bystander."

He leaned in to kiss her, but she turned her head. "Not on the rock," she said. "When I'm here, I climb. That's all."

"Really?"

"Really." She gave him a steady glance. Surprised, he held up his hands and backed off. She looked at me. "You ready?"

"Um..."

"I won't let you fall," she said. "The boobs won't get in the way, I promise. You don't have to talk. Just climb."

Heat rose in my face again and I knew I was blushing. I turned to the rock and started up. As I searched, reached, grabbed, moved upward, I started thinking about Winsley's style of climbing. After the first few moves, I made an effort to change my approach.

I stopped looking for handholds. Instead, I looked for any ledge I could stick the edge of my foot onto, any crack I could jam my toe in, or any edge I could hook my heel on. I used my legs for propulsion and my arms to anchor my weight, instead of the other way around.

It felt so much smoother, and my arms didn't tire out nearly as fast. I literally got into the swing of it, and before I even realized it, I was at the top. So often by the end of a route, my arms would be pumped and useless, but not this time. I felt like I could do this all day long.

I didn't think I could feel any more euphoric about climbing, but this was a whole new level. I felt like I was dancing with the rock, moving with what it gave me instead of straining to get that next hold. I took a moment, looking out over the valley, then I let Winsley ease me back down.

I reached the bottom and she held up her hand for a high

five. I slapped it.

"That was pretty," she said.

Gage was staring at the rock like he didn't know what he'd just seen, and he was trying to work it out. "What was that?" he asked.

I glanced at Winsley, hesitated, then decided I totally needed to get over this bullshit stuttering thing when I was around her. "I watched her," I said simply. "She uses her legs a lot more than we do. So I tried it."

"And?" Gage asked.

"My arms weren't blown out when I got to the top. It was..." I gave a shy glance at Winsley. "It was great."

He looked up at the rock again and said, "Huh."

On the very next climb, Gage started trying to use his legs more. What I took to like a fish to water, he struggled with. But in true Gage fashion, he didn't give up. He kept at it. He got better.

For me, it was like I'd been climbing with only one eye open until today, and now I could see through both. I could finally see the whole picture. New possibilities opened up. When I needed to switch to a pure grunt maneuver, I did, but Winsley's way soon became my way. I felt I'd shifted into a whole new gear.

We called it quits when the sun was low in the sky and we hiked back to Curry Village.

"That was...worthwhile," Winsley said, and she sounded surprised. "Thanks for the climb."

"Worthwhile?" Gage said.

She shrugged. "We get a lot of posers in the valley. They talk big, then I get them on the rock and they flail. But you guys..." She shrugged.

"Thanks," I said.

"So, dinner at The Shack, then?" she asked.

"The what?" I asked.

"The employees don't call it the Pizza Patio," Gage explained. "It's The Shack. Which makes way more sense because they don't just serve pizza."

"So yes, then?" Winsley asked.

"Yes," Gage said.

"You can tell me all about this miracle road trip," she said. "Now that I've met Thunderstruck here, I'm into it."

"Right now?" he asked.

"Shower first, boys. Dinner after." She walked away, shouldering her pack. We both watched her hips swing as she went. She waved over her shoulder like she knew we were staring at her.

I looked away, but Gage just kept staring. "God damn," he muttered under his breath.

I completely agreed, but I didn't say anything. A deep guilt had settled into my belly.

Gage had a new girlfriend, and I was completely, head-over-heels in love with her.

CHAPTER 14

We dropped our stuff at the tent cabin, grabbed our somewhat clean towels, then headed to the shower stalls in the long cinderblock building at the end of the row.

Once we were clean and as presentable as we were going to be, we went to The Shack.

I couldn't help but wonder—if I'd gotten here first last night, if Gage had parked the car and I'd ordered burgers, maybe Winsley would be with me now instead of him.

I shook my head. It was a crappy-ass thought, and I tried to forget about it. She was with him, and I was out of luck.

We got a table after about a ten-minute wait. Gage tried to order a beer, but they carded him and told him no way.

"Can't blame me for trying," he said. He ordered a Coke instead.

Winsley showed up about ten minutes later in cutoff jean shorts and a tight green tank top with a zipper pull-down on the front. I'd resolved not to look at her in any kind of lustful way, but the sight of her stunned me. I had to glance away. This was going to be a painful dinner. What the hell was I thinking, agreeing to be a fifth wheel on this date?

"Boys," she said as she came up to the table. Gage stood up, slipped his arm around her waist and she fell into him. I think I was hoping she'd turn her head again like she had at Moonpath, but she didn't. He gave her a long, serious kiss. She pushed her fingers into his hair and everything. When he pulled back, she nibbled his lip and said, "Mmmm."

I looked down at the table.

She sat and waved for one of the servers. A short brunette with a super-cute smile came over, order pad in hand. "Winsley," she acknowledged with a nod and a smile. She glanced at me, then at Gage.

"Lisa, these are my boys." Winsley reached out and put a hand on each of our arms. "We just spent the day on the rock and we are ravenous."

"Really? Our Winsley doesn't climb with posers. They're good?" She gave an expectant look to Winsley.

"They kept up," Winsley said. "And at least one of them can kiss." She winked at Gage. "We'll try again tomorrow and see if they can repeat."

Lisa laughed. "Well, Gary just singed a pizza. It's free if you want it."

Winsley arched an eyebrow at us. "What'll it be, boys? Free burned pizza or something off the menu that costs money?"

"Pizza is like sex," Gage said. "Even when it's bad, it's still pretty good."

Winsley chuckled at that. "Gage says burned pizza. Thor?" She turned to me.

Thor?

"Um, yeah. Uh, sure."

She grinned as I fumbled over the words, and she turned a winsome smile to Lisa. "Thor gets tongue-tied talking to girls," she said. "But he's a rock god, so be nice to him."

Rock god?

"I'm always nice." Lisa pointed at us each in turn. "Coke? Coke? Coke?"

I nodded. I could feel my blush rising again.

"Thanks, Lisa," Winsley murmured, touching her arm, too.

"I gotcha covered all night," Lisa replied. "Have fun." She bustled away.

Winsley turned her blue-eyed gaze on us, and she leaned back in her chair. "So. A road trip story."

"It's better with beer, but the guy I asked turned us down. Maybe Lisa could hook us up?" Gage asked hopefully.

Winsley shook her head. "Manager's here until eight. Maybe after that?"

"I say now is better than later," Gage said, pulling a flask-sized bottle of Jack Daniel's out of his cargo-shorts pocket. He showed it to us, then lowered it and his Coke cup beneath the table with a wink. He set the cup back on the table, looked at Winsley, eyebrows raised.

She pushed her cup at him. "Do it up," she said.

He doctored her drink, gave it back, then cocked an eyebrow at me.

"Where'd you get that?" I asked.

"Do you fucking care?" Gage said.

I pushed my Coke to Gage. He took it and lowered it beneath the table. I'd never drunk whiskey before. In fact, I'd had a total of seven beers in my life, four of those at Canyonlands with Gage.

We sat back and sipped, and the taste burned down my throat.

"Okay, boys," Winsley said. "Last night Gage was talking about this epic road trip, all the way from Colorado. So spill."

I was trying to work up a version of the story that didn't involve the fetch when Gage popped off.

"Tell her about the fetch," he said.

I could have smacked him. I glared, but he just shrugged. This was Gage, after all. I wasn't going to back him down with a glare.

"What's a fetch?" Winsley asked.

I felt a foreboding in my belly, like I was in some cautionary Greek myth where if I revealed the existence of the fetch she'd vanish forever. When I'd told Gage back in Durango, I hadn't really believed in her myself yet, so I hadn't considered that I could lose anything. Now I did believe and I didn't want to mess anything up.

"Come on," Gage said. "Winsley's one of us. And the story is fuck-all without the fetch."

"I don't know if I'm supposed to talk about it," I said.

"Did she *tell* you not to talk about it?" Gage asked.

"Gage, I don't think—"

He turned to Winsley. "All this happened because some hot chick told him to follow his heart."

"Oh?" Winsley said, interested. "There's a Mrs. Thor?"

"No, she's imaginary," Gage said.

An amused smile spread across Winsley's face. "Like you have a fetch but she lives in Canada?"

I was certain my face was bright red again, but I swore I wasn't going to stumble and stutter anymore. I looked Winsley straight in her honest eyes and said, "Fine. I'll tell you. Gage would just fuck it up anyway."

He shrugged, smugly satisfied that he'd forced me into telling the story.

In a hushed voice, I told her everything, starting with the fox in my window and ending with our arrival in Yosemite. By the time I was done, we'd polished off the flask of Jack, and I was holding my fingers up in front of my face, touching the tips together and feeling how they were numb-but-not-numb at the same time.

I also wasn't worried about telling the story anymore. I was in love with Winsley, wasn't I? And if I was in love with her she ought to know about the fetch, right?

When I'd started the story, Winsley had been leaning back in her chair. Now she leaned all the way forward, elbows on the table, chin on her hands, completely focused on me. I liked the way that felt.

Winsley was quiet for a moment, then she leaned back in her chair again. "Wow."

Even with the alcohol making everything seem warm, fuzzy, and happy, I felt a stab of regret. I was suddenly sure she didn't believe a word of it. Now I wasn't just the stuttering geeky boy who blushed at the mention of boobs, but I was some big time liar too.

My euphoria faded, and I waited for her scoff like I was waiting for a hammer to fall.

She stood up, leaning over with her fingertips touching the table. The pose gave me a full view of her cleavage as she drilled me with that blue gaze. I swallowed.

"That's the sexiest thing I've ever heard in my life," she announced. She turned to Gage, took a fistful of his shirt, and pulled him to his feet. "Gage, 'you big stud, take me to bed or lose me forever,'" she said, mimicking the quote from *Top Gun.*

"'Show me the way home, honey,'" he finished, and she tugged him forward into a kiss. When they came up for air, she hooked her pinky around his and led him away from the table.

As they reached the steps, she turned and pointed at me. "Wow," she said. "Just wow."

And then they were gone, and I was left alone with an aching in the pit in my stomach.

CHAPTER 15

The next few days in Yosemite turned into the next few weeks, and they all went much the same. We got up early. All three of us went climbing. On the days that Winsley had to work, she'd kick off around noon and we'd visit her at The Shack when we finished up, always taking a table in her section. On the days she didn't have to work, we'd climb until the sun went down, then walk back to our tents exhausted and glowing.

More often than not, Gage would head off to Winsley's tent to stay the night. Sometimes she'd come to ours, but only to hang out before heading off to her own bed. I thanked the stars they did their saliva-swapping somewhere else. I don't think I could have handled that in the bed right next to me. I'd have had to spend the night in the woods.

Nights were torture, so I focused on the days, on climbing. Toward the end of the first week, at Winsley's insistence, Gage and I climbed the first few pitches of Half Dome and learned how to stay overnight on the rock face before rappelling back down. Winsley had to work, so she couldn't do the overnight, but she'd already climbed Half Dome once. She was happy to bow out.

"For now," she had said. "But we should hit it before the

end of the summer."

The first night I clipped that little portaledge into the rock face and gingerly climbed inside, I must have lain there rigid, eyes wide open, for a good hour before I relaxed enough to sleep. I felt every breeze, and though I'd trusted my weight to the ropes and carabiners day after day for weeks, I suddenly doubted them when I was hanging inside a fabric house thousands of feet off the ground.

By the third week, I led my first 5.12. I'd gotten into a groove. It was like the rock was talking to me in a foreign language I had somehow learned, and now the only place I could speak that language was when I was climbing. When I woke up, I didn't feel right until I pulled on my climbing shoes. And at the end of every day on the rock, as I stuffed my pack and started walking away, I felt a keen loss. There was simply nothing more fulfilling than climbing.

And of course, when we were climbing, Winsley was not Gage's girlfriend. That was another plus, another reason to spend every moment out there. Every now and then, he would try to cop a feel or move in for a kiss, and every time she'd rebuff him. She wasn't playful about it, either. She got dead serious and reminded him firmly that they weren't lovers when she was climbing.

In those moments, Gage was no more or less important to her than I was, and for me, a weight lifted. He and I were on equal ground as long as we were climbing.

Believe me, I was fully aware of how fucking stupid that was. She wasn't mine, and my fantasies to the contrary could never go anywhere. She still went to bed with Gage every night. And I tried—oh, I tried—to kick my desire to the curb. I tried everything I could think of.

I imagined horrible secret flaws behind her seemingly lively, open personality, like she was actually a crazy psychobitch in disguise who would end up boiling Gage's rabbit. I imagined her with warts and rashes on her perfectly smooth tanned arms, shoulders, and face.

When that didn't work, I imagined her and Gage married, a

ring on her finger. Absolutely forbidden.

I even tried to invoke Tina Cartwright, tried to remember how perfect I'd thought she was. But I could barely picture her face now. The only face that popped into my daydreams was Winsley's.

Every day I spent with her only showcased how awesome she was. I lived for the next piece of information she'd drop about her past. Climbing lit me up like nothing I'd ever experienced before, but a close second was standing with Winsley on the ground as she told me about her life while Gage was on route.

She was from Montana, the only daughter of a ranching family. She had four older brothers, and she said that was probably why she was more comfortable around guys than girls. She confessed that Lisa was the exception to that rule because Lisa didn't play emotional games like most girls did. Lisa and Winsley had been best friends since her first week in Yosemite.

She'd just finished high school like Gage and I. She'd mentioned that her school friends were beach-hopping for their last high school summer. But Winsley had decided, rather than spending sun-soaked days in a bikini on some Mexican coast drinking herself stupid, to spend her summer in Yosemite, which she kept referring to as "the most beautiful place on Earth."

And then there was the day that she dropped my jaw and told me that, after her last hurrah in the "most beautiful place on Earth," she was going to attend CC in the fall.

It hit me like a brick. Winsley and I were so alike we'd picked the same school as our top choice before we'd even met. In a different life, we would have gone to the same college, moved into our next stage of life in the exact same place.

But everything was different now. I wasn't going to college. I didn't get a "next stage."

Up until that moment, I'd kept myself blissfully blind to the inevitable end of my summer pact. But knowing that Winsley would be at CC in the fall shone a light on my decreasing number of days. In a little more than two weeks, I'd be eighteen. And I'd be dead.

I'd bargained with the fetch for a perfect summer and she had delivered. With the exception of my ill-fated crush on Winsley, this entire journey had been a legendary rush. A monument to breaking limits. I marveled that it had already been two and a half months since I'd started this. Two and a half months... It had gone in a flash.

And soon it would be my turn to pay up.

Today was Tuesday. My birthday was exactly two weeks away. Wow. Two Tuesdays from now, I'd be dead. I reflected on all of this as I crested the end of my last climb of the day, which was Moonpath. We had returned to the hidden route Winsley had shown us that first day I'd met her. Currently, she was belaying me, and I took a moment to soak in the view, just resting on belay. That fleeting moment of invincibility filled me. I was part of everything I looked at. I was larger than life.

Winsley held the rope. She had a sense for when I needed a moment up here, soaking it all in. I think she appreciated my top-of-the-route introspections.

Finally, I glanced down. It was an unspoken sign between us. She began to lower me. When my feet touched the ground, I worked at the knot, and I noticed Gage wasn't there.

"What happened to Gage?" I asked.

"His beloved," she said.

Gage called his favorite cam—a #1 size Camalot— his "beloved." One of the wires inside the release mechanism had broken two days ago. He'd been in mourning ever since.

"He's beating it with a rock?" I asked, looking around.

"Harm his 'beloved?' Perish the thought." She worked the rope out of her figure 8. "He bailed to see if he could get it repaired at the rock shop."

"Before it closes," I said, finally getting it. The sun was almost down.

"It's good, though," she said. "It'll give us a moment alone. I wanted to tell you something."

My hands froze on the knot.

She looked pensive, staring at me like I was a puzzle she wasn't sure how to solve.

Oh God. My throat tightened. This was the moment she gave me "the talk," some well-meaning words about how she knew that I liked her, but that she was with Gage. That she was so sorry. She just didn't think of me that way and could I please stop mooning over her and staring at her breasts whenever I thought she wasn't looking?

I swallowed, and my heart constricted. I cleared my throat. "O-Oh, you wanted to talk to me?" I stammered.

Oh great, Stuttering Stanley was back.

But she didn't seem to notice. She'd turned her gaze to the rock, hands at her sides, her beautiful neck stretched out as her chin pointed upward.

"I wanted to say that...you're amazing up there," she said softly. "I've never seen someone who feels the rock like you do."

"Oh." I blinked. "You mean the 5.12 lead?" That had been an amazingly fortunate lead. Everything had flowed my way. It was like the fetch had hovered over my shoulder the whole way.

"No." She shook her head as though mildly annoyed. "I don't mean the 5.12 lead. I know the ratings are a big thing for you and Gage, but I don't like them. A rock face isn't numbers." She pinned me with her blue gaze and cocked her head. "Sometimes I think you're two different people. One is this stuttering high school boy who keeps trying to prove he's good enough. Like leading a 5.12 is going to show everyone." She glanced up at the rock again. "And then there's this other you. This...true climber. Confident and fluid and amazing." She paused. "You breathe it all in. You feel the rock. You talk to it and hear it talk back." She hesitated, as though she was about to say something else, but then didn't.

"Winsley—"

"Anyway." She waved her hand. "I wasn't going to say anything because I was sure you already knew how good you are. But then I realized you're kind of an idiot, too, and maybe you *didn't* know. So what I wanted to say is: whatever that special thing is that makes a legendary rock climber, you've got it. I see you up there, and it's like I don't even see your body. You're just pure soul. It's like...this is your religion. And I needed to tell you because...it's my religion, too." She looked at her feet. It was the first time I'd ever seen her act embarrassed. She cleared her throat and flashed that blue gaze again, reached out and touched my arm. "You're the best climber I've ever seen, Eric. Hands down. And it's not about the numbers. I'm talking about soul. Nobody else even comes close."

A thrill went through me at her touch and I suddenly realized that without even meaning to I'd taken hold of her arms, one in each of my hands.

She looked up at me, seemingly in a daze, like she was opening her eyes after a prayer.

I pulled her to me and leaned toward those parted lips. Her hands slipped around my waist, and I could feel her fingers— strong and sensitive—slide around my waist and up my back.

"Eric..." she murmured, rising to meet the kiss. Our lips almost touched, and then she blinked. The daze vanished from her eyes and she gave a little head shake. She pushed gently on my chest. "Eric, wait," she breathed, as though those two words had taken all of her strength.

I let her go, and the spell broke. Horror rushed in. I stepped away. "I'm sorry," I said. "No, you're right. I'm so sorry. That was fucked up."

"Eric," she said. "I-I can't...."

"I'm sorry," I said again, going to my pack. I felt like a piece of dog shit. I grabbed a pile of quickdraws and a coil of rope and began shoving them inside the pack. I didn't even know if they were mine or hers.

She came toward me. "Eric..."

I leapt away from her like she was a live wire, rope trailing from my pack. She held her hands out like she was trying to calm a skittish animal.

"Eric, please wait," she said.

125

"I'm sorry," I said again, stepping further away from her.

"Please," she said, and her voice broke. "Don't go."

But I ran. I ran into the woods like the betraying ratfink bastard coward that I was.

CHAPTER 16

I got back to the tent cabin, flung open the door and threw my pack across the floor, scattering equipment. Stupid stupid stupid!

I'd just ruined everything. I'd never imagined things could be worse with Winsley than they already were, but I'd just made it happen. At least before, I could still hang out with her. And in between my moments of mooning, I could actually talk with her.

She'd just opened herself up to me. She'd reached out to me. She'd described what being on the rock really meant to her. She'd made a bridge to me as a friend, and what did I do? I'd tried to kiss her.

"Stupid stupid stupid!" I said, dropping onto the bed like my legs had been cut. I banged my fists against my head, and desperately tried to think of a way to walk back what I'd done.

I thought about going to the rock shop immediately, finding Gage and coming clean. He might even understand.

Or he'd punch me in the face.

Or maybe I should go back to Winsley, tell her not to tell Gage, to pretend that it had never happened.

The idea twisted my guts. I'd never hidden anything from Gage. I'd been open with him about the fetch, about everything, and he'd had my back from the start. If I hid this, it would betray that trust.

But what the hell else could I do?

I stared hopelessly at the floor, and that's when my gaze caught the glimmer of the handle of Jack Daniel's under the bed. It was still about half full.

I pulled it out and spun the cap, which flew off and clacked to the floor. I took a long swallow.

It burned like hell. I gasped, took another pull and lay back on the bed, bottle clenched in my fist.

"What am I doing?" I said to the tan canvas overhead, which was growing slowly darker.

Was this how everything was going to end? With Winsley just out of reach and Gage punching me in the face? Why couldn't I have just held on for two more weeks? Then everything would have ended like it should have ended, with the three of us still friends.

Now there was no step I could take that didn't end in disaster. Disaster with Gage. With Winsley. With myself. I had two weeks left to live and I'd backed myself into a corner that promised only misery.

I'd fucked it all up by trying to kiss her.

But even now Winsley hovered in front of my eyes like she was actually standing in my tent. Her careless ponytail, those blue eyes, her amazing arms and...

"Goddamn it..." I said.

I sat up enough to take another swig of the whiskey, then lay back down, letting my arm settle until the bottom of the bottle thunked against the wooden floor.

"It's so fucking stupid," I said.

"Who's so fucking stupid?" Gage said, pulling open the door.

I sat up, eyes wide.

"Talking to yourself again?" He stepped inside and the spring door banged behind him. He held up his #1 Camalot and thumbed the mechanism three times. It twitched as the little half-moons rotated. "My beloved lives," he said in satisfaction. His gaze fell on the bottle of Jack, and his eyebrows raised.

"The fuck is this?" he asked.

"I..."

"You starting without me?"

I swallowed. The fear trickled into me like cold water. I wanted to tell him about Winsley, but my mouth suddenly seemed filled with cotton. "Two weeks," I said hoarsely. It was all I could manage to push out.

"Two weeks to—" He cut himself off. "Oh. Right. Time to turn up the volume?"

"Gage..." This time I really tried to tell him. I tried to say: *I almost kissed Winsley tonight. And she's going to tell you when you see her. And I'll understand if you hate me. I couldn't help it. I've been in love with her since the first day I met her. I'm a horrible friend. And I'm sorry.*

But I didn't say that. I didn't say a damned thing.

He hesitated a moment, then reached out with his free hand, fingers clasping air. "Well, fuck you, getting started without me."

I passed the bottle to him, and he took a long pull. He stamped his foot like a jackrabbit, then let out a rasp. He passed the bottle back. "That'll wake you up."

I took another drink.

"Better get Winsley," he said. "We drink without her, she's going to jack slap us both." He winked and started for the door.

"Have you talked to her?" I asked.

"What, since the climb?"

"Yeah."

"I was at the rock shop. Why?" He paused.

"Oh," I said. "We just... We came back from the route separately. I thought maybe you'd seen her."

He cocked his head. "Separately? Why?"

"I just..." I swallowed, and I knew this was the time. I was going to man up and just do it. I tried to make the words come out of my mouth. I felt my face going red from the effort.

But the words didn't come.

He saw my expression and he frowned. "Fuck's wrong with you?"

I took another deep drink from the bottle. The harsh burn in my throat turned to heat that spread from my chest to my arms and legs.

Gage stepped toward me. I got ready for him to hit me. I was sure he could see the guilt on my face.

Instead, he knelt in front of me, put his hand over mine on the bottle. "Hey," he said softly, and his digging sarcasm vanished. He looked me in the eye and wrapped his other hand around mine like we were gripping the hilt of my wooden sword, like this was some knight's ritual.

"You were the one who told me to stay in the moment," he said. "That's what this whole thing is about, right?"

"Right," I said. Tears burned my eyes.

"There is no tomorrow, man. This is where we stay. Right here. Right now. All that matters is now—you showed me that. Don't think about tomorrow. Fuck tomorrow."

"Gage..."

"Don't pussy out on me now."

"Yeah," I said through a tight throat.

I wanted to crawl in a hole and die. Right here. Right now.

He stood up, let go of my hands. "All right then." He stooped and looked under his bed. "Where the fuck is that flask? We can't go to The Shack with that big honking thing in your hand."

"Cargo shorts," I said in a monotone.

"Oh yeah." He rummaged around in his pile of laundry until he came up with it.

The whiskey's warmth reached every part of me now. As Gage began to carefully pour from the handle into the flask, the sharp need to tell him about Winsley softened. And I knew I wasn't going to. Not tonight. Not ever.

Gage changed out of his climbing gear, and I numbly did the same. By the time I pulled on my ratty jeans and a freshly laundered T-shirt, I was so tipsy I didn't even think what had happened at Moonpath was that important.

Gage and I started swapping quotes from *The Princess Bride*, the amazing new movie that our friend group had latched onto last year. We'd all seen it about a dozen times already.

"Ho there, brute! Give me that flask," Gage said as we headed to the door.

"I do not budge. Keep your 'ho there.' I am waiting for Vizzini..."

He laughed and snatched the bottle away, tucked it into the pocket on the side of his shorts. We headed to The Shack and sat down in Lisa's section. She showed up with her cute smile that put a delicate little dimple on each cheek. She cocked her head and looked at us curiously.

"Early start, boys?" she asked.

"We have come to storm the castle," I said too loudly, holding my fist up in the air.

She looked over her shoulder, then back to us and said in a conspiratorial whisper, "Maybe storm the castle quietly for an hour or so until the manager takes off?"

"I admit it," I said in my best Inigo voice. "You are smarter than I am."

"Then why are you smiling?" Gage fed me the line.

"Because I know something you don't know. *I* am not left-handed!"

We burst into laughter.

She sighed. "You can't say I didn't try," she said. "How about some food? Same same? Two Cokes. Basket of fries?"

"Yes," I said. "And cheeseburgers. We must have cheeseburgers."

"You got it."

The Cokes came and Gage doctored them both.

"That little splash?" I said. "Are you just fiddling around with me or what?"

He affected his best Andre the Giant voice and said, "I just want you to think you are doing well."

I drank, and for a moment all was right in the world. The cool evening breeze blew over us. The valley darkened and a hundred crickets chirped in the bushes around the deck. Gage seemed to feel the sublime moment too. He took a deep breath, looked at me, made a fist and grinned.

That was when we both looked up and found Winsley standing next to our table.

"Hey babe," Gage said, standing up.

"What's happening here?" she asked.

"Storming the castle," I said, raising my Coke, but I didn't look in her eyes.

"I see." She hesitated, like she was trying to get me to look at her, but I wouldn't. "Well, I assume you're going to need someone on this quest who can climb. It *is* a castle."

"And we have no boobs," Gage said. "Every good quest needs boobs." He slipped into a bad English accent. "There's a shortage of perfect breasts in this world," he said in his best Westley. "It'd be a pity to leave yours behind."

She seemed to give serious thought to the proposal. "Boob sherpa and castle climber...?" She nodded. "Okay. I can handle that. I will join this quest on one condition."

"Anything," Gage said.

She grabbed the bulge of the flask in his pocket like she was grabbing a different bulge. "I'm going to need to catch up," she said, slipping the whiskey flask out. She took a less-than-discreet drink.

Gage kissed her.

I turned my attention to Lisa, who was picking up our basket of fries and bringing them our way. "Let the quest begin!" I said.

We ate our burgers and fries, and continued drinking Gage's special Cokes. Winsley appeared to have completely forgotten what had happened earlier today. She never once looked at me expectantly, waiting for me to fess up.

We laughed, we talked rock climbing, and the night deepened. The families soon trickled away, and only the younger crowd remained.

Lisa's shift ended and she joined our table, tossing back special Cokes and working hard to catch up. There was so much laughter that the pain I'd felt earlier vanished.

At some point in the night, Lisa found her way onto my lap. As Gage regaled us with yet another climbing story, Lisa ran her fingers through my hair, softly combing out tangles. I hadn't cut it since I'd left Durango, and it was almost down to my shoulders.

Winsley was in Gage's lap now, and she whispered into his ear. He laughed. "Well," she said suddenly, standing up. "We've stormed this castle. It's fucking stormed."

"Overrun!" Gage held up his cup, sloshing Coke onto the table.

"We've so thoroughly overrun it they're building new walls." Winsley jerked a finger over her shoulder. Tie-dye guy, whose real name was Gary, was pulling the gate down over the counter. All of the tables were empty except ours.

"I bid you goodnight." Winsley bowed to Lisa and me.

"I'm with you." Gage stood up, and he was so unsteady he stumbled. Winsley caught him and righted him. Once he had his feet, he swayed into her and kissed her on the cheek. I think he was aiming for her lips.

She laughed. "Yeah, I think you're done."

"Inconceivable!" he said.

She slipped an arm around his waist. "You keep using that word," she affected her best Inigo Montoya accent. "I do not think it means what you think it means."

We all laughed and Winsley steered him toward the steps. I watched them go, and that ache in my heart twisted again, distantly, like it was deep under a lake of Jack 'n Coke.

At the top of the steps, as she was guiding Gage, Winsley turned and looked at me. It was just a quick look, but I thought I saw sadness in her eyes. I thought I saw an ache in her too.

But I was drunk, so what the fuck did I know?

"I think it's time for us to be going, too," Lisa said. She got off my lap and pulled me to my feet.

"You're helping me like Winsley helped Gage," I noted.

She chuckled, put one of my arms over her shoulders and held it there, steadying me. "You're perceptive."

"And you're sweet," I said. "But I actually have better balance when I'm drunk."

"You and every drunk driver who's ever been arrested."

"I'm not talking about driving. I'm talking about..." I gently took my arm back from her, and then jumped straight up onto the flat wooden rail that bordered the deck. I stuck the landing.

It was satisfying to see her eyes go wide. She moved forward to grab my hand to steady me, but I held up my palm like a traffic cop. I felt invincible, like I could attempt any physical challenge, whether filled with Jack Daniel's or not.

I walked the rail, one foot in front of the other, all the way to the steps. When I reached those, I walked down the slanted rail to the bottom of the stairs, then hopped to the ground.

"Are you trying to impress me?" Lisa asked.

"Yes," I said, extending my hand. "Yes, I am."

She took it. "Well, it worked."

"Good. Because I'm not very good with girls."

She laughed and pulled me close to her, wrapped my arm over her shoulder again and put her arm around my waist. "You're better than you think."

"Winsley says I get tongue-tied."

"She did say that." Lisa steered me down the path that went to the tent cabins. Together we made our way to #27, pushed through the spring door and tumbled onto my bed together.

She rose up, straddling me. Her palms pressed against my pecs as though they had been molded for that purpose. Her brunette hair cascaded around my face.

"You're...on top of me," I murmured.

"Again, perceptive." She leaned down and kissed me. Her lips were so soft, and she tasted like something tropical. I kissed her back. She broke the kiss and rose up again, mouth slightly parted, watching me. That tropical taste lingered on my lips. Some kind of Chapstick.

"Wow..." I said. "What...are you doing?"

"Seeing if you really are tongue-tied." She leaned down and kissed me again, this time longer. "Thor, indeed..." she murmured.

"Thor?" I'd never understood why Winsley called me that, or why Lisa had picked it up. "Why do you call me Thor?" I asked.

"Norse God of Thunder," she said.

"I know who he is," I said. "I just don't know why Winsley calls me that."

Lisa blinked at that. "I think it started because of that sword." She indicated the wooden sword leaning against the tent by my bed. You know. You carry a sword. Thor carries a sword."

"Thor carries a hammer."

She hesitated. "Really?"

"It's a hammer."

"Whatever." She shrugged. "Sword. Hammer. Same thing."

It was *so* not the same thing. But I wasn't about to go all D&D geek on her right now.

"But it stuck because you're a god of the rock and, you know, you're tall and ripped and blond and... I mean, you look like him."

"I do?"

She shook her head fondly. "So cute. You have no idea how hot you are..." she whispered. "That's adorable."

"I'm hot?"

"Hmmm." She seemed to contemplate. "Let me see." She worked at the edge of my T-shirt, which was pinned under me. I sat up a little and she pulled it over my head. She gazed at my chest, then descended on me again and kissed me. "Yes," she murmured.

I touched her shirt, and she raised her arms for me to pull it off. She had a pale pink bra underneath.

She fell on me and we made out.

We stopped for a moment, breathing hard and lying side-by-side, facing each other in the dim light.

"You have the cutest smile I've ever seen," I said.

As if to prove it, she brought those dimples out.

"It's even cuter than Winsley's smile," I said.

"She does have a great smile," she said. She rose up,

straddling me again. Her hands went behind her back and her bra came loose. She tossed it to the floor. I stared.

She descended on me again, her fingers in my hair as she kissed me. Her bare breasts pressed against my chest, and I'd never felt anything so warm and soft and amazing.

"You're...with me," I said.

She pushed her long hair away from her face, grinning. "That's the idea," she whispered. "If you want me to be."

"And Winsley is with Gage," I said.

She went stiff in my arms, and her smile faded to a frown. "Yeah," she said softly. "Winsley is with Gage."

"I mean, I know that," I said, too quickly. My sodden brain suddenly realized I'd been talking about Winsley a lot. "Of course I know that. Never mind what I said."

"Oh god," Lisa breathed. She sat up. Her eyes searched mine, and then she hung her head. Her long, straight hair dropped into a curtain over her eyes. She left it there for a short moment, then brought her head up, flinging her hair back. She drew a breath, then let it out through puffed cheeks. "That explains a lot, actually."

She moved to sit on the edge of the bed, casting about. Finally, she found what she was looking for—her T-shirt—picked it up, spun it around, turned it right side out.

"What are you doing?" I asked.

She let out a sigh. "It's not what I *am* doing. It's what I'm *not* doing." She shook her head. "I should have called that. Really should have seen it."

"Called what? Seen what? Lisa, what's going on?"

She turned to me, hands in her shirt without having put it on yet. "You're in love with Winsley," she said. She dove into the T-shirt and pulled it down over her glorious breasts.

"I-I'm not in love with Winsley. She's with—"

"With Gage. Yeah. We established that." She stood up. "Look, I have to go."

"I don't... I don't know why you're leaving. It's not... I'm not..."

She paused, and her urgency vanished. She cocked her hips

and considered me wistfully, then she came to me, leaned over and put her hands on my cheeks. "In the morning you'll be glad I walked out that door. We both will. You don't want me. You want Winsley."

"I think maybe I do want you." I ran my fingers up her side. She put her hand over mine, seemingly about to stop me, but she didn't. She just followed my hand with hers, closing her eyes and luxuriating in the touch. But when I reached the edge of her breast, her hand tightened. She stopped me and took my hand gently away from her body.

"Yeah," she breathed. "Me, too. But I don't play a good second fiddle." She walked to the door, turned. She watched me for a long moment like she was memorizing me.

"God, so hot," she murmured, and she left. The spring door banged shut behind her.

I sat in the quiet of the tent cabin. My thoughts were hazy, but the pleasantness had faded. Even drunk as I was, I could feel the heaviness of the moment. If even Lisa could see that I was over-the-moon about Winsley, how the hell had Gage not seen it yet? How long until he did? How long until everything blew up in my face?

"Fuck this," I said, and I burst out the door. I took the marked path for a few minutes, then headed into the woods. At first, I could feel the whiskey in my veins. I swayed a little, pushed off a tree or two, but the cool night air cleared my head somewhat. After half an hour of following a little dirt path, I came out onto the open valley with a full view of the moonlit majesty of Half Dome.

"What the fuck am I doing?" I shouted. "Why am I even here?"

"Because it's the most beautiful place on earth?" The voice came from behind me.

I thought Winsley had followed me, but when I turned, it wasn't her.

The fetch wore jeans with a hole in one knee, hiking boots with loose laces, and a jog bra. Her pale skin glowed in the moonlight, and her hair seemed like a flame in the dark.

My gaze raked over the jeans, the boots, the bra. My temper rose. "What are you doing?"

She raised a curious eyebrow. "What do you mean?"

"You're dressed like Winsley. What the hell is that supposed to mean?"

"You're angry."

"You're goddamned right I'm angry!" I said.

"Well," she said. "You're not angry with me. So who are you angry at?"

"Why do you look like her?"

"I respond to your desires, Eric," she said, and a wry smile turned up the corners of her mouth.

I turned away, letting out a frustrated breath. I didn't say anything for a long time, and neither did she.

"I'm lost," I finally said. "I came here to find myself, and I'm more lost than ever."

"Are you?"

"I'm in love with my best friend's girlfriend."

"I know," she said.

"Well that's about the worst thing that can happen!"

"Hardly the worst thing. You could be in Malaysia. Or in a Turkish prison."

"Is that supposed to be funny? Am I supposed to laugh at that?"

"You're upset because you know it's coming to an end," the fetch said, putting her finger right on the wound.

I choked on the catch in my throat. "No, I'm not... It's because... It's because I screwed up today. I messed everything up." But suddenly, I wasn't so sure anymore.

"Eric—"

"I'll never get to know a girl like Winsley," I said hoarsely. "Two weeks, and that's it for me."

"If that is how you see it."

"How *else* am I supposed to see it!"

"It's an illusion. Time."

"So I'm *not* going to die in two weeks?"

"Two weeks from now. One hour from now. Time is a

construct of your mind, and you've chosen to believe in it so strongly it's torturing you. But the truth is, there is only one time. *Now.* There actually isn't anything else. And you can ruin your present with these illusions." She paused. "Or you can live."

I fell silent, and I felt her move quietly through the tall grass to stand behind me.

"Eric," she said, but I didn't turn around. "What do you want to do right now? If you didn't have a future, what would you do right now?"

I turned, and she was so close to me we were almost touching. She wasn't taller than me anymore, and I looked down into her green eyes. I reached out and touched her cheek with my calloused fingers, pressed my palm against that smooth skin.

"What happens if I kiss a fetch?" I murmured, feeling reckless.

She didn't look surprised, didn't back away, didn't look down and blush. She held my gaze. "It's dangerous," she said.

"Unlike everything else about a fetch," I said drily. She just watched me with those green eyes. "Why is it dangerous?"

"If you kiss a fetch, you'll never fall in love with a mortal woman."

"That would solve all my problems," I said.

She didn't say anything. Her eyes seemed larger than before, green cat's eyes glowing in the dark. For some reason, I thought of those white, sharp teeth behind those red lips.

"I'm dead in two weeks anyway," I said.

"Then kiss me if you dare," she said.

I pulled her to me, and she came willingly. Her pale, slender arms wrapped around my neck. Our lips met, and all the passion I'd wanted to give to Winsley, I gave to the fetch.

I don't remember how long the kiss lasted. I only remember her red hair surrounding us like a halo. I remember the moon moving through the sky. I remember the wind caressing my face. I remember feeling fuller with every moment our lips stayed together.

When we finally parted, she drew a deep breath like she was pulling all the air from my lungs.

I gasped, dizzy. I looked for the moon, but it wasn't where I remembered. It now hung behind Half Dome, lighting up the valley like a searchlight. My head swam at how much time must have passed for the moon to go from one horizon to the other.

"You know what you need to do," the fetch whispered, but I couldn't see her. All I could see was the moon. The fetch's whisper became the breeze, the rustling grass, the swaying trees. "I will be with you. Always."

The world spun. I tried to catch myself, but I couldn't seem to find the ground. Everything went black.

CHAPTER 17

I woke up in that field, and my head felt like someone was squeezing it in a vice. The sunlight was too bright, and my arms and face had already become uncomfortably hot. I heard someone off to my left, and my first thought was that Gage had come to look for me.

I sat up and came face-to-snout with a black bear.

"Holy fuck!" I scrambled to my feet.

The thing was as big as I was, round as a barrel, with dark black fur and a giant head. Surprised by my sudden lurch to my feet, it gave a thunderous "gronk" and rose up on its hind legs. I froze.

My hesitation probably saved me from a mauling, because as I gaped at the bear, I remembered you aren't supposed to run from bears. And if I hadn't remembered that, I'm sure I'd have booked it into the woods as soon as my limbs started working.

Another memory flashed through my head in that panicked instant. My grandmother had lived in Minnesota, and she had once told me about rushing out onto her deck and scaring away a bear by banging two pans together.

So I shouted.

I stuck my hands up in the air and waved them like a crazy

man. I was sure it was going to charge me and smack the head right off my shoulders. But it gronked again, this time a little softer, and fell back to all fours. It turned, like it was disinterested in me, and moved off toward the trees.

I thought maybe I was supposed to chase it, make a big show like I was tougher and meaner, set it to running, but I didn't have the guts for that. I just stood there, wide-eyed and shaking from fear and adrenaline. Once it had headed into the trees and I couldn't see it anymore, I fell to my knees.

I breathed steadily in and out until my heart rate returned to normal. On the upside, the shot of adrenaline had totally made my headache vanish. As soon as I was sure the bear wasn't going to come charging back, I turned and headed toward Curry Village.

It had to be about 10 o'clock when I got back to the cabin, so I was surprised to find Gage there. He was lying on the bed playing a Simon's Quest portable video game he'd brought from his house. He looked me over—rumpled clothes, messed-up hair, untied tennis shoes. He sat up, grinned, and tossed the game on the bed.

"Nice," he said. "Walk of shame, slut." He pointed a finger at me.

"What?"

"You and Lisa. The big boom-boom."

"What? Oh. No."

"Fuck you, liar." He picked up Lisa's pink bra from the floor of the tent with his toe. "What's this?"

"No, we didn't..." I shook my head. "She took off after she walked me home."

"She walked you home, stepped into the tent for one last drink and her bra fell off. 'Cause bras just do that." He twirled it on his finger. "You're full of shit. You totally nailed her. Did you guys tumble out of the tent and sleep in a field or what?"

"No, it's not..." I trailed off, and Gage got a curious look in his eye.

"Oh my god!" he said, dropping the bra and bringing his hands up to the sides of his head. "Did you fuck it up?" He started laughing. "Did she start to strip and then bail? I can't believe you. Easiest lay of the century, and you fuck it up. What did you do, Romeo?"

"I don't want to talk about it."

"Classic." He continued chuckling, shaking his head. "Well, it's probably for the best. Now we're both single."

My gaze locked on him with a laser focus. "What?"

"Yeah. Winsley broke up with me last night."

"What?" I repeated, stunned.

He waved a hand. "It was the 'I just want to be friends' speech. Said she'd had a good time, that it was fun for the summer but she just didn't see it going anywhere long-term."

I swallowed. "Uh... You okay?"

He shrugged. "I was kind of expecting it. Vibe's been weird between us lately. And, you know, the summer *is* coming to an end. Makes sense. Clean break. Do it with style."

"I..." My throat was tight, but I knew I had to say something, so I pushed the words out in a dead monotone. "I'm sorry, man. That sucks."

"Chick was totally sane about it. Best breakup I ever had. No yelling or throwing things. She said her piece, then she was done. We talked for a while, then I came back here. But you were gone."

I sat down on the bed, numb.

"Anyway, it's just you and me again," he said. "Way it should be."

I swallowed. Part of me wanted to rush to Winsley's tent right now and profess my undying love for her, but I shoved that thought to the back of my mind.

This summer wasn't supposed to be about her. And it sure as hell wasn't supposed to be about some fucked-up love triangle. It was about following the fetch. So no. I wasn't going to Winsley. I had two weeks. And I knew exactly what I was going to do with them.

"I'm going to climb Half Dome," I blurted.

"Yeah?" Gage said. It was something we'd said we were going to do before the end of the summer, but I wasn't talking about that.

"Free solo," I said.

Free solo meant no ropes. No fall protection. And *no one* had ever done it on Half Dome.

The silence in the tent was absolute.

"Fuck you, you're free soloing it," he finally said.

"I am."

"You can't free solo and carry a portaledge, and it's a two-day climb, dude."

"Not without ropes." Without placing pro, setting up anchors and top ropes, cleaning the equipment, waiting for a belayer, I figured I could get up in half the time. If I could get up it at all. "I'd just need some water, a few snacks. Some quickdraws to clip in and rest every now and then."

"Fuck you."

"You already said that."

"You're going to kill yourself."

"I'm dead in two weeks anyway."

He opened his mouth to retort, but shut it. He paused, like he was debating whether or not to say something, and I could guess what it was. He didn't believe in the fetch, didn't believe I was going to die at the end of this. He'd been happy to go along with the story while it meant adventure, but not when he saw it as suicide.

But he didn't say that. I wondered if Gage thought the magic of the road trip might be shattered if he admitted there was no fetch. Maybe he thought it would destroy my psyche or something.

"It's stupid," was all he said.

"I know."

He leaned forward, elbows on bent knees with his head hanging down between. Finally, he looked me in the eye. "Fine, fucker. I'm going with you."

"No, you're not," I said. Something had been turning in the back of my mind since L.A., and it finally worked its way to the front.

He raised his eyebrows and straightened up, his shoulders

going back. "Fuck you I'm not. You don't tell me what I'm going to do."

"I'm not sure the fetch is looking after you. The speeding ticket outside of Joshua Tree? You said it yourself. Where was the fetch then? I think it's because she's not looking out for you, not making you invincible. I don't want to risk it."

"I got a speeding ticket. So what?"

"So that was a speeding ticket. This is falling a thousand feet. You could die."

"The fetch is in your head, motherfucker!" he said. "There is no fetch. You got to this point because of pure balls. And if you're going to push the envelope, so am I."

Gage was like a bulldog with a bone once he'd made up his mind, and nothing could make him let go. Or...almost nothing. I knew what I had to say to protect him, to make him break away from me right here and now.

"I'm the reason Winsley broke up with you," I said. "I'm in love with her. I have been since I first saw her."

He looked confused, like I'd spoken in Greek. "What?"

"It happened yesterday, when you went to fix your cam. She and I got to talking and I..."

He finally realized what I was saying, and his brow furrowed. "You what? What did you do?"

"I kissed her. Or... I almost did. I pulled her to me and—"

"What the fuck!" He stood up.

I wanted to explain to him that it didn't go that far, that I jumped and ran even as she asked me to stay. But I didn't want to soften the blow. I wanted him to hate me. His endless summer had to end here because mine was going to end on Half Dome, and I didn't want him with me when it happened. I didn't want to put him in more danger than I already had.

He breathed harder, clenching his fists. My heart hammered. Gage had always been quick to violence, and I waited for the punch that would knock me senseless. But he just stood there, muscled chest pumping, his fists trembling.

"That's fucked up, man," he growled.

I really thought he was going to hit me, but he spun and hit the spring door instead. It slammed open, and he stalked out. It slammed shut behind him.

"Motherfucker," he shouted.

I hung my head, trying to control my breathing. "Good," I whispered to myself. "Good. This is the way it should be."

But I didn't believe it.

CHAPTER 18

Slowly, I gathered up my stuff, packing what little I'd need for the climb. My harness, water bottles. We'd just gone shopping the previous day, so there was plenty of food. I used an old stuff sack and crammed it with granola bars, almonds, and a peanut butter and jelly sandwich. I put everything into my day pack.

After I was done, with the pack cinched up tight and leaned against the bed, I left the tent and walked up the marked paths to the parking lot where I'd left The Pumpkin almost a month ago. It was covered with a thin coating of dust. I felt a strong pang of nostalgia. The road trip was over. There was just one more adventure, the biggest of them all, and The Pumpkin couldn't go with me. I opened the door, got the pink slip from the glove box and brought it back to the room.

Gage hadn't returned, which was good. By the time he came back I wanted to be well into the woods where he couldn't find me. I'd sleep under the stars tonight and start my climb tomorrow before first light.

I pulled the pink slip from its yellowed envelope, set the envelope aside and flipped the pink slip to its back side. I signed it over to Gage, then stuck it under his water bottle on the nightstand so it wouldn't accidentally blow away. Then I wrote a note, put it beside the pink slip and the yellowed envelope, and placed my keys on top.

Gage,

I don't have much to give you in return for all you've given me, but I hope this will balance the scales a little. The Pumpkin is yours. No one ever loved that car as much as you do, and you should have it.

Thank you for pushing me, for teaching me, for staying by my side through all this crazy shit. You made this endless summer happen. I couldn't have done it without you.

I'm sorry about Winsley. If I could have stopped myself from loving her, I would have. In the end, I chose you over her, even if I didn't do it fast enough.

You're my hero. You have been for years. Thanks for everything.
-Eric

I grabbed my pack and left the tent. With every minute that passed, I got jumpier, thinking if I didn't get my ass out of Curry Village fast enough, I'd run into Gage or Winsley or even Lisa. I didn't want to have any one of those conversations.

But perhaps the fetch was watching over me, because I didn't see anyone until I got to where the woods bordered the path. I stayed away from the little game trails that branched off, paths that Winsley had introduced us to, and I chose a random place to bushwhack. Only when I was out of sight did the muscles in my shoulders start to ease. The weight I'd been carrying dissipated.

I hiked for more than an hour, feeling clearer and more focused with each step. This was simple. I was going to spend the day and the night focusing my thoughts on one thing, and one thing only.

There would be no sarcastic banter with Gage. When my fears rose about what I was contemplating, he couldn't be my crutch this time. And there would be no mooning over Winsley, no hopeful thoughts about spending the night in her tent, about some future with her that didn't exist.

Soon there'd be nothing but me and the rock and the fetch. And we would dance.

I hiked until I was hungry. I stopped to eat, then I continued on, finally hitting the slope that headed up to the face. I spent most of the day hiking, until the sun started to sink in the sky. Then I cleared out a little spot among the rocky talus slope leading up to the Half Dome face, and I set up my makeshift camp. I plopped down my pack and rolled out my sleeping bag on the incline. I just lay there for the remaining hour or two of daylight, looking up at the sky, soaking in nature. I let my muscles settle. I imagined myself on the rock as I relaxed. I drank most of my leave-behind water bottle and I even napped a little, imagining last night's alcohol flowing out of my bloodstream.

The sun slowly dropped beneath the horizon, and I stayed up late enough to hear the crickets and other night creatures come to life, to watch the stars shine high above. I thought about how this could be my last night alive. There was no guarantee I'd make it to the top. Half Dome was almost 9,000 feet tall. What were the odds I could climb 9,000 feet and make zero mistakes?

I let those thoughts go, felt the warm summer breeze, listened to the crickets and the rustling grass. An owl hooted deep in the nearby forest. I focused on the bright, bright stars overhead. They'd never seemed that bright in Durango. God, they were beautiful.

Soon, I fell asleep.

I woke in the pre-dawn darkness, as though the fetch had stroked my neck. I blinked and sat up, looking for her, but no fox darted away. No flash of red made itself apparent. I let out a breath, blinking, and everything rushed back in. I was free soloing Half Dome today. That brought me wide awake.

I put on my harness, then pulled everything I'd prepared out of my backpack and clipped it to my harness. I left the sleeping bag and the backpack on the talus. I wouldn't need either on the face, and they would only weigh me down.

It took me a while to meander up the talus. The chunky slope of rock leading up to the north side of Half Dome was formed from all the rock falls that had come off the face over the centuries. I remembered Gage telling me that those rock falls smashed into the ground with such earth-shattering force they snapped trees like matchsticks as they rolled down into the valley, some going incredibly far. The house-sized, moss-covered boulders in Curry Village had all come from massive rock falls centuries ago. I could only imagine what it would look like to watch thousands of tons of rock shear off that mountain.

I made it to my chosen spot, breathing hard and already sweating. I turned to take in the view. The valley stretched out before me, the swaths of pine trees and grass looking gray in the pre-dawn light. I saw the squarish roofs of Curry Village peeking out in the distance. And...

I squinted. Two odd-looking shapes caught my interest below. At first, I thought they were shadows of the irregular rocks of the talus, but these shadows were moving. These shadows were people.

I was about to turn and ignore them—just two more climbers looking to get on Half Dome—when I recognized the gait of the one in the lead. His big shoulders twisted this way and that as he worked his way up the slope. My gaze snapped to the second figure, and I recognized her as well, the graceful swaying of her hips, the swing of her messy ponytail.

It was Gage and Winsley.

CHAPTER 19

"What the hell are you doing?" I said when they got closer.

Gage looked up at the rock, then back at me.

"Free solo, huh?" he said.

"You're not going," I said.

"The day a cheesedick like you tells me what I'm doing...."
He shook his head and looked up at the rock.

"We're with you," Winsley said calmly. "We're going."

"Gage..." I said, and my emotions twisted up. I didn't want
to face him. I didn't want to face Winsley, either. I just wanted
to concentrate on the rock. "I don't want you guys here."

"It's been the three of us all summer," Winsley said. "And
now it's just about what *you* want? Is that how it is?"

"I came out here alone," I said.

"And we followed you," she said back.

"Look, I made a wreck of things," I said. "Things would
have been fine if I hadn't... You know, if I didn't... I mean we
were fine until I—"

"No lovers on the rock," Gage interrupted. "None of that
shit when we're climbing. Winsley's rule. Neither one of us
came here for that."

"He's right," Winsley said. "We came to climb."

I swallowed the lump in my throat. "Then we're not free

soloing. We're bringing ropes," I said hoarsely. "We tie in—"

"So you can come back another time to try without us?" Gage shook his head. "Fuck that."

"Gage—"

"We started this together, you and me," he said. "Fuck if I'm walking away now. And Winsley's right, this last month it's been all three of us. She's as much a part of the Summer of the Fetch as me. We're all doing this."

I stood there looking at them helplessly. I turned to Winsley, and her eyes were determined.

"Then I'm not doing it," I said.

"Fuck you," Gage said.

"You could die," I pleaded with him. He crossed his arms. I turned to Winsley. "Winsley, you could die."

"I could live." She winked. "I don't need you to protect me."

"And I sure as fuck don't," Gage added.

I tried to gather my thoughts. Winsley and Gage had banded together, put aside whatever stuff was between us, and they'd come after me.

Gage was right. Whatever *this* was—this Summer of the Fetch—they were a part of it. I wouldn't even be here if it hadn't been for them. Gage had taught me to climb. Winsley had taught me how to make it my religion.

I let out a long breath and looked up at the tall flat rock face above us. My will galvanized around one single thought: I was holding back because of fear. Fear for my friends. Fear of making the wrong decision. But this summer was about moving past fears, about breaking boundaries no matter what. It was about dancing with the fetch.

"All three of us?" I said.

"As it should be," Winsley said.

"Fuckin' A."

"To the end," I said.

"To the end," they said together.

"Okay. Let's do this," I said.

Gage slapped me on the shoulder. I wanted to hug him. I

wanted to hug Winsley, but I did neither.

Instead, I stuck my hands into my chalk bag, chalked up, and looked up at my chosen route.

"On belay?" I said. Gage smirked and Winsley smiled.

I put my hands on the rock.

I took the lead with Gage behind me and Winsley trailing, and we started up.

Ten feet. I could fall now and still survive.

Twenty feet. Less likely.

I mentally marked the spot I'd have placed my first piece of pro, and the hairs on my neck stood on end as I passed it. It was one thing to talk about free soloing. It was another to be here, on the rock, and consciously choose not to protect myself.

I mean, I'd bouldered a lot, never using protection. I'd even free soloed a couple of 5.9s, but nothing approaching this level of commitment. On a free solo well within my capacity—like a 5.9—it's all about focus. I know I can do the moves. There's no uncertainty about my skill, just the head trip of knowing that if I fall, I'm going to die.

But on a route that pushed the edges of our abilities, Gage, Winsley, and I had to beat the head game *and* climb at our very best.

Most of the time, climbing was about falling. To learn, I'd had to fall more times than not. We had all three fallen many more times than we'd flawlessly finished routes. But this time there would be no ropes to catch us. We didn't get to suffer a "bad move" or make a "bad choice." Not even once. We didn't get a single do-over. One mistake, one slip, and we were dead.

That thought plagued me at the first point I would have placed pro. I almost panicked at the second point, like my brain was saying, "Last chance!"

But by the time I got to the third point, I had acclimated. It was as though I'd gone so far beyond ridiculous that my nattering fears didn't know what to do. They just got quiet.

It's amazing how fast a person can adjust to something,

even a constant fear of death. As soon as my whole world became making sure that every single move I made was solid and certain, that's just the way it was. It became the new normal.

I didn't daredevil it. Not once. There was no jumping for a hold. There was no "I bet I can make that" attempts. I saw every move in my head before I did it, and then I did it, smooth and sure. We all fell into a groove, working the rock, dancing with it, sweating and straining and resting.

The sun rose high in the azure sky, and the rock warmed. It was the perfect weather for a climb. Warm but not hot, and not a lick of wind. We were young, strong, our fingers calloused and ready, our muscles toned, our skin browned from the sun. We climbed, and every move felt like the only move that mattered. I didn't think about falling, about dying. I only thought about that next problem and how to solve it.

When the sun hit its zenith, Winsley called up from below.

"Lunch anyone?"

"Fuckin' starving," Gage said.

"I see two belay station bolts a few moves ahead," I said. "Lunch there?"

"Yummy yummy," Winsley said.

I found an off-width crack to follow up to the bolts. I got there, executing a smooth crossover on a tasty ledge beneath the bolts. I created a quick anchor on the bolts for Gage and Winsley, then I double-cammed a nice little crack nearby and clipped in. I sank into my harness.

God, that felt good.

Gage came next, duplicating what he'd just seen me do, and clipped into the anchor I'd made.

Winsley clipped in last. "Nice little climb, boys."

Gage shook out his arms. "Fuck me in the ass," he said, looking out over the ridiculously long drop beneath us. "I've never been so scared in my life." Then he whooped at the top of his lungs.

"God, what a view," I said.

"Only us and the hawks," Gage said, rummaging around in

his food bag. Winsley and I did the same.

As I chewed on my PB&J, I thought about how we were all committed now. There was absolutely no going back. We couldn't downclimb this. That would be more dangerous than pressing on. It was three times more likely we'd fall.

Our only real choice was to finish the climb up to the top and take the easy route down the backside. We had to make it to the top.

It occurred to me that this was the ideal time to freak out, to let the head game get to me. We were literally trapped on the face of a rock with no way out but up, and no safety net. But I felt calm. I felt like this was exactly where I was meant to be. I was a part of this rock.

It wasn't so much like I felt I was invincible, but more like I felt this was my life, this was where I belonged. I couldn't run away from it even if I tried. And I didn't want to.

I glanced over at Winsley. Her eyes were closed and her chin was slightly elevated, like she was luxuriating in the sun on her face. She took a bite of her sandwich and chewed, still with her eyes closed, and I knew she was feeling what I was feeling.

We finished our eats and clipped our snack bags back onto our harnesses.

"Switch lead?" Winsley asked.

"Sure," I said.

She nodded and started up, working that off-width crack a little higher, doing gorgeous laybacks. I watched the muscles work in her calves, in the divots above her shoulders and along her back, in her beautiful arms. Gage waited a moment, unclipped and headed up after her without a word. I took the rear this time, and I found it easier and harder in different ways. It was easier because watching Winsley do things her way gave me alternate options, things I might not have seen before. It was harder because I could see my friends ahead of me. I worried for them, and that could break my focus.

Not to mention the fact that watching Winsley was gorgeous and distracting all by itself. I had to remind myself to watch her clinically.

No lovers on the rock.

We climbed for another hour, just making our way coolly and confidently, resting when we found a good spot, downing water, then continuing on.

It was early afternoon when the wind picked up. At first, it was nice. A cool breeze to chill the sweat on our bodies. But it got stronger.

Once it was strong enough to really notice, Winsley found a nice fist-sized crack, worked it high enough to give us each some room to get into it, then did a fist jam and a foot jam at the same time. We followed suit. It wasn't as good as clipping into a bolt, but we could all rest long enough to have a talk.

"Storm," Winsley shouted down over the wind. She pointed.

Gage and I both looked north to see ugly black clouds on the horizon.

"Goddammit. What the fuck? Weather report said all clear," Gage said. His eyes were wide as he looked at that storm.

The storm meant more wind, which could tear a climber off the side of a wall with ease if a gust hit at just at the right moment. But worse was the rain. So much of climbing relied on friction. Once this rock got wet, a 5.10 could suddenly become a 5.12 because half the holds you'd use wouldn't work anymore.

Or it could just become impossible.

"I think we need to make a decision, boys," Winsley said.

"What do you think?" I said.

"We've been moving slow. We're only about two thirds of the way up."

"So what's the choice?" Gage said.

"Try to make it up before the storm. Or...or we find a place to clip in and hang there for the night."

We were pretty well fucked either way. Trying to rush it, make it to the top before the storm... That was just asking for a mistake to happen.

But camming a crack, being sluiced with water, and hanging

there in a lightning storm—that just sounded like a different flavor of shit. What if we had to sit there all night? What if the cams slipped out because of the water?

I glanced back at the storm. It was moving fast. A moment ago, it had just been a bit of darkness on the horizon. Now it filled up a quarter of the northern sky. Even if we took ridiculous chances, we couldn't make it to the top in less than two hours. That storm wasn't even going to give us half an hour.

I looked around for a place to stick a cam or a nut, but I couldn't see anything.

"Well, we can't stay here," I said. "Let's get to somewhere we can clip in, then go from there."

"Yeah," Gage agreed, also looking over his shoulder at the storm.

"I think there's a bolt set not too far up," Winsley said.

"How far?" I asked.

"See that ledge?" She pointed.

"No," Gage said.

I couldn't see a ledge either, just a smooth-looking rock face that was getting harder to see by the minute.

"I think it's there," Winsley said, but she didn't sound very confident. "Make for it?"

"We'll follow you," I said. "Let's hurry before it gets wet."

"Fuck," Gage said.

"One move at a time, man," I said. "It's not wet yet. Don't let the head game get you."

"Fuck, you're right. Of course you're right." He let out a breath, shook his head, and that determination came back to his eyes. "I'm good."

We started up.

Winsley's ledge turned out to be almost thirty moves away. The wind kept getting stronger, which meant we all took more time, made sure we had what we needed before we executed. No dicey grabs. No graceful swings to a secure spot. Everything had to be solid.

Gage started saying "fuck" every thirty seconds or so, and

the sky darkened.

Intermittent droplets began to hit the stone. It was just a few, but those droplets brought panic, like we were all in a small room with the walls closing in. Once that sky opened up, if we hadn't reached those bolts, we were screwed.

"One move at a time," I said to Gage. "Focus on the rock."

"Fuck fuck fuck..."

The rain was still just a sprinkle when Gage caught up with Winsley. I made it moments after, and I pulled up to join them. Her "ledge" was only about two inches deep, and about four feet long. Unfortunately, it was right below a gradual overhang, which meant we had to crouch to hold ourselves on it.

And there were no bolts.

"Where are the bolts?" Gage demanded.

Winsley shook her head, and I could see the whites around her eyes. We were all breathing hard. We were all tired, and there were no bolts.

"No bolts," I said.

"I'm sorry," she said. "We must have gone off route. Or I remembered wrong." She shook her head like it didn't matter. "Anyway, they're not here."

"Well what the fuck do we do now?" Gage said.

I could hear hysteria creep into his voice, and it threatened to infect me, because he was right. We were screwed. We couldn't stay on this ledge through a storm. We'd get tired. Our muscles would get cold. We'd slip.

"We have to use our own pro," I said. "Gotta find a place for that. It's all we can do now."

"And how the fuck are we going to do that?" Gage demanded. "It's so fucking dark I can barely see anymore."

"Gage, chill. We're going to find a place," I said.

"How do you know?" he said.

"Because we have to."

He swallowed. "Yeah, okay," he said, and his voice sounded a little calmer. "Okay."

"Winsley, we have to move," I said. "The rain."

"Yeah," she said.

"Up, down, or sideways. What's our best bet?"

"There's nothing down," she said.

"Agreed. Sideways?"

"I... I can't see. It'd just be a shot in the dark."

"Okay."

"But..." She hesitated.

"No time, Winsley. But what?"

"The way this rock is going." She made a little curve with her free hand. "I think Big Sandy Ledge isn't far above us."

"Bigger than this ledge, I hope," Gage said.

She gave a quick smile. "Big Sandy is a highway. You could pitch a tent on it."

"If it's there," Gage said.

Her mirth vanished. "Yeah. If it's there."

"And if it's not, we're climbing in the rain," he said.

She paused, then nodded. "Yeah."

We all hung there in silence. I could see Gage's arm trembling from where he pushed against the undercling.

"We go up," I said. "And nothing changes. Shake the demons out. We either die or we don't, but it's not going to be from making a stupid mistake, okay?"

"Yeah," Gage said.

"Okay," Winsley agreed.

"Winsley, you lead."

She looked at me, and I could see the fear in her eyes. Not of falling, I think, but of being wrong about Big Sandy Ledge and letting us down.

She blew out a breath, then said, "Walk in the park, boys." And she started up and over the overhang.

The rain started to come down a little more. Spots appeared on the rock. There was still more dry rock than wet, but it wouldn't stay that way. Gage started his mantra again as we both went up and around the overhang.

I stayed right behind him. I had no idea what I'd do if he fell, except make sure he didn't go down alone. If he went, no way I could hold my body up and break his fall without coming off the rock too.

The rain came harder, and soon the entire face was wet.

"Jesus Christ," Gage said. "We're fucked."

"One move at a time," I said, but even I was getting uncertain about my grabs.

"It's here!" Winsley shouted from above. "You guys, it's here!"

Relief flooded through me, but I reminded myself to stay focused. Big Sandy was above us, but we still had to get there.

Inch by inch, we tried to reach her. She stood above us, looking down, and she was hastily pulling quickdraws off her harness, snapping them together.

The rain came harder now. We were only about five feet from the ledge, but Gage had locked up. He'd completely stopped, legs shaking. The rock was entirely wet now, and rivulets were starting to form, running down the face.

"Gotta go, Gage. Gotta go now," I said, in as calm a voice as I could.

"Fuck man," he said. If his legs shook much more, he was going to slip off the face, and we'd both go down. "I don't think I can. I can't see the move. This fucking rock feels like slime."

"You got this. Above your head and to the left."

"It's fucked, man. That's too narrow. I'll slip right off."

"You won't," I said. "Make it your best move. Make it now."

He nodded his head, took a deep breath and got the hold, pulled himself up, his biceps quivering.

"Get the next one," I said.

He reached, got the next hold—

And slipped.

He let out a guttural scream, like he'd been punched in the stomach. His arms winged out—

And caught a flying piece of webbing.

Gage pulled up short, smacked into the rock, but he held onto the carabiner at the end of the webbing.

Unbelieving, I looked up, trying to figure out where the miraculous webbing had come from. The rain came down hard now, and it was hard to see, but I suddenly realized what had happened. Winsley had clipped in, taken four quickdraws and linked them together to form a webbing-and-carabiner rope about four feet long. She'd thrown it to Gage just as he'd fallen.

He clung to the thing, then hauled himself up to the ledge. He heel-hooked the top and rolled onto the ledge and out of sight. The makeshift rope came down immediately after, and I grasped hold of it.

I'd never felt a greater rush of relief in my life. Once I had the rope, it was easy—even on the wet face—to clamber up and roll onto the ledge. Winsley had been right. It was enormous. If we'd had sleeping bags, we could have spread them out here: one, two, three.

"Well," I said as water streamed down my nose. "Good find, yeah?"

Winsley looked at me as the skies opened up and the deluge soaked her. She started laughing.

CHAPTER 20

We huddled together in the rain, clipped in to an anchor and as far away from the edge as we could manage. Lightning forked down in the distance and thunder boomed. The wind raged, and we gripped each others' hands, watching in stoic silence. The squall hit hard, and we waited in limbo like that for hours, shivering and staying together to keep warm.

Then, just as quickly as it had come, the storm was gone. The rain slackened, then stopped altogether, but by the time it did, it was night. The moon rose, mostly full but waning. We weren't going to make the top tonight. My one-day adventure had turned into a two-day odyssey. We were going to spend the night right here.

Winsley seemed in good spirits, even though we were all cold and wet.

"We couldn't have cut that any closer," she said.

I shivered a little, from the cold or from our near-deaths, I couldn't say. The full truth began to hit me. If we hadn't gotten lucky, if we hadn't found Big Sandy Ledge just at the right moment, Gage would have died. We all would have, if that storm had caught us anywhere else.

I gave a silent thanks to the fetch, wherever she was, and tried to shake this feeling of doom away. I turned my attention to our little ledge of salvation, a moonlit stairstep of ledges, silver in the dark. We stood on the lowest and biggest ledge, but smaller ledges reached up from our perch to where the rock face went flat again. The place was true to its name, with a dusting of sand like ten people had visited a beach and come here to brush off their legs. I wondered if the stairstep formation, cracks between each, had somehow caused this sandy effect.

The lowest ledge, where we stood, was roomy. Well, roomy compared to everything else on the face. It was about twenty feet long, starting with the western edge—about four feet wide—and tapering to three feet wide on the other side, where it ended in a cluster of craggy rock pillars forming an arête. The widest edge looked like the prow of a stone ship that had been cut in half by the mountain, looking out daringly onto the western stretch of pine forest far below.

Winsley had claimed we could pitch a tent here. Heh. A very small tent, maybe. But it was long enough that we could each lie out head-to-toe without touching.

Gage had clipped in and propped himself up against the wet rock pillars on the eastern edge, and since I was gazing off the "prow" of the stone half-ship, our sleeping spots were decided. Winsley took the middle with her "boys" on either end, and we all settled down. The breeze had died, and the rock radiated the lingering warmth of the day. We were soaked, but not cold. I had hope that maybe it wasn't going to be a totally miserable night.

The danger was over for now, but none of us could sleep right away. We were jacked on adrenaline and starving. We chomped sandwiches and nuts, then lay down and started talking, mostly about stupid normal stuff like TV shows. Winsley confessed to being a fan of *Night Court*.

"*Magnum P.I.* is good," I said. "I mean, since they cancelled *Knight Rider*."

Winsley laughed. "Are you kidding me? *Magnum P.I.?* All those hairy chest scenes with Mr. Sensitive-Soft-Brown-Eyes. It's a soap opera with guns and a Ferrari."

"It is not!" I said.

"Totally made for housewives," she said.

Actually, my mom *had* been crazy for *Magnum P.I.*, and I felt a blush heating my skin.

"Hey," I said defensively. "Magnum was a good guy. He, you know, he tried to do the right thing."

"You're adorable," she said.

"Screw TV. Movies rule," Gage said. "*First Blood.* That's something worth watching."

"Can you tell Gage hates authority?" I asked.

"I hadn't noticed," she said.

"Hey, the cops ran Stallone out of town," Gage said. "And he, like, blows up *everything*."

"Simple. Straightforward," I said.

"Dude never gave up."

"Here's to never giving up," I said, intending for it to be inspirational, but I think it was a little too close to the mark.

Everyone went quiet, and after a few more stuttering attempts to start up a conversation about movies, we all fell silent. My adrenaline had finally died down, and I began to feel the exhaustion of the day.

As if on cue, Gage said, "I'm fragged. I'm going to fluff my pillow here and get some sleep." He thumped his fist against the solid granite, then slid down to a prone sleeping position, at an angle with his legs and butt facing me and Winsley. He shifted around a little before going still.

I looked to the north. The clouds had parted and the moon rose over the horizon. Moments later, I heard Gage snoring.

Winsley lay down, pretty much in the same position as Gage, and soon she seemed to be asleep too.

I had no idea what time it was, but I didn't really want to know. I just watched the moon and soaked in this surreal moment. I was sitting on a ledge on a cliff face towering over Yosemite Valley. We were more than halfway up. We'd done it free soloing, in a rainstorm, and nobody had died. My god. We'd actually made it this far. It was a miracle, and I wanted to stay in this moment forever.

Finally, the events of the day pulled at me, and my eyelids started to slide closed.

"Hey," Winsley whispered. "Got room for two?"

I blinked my eyes open, and realized that Winsley had come to my part of the ledge.

Stunned, I shifted to the side and she scooted dangerously along the outer edge, wedging in next to me. I scrunched up against the rock face to give her room. There was barely enough room for one, and I swear her ass had to be hanging over the edge. But she managed it gracefully, clipped her harness into my anchor, and sandwiched up against me.

"Cozy," she said.

"Haven't you had enough excitement for the day?"

"Never."

"You want to sleep with your back over the edge?" I said, but I was grinning from ear to ear.

"It's warmer here," she said.

"You're crazy."

"You ran away so fast at Moonpath, we didn't have a chance to talk. Then you stonewalled me with Jack Daniel's and Lisa on your lap. Then you made me chase you halfway up Half Dome. I mean, I've heard of playing hard to get, but you really raised the bar."

"I tried to stop you."

"You did, huh?" she whispered. "Like a girl tries to stop a boy by flipping her hair and swinging her hips as she walks away? That kind of trying to stop me? 'Hey, don't follow me up this sweet cliff and do something daring.' I thought you were flirting."

"I wasn't flirting."

"I know, jackass," she whispered. "You're an idiot. And now look where we are."

I chuckled. "I *did* try to stop you."

"Yeah," she said. We both looked out at the moon. "But was I going to miss this?" she said softly.

We went quiet, and I was very conscious of her body pressed up against mine, her thigh draped over mine.

"You know," she said softly. "I've never kissed anyone while I was working the rock. My only rule. And you made me break it."

"We didn't kiss."

"Our lips touched," she said.

"Totally didn't."

"It felt like they did. I really wanted to kiss you. I don't know what stopped me."

"We didn't kiss," I repeated.

"You sound sad about that, honey." She pushed a lock of my hair off my forehead.

"Winsley..."

"Yeah?"

"I know you broke up with Gage, but that was like two seconds ago. He's my best friend and he's, you know, two feet away."

She let out a breath. "I swear you're too sweet to be real," she said. "Gage and I had a good long talk before we went looking for you. We worked it out."

"Don't be a pussy," Gage said from his eastern perch.

I started, then peered over at him. He hadn't moved, curled up in a ball, his butt to us. "I thought you were asleep," I said to him.

"I was," he said. "I was having this dream about a cheesy soap opera. Then I woke up and realized it wasn't a fucking dream."

"Gage—"

He raised his head and looked at me. "I'm the one who told her to visit you," he said, then went back to his huddle. "Bitch saved my life. She can kiss whoever she wants."

Winsley grinned. "Hear that? Bitch can kiss whoever she wants."

I was overwhelmed with emotion. I didn't know what to say.

"Gage—"

"Just don't start fucking," he said over his shoulder. He shifted again, like he was going to find a more comfortable spot on the rock. "There are no walls on this damned thing."

Winsley chuckled into my shoulder, then said, "We promise."

"We do?" I joked. "Don't I don't get a say?"

"You get a kiss," she said. "If you want one."

I looked into Winsley's eyes. Her face glowed in the soft moonlight. She raised her lips to mine and I kissed her. Electricity raced through my body, and she trembled like it was racing through hers, too. She tasted like mint. Even after a day on the rock, her lips somehow tasted like mint.

"Oh my god," I whispered when our lips finally parted.

"I think I've found a new religion," she said.

I kissed her again and again, and that electricity hit me every time. I didn't want it to ever end. But eventually, our exhaustion took hold of us both. She nuzzled into my shoulder, and we fell asleep.

I don't know how long I was out, but at some point my eyes opened for no reason.

The nearly full moon was high and huge, shining down over us. An aura surrounded it, as though it was pushing back the dark sky.

The fetch perched on the edge of the ledge with her legs dangling over the abyss. She was grinning, and her green eyes glowed in the dark.

She pushed out a breath between pursed lips. "Oh Eric, you do not disappoint."

I sat up, glancing at Winsley, but she was sound asleep.

"Don't worry. They won't hear us," the fetch said.

I was completely disoriented. I'd woken up in a moonlit darkness on the side of a cliff, and I was talking to a magical fetch. But more than that, as soon as I saw her, I thought about the last time I'd seen her. When I'd dared to kiss her.

If you kiss a fetch, you'll never fall in love with mortal woman.

I suddenly wondered if the fetch was going to do something horrible to Winsley.

"Why...are you here?" I asked.

"I'm with you always." She winked. "But you knew that. So

what do you really want to ask me?"

I glanced at Winsley again, and at Gage beyond her. "I didn't mean for them to come with me," I said. "I was going alone."

"But that's not your choice anymore is it? I told you what would happen when you dance with a fetch."

My throat constricted.

"*Give me your passion.*" She echoed the first words she'd ever said to me. "*And I will make such a fire that those around you won't be able to turn away.* Remember? They're here because of you. Your light pulled them like moths."

"But they're dancing with you, too," I said, and my heart was in my throat. I wanted her to say that she was protecting them, too. That they were invincible, that I hadn't just led my best friend and the woman I loved to their deaths. I wanted her to promise me.

"They're dancing with *you*, Eric."

"But you're protecting them. Like you're protecting me."

A touch of sadness glimmered in those emerald eyes. "I'm *your* fetch, Eric."

"What does that mean?" I demanded.

"You know what it means," she said, then paused and cocked her head. Her pale slender fingers caressed the edge of the rock, and she watched them like she was watching sparkling lights. "Oh, you've inspired me, Eric. *You.* You've taken a summer and made it a legend. Don't stop." She turned her emerald gaze back on me.

"Don't play games with me!" I said. "What about Gage and Winsley?"

"Live, Eric," she whispered. "Like you've never lived before. This is your moment. And it will never come again."

"I want you to protect them—"

"Eric?" Winsley murmured, shifting beside me. I glanced at her and she blinked, rising up on one elbow. "You okay?"

I shot my gaze back to the fetch, but she was gone. There was nothing except the moonlit night staring back at me, cold and unforgiving.

CHAPTER 21

"Bad dream?" Winsley asked as I stared at the night.

"Yeah," I lied.

I dreamed we were stuck in the middle of Half Dome with a fetch who just told me she was going to let my friends die, I thought.

I felt sick.

"Time is it?" She yawned and brought up her watch, an all-black swatch with no numbers and glow-in-the-dark hands. "Just a few minutes before light. Wow. Good internal clock there, Thor. Ready to hit the rock?"

"Mmmm hmmm," I said.

She took my chin in her hand. "No," she said, as though she'd expected me to catch something.

"What?"

"Wet rock? We'll probably have to wait most of the day, let the sun do some evaporating."

"Yeah. Right."

"Hey," she said. "You okay?"

"Yeah. Yeah, I'm fine."

She pulled me to her, kissed me. "Bad dreams begone," she whispered.

That made me smile.

"Hey Gage," Winsley called to his unmoving form. He

169

didn't respond. She turned to me. "I think he likes his bed."

"Fuck off," Gage mumbled. He grunted and sat up. The right side of his face was red, imprinted with the texture of the granite it had rested on.

"Sleep well?" I said.

"Almost as good as sleeping with a log shoved up my butt," he said, blinking.

Winsley chuckled.

Together, we waited as the sun rose into an overcast sky. Just hanging around waiting for the rock to dry was torture, but hour after hour went by, and it didn't seem to be getting much drier. We still had a ways to go before we were done, but none of us were in a hurry to climb on wet rock again. I started wondering what would happen if we were forced to spend another night up here. That prospect created a little fist of fear in my stomach. We'd eaten the last of our food, though we did have plenty of water. We'd had the foresight to refill our water bottles during the storm.

The sun continued to climb, but it was obscured by clouds. For a time, I thought maybe it was going to rain again. We waited for hours, wasting the day as we checked the dampness every fifteen minutes out of impatience.

But Gage seemed to have lost the panic he'd had last night. He joked around. He even found a crumpled old piece of paper in the bottom of his stuff sack, flattened it out and took great pains to make a paper airplane out of it. He tossed it into the wide expanse and watched it float slowly downward.

Winsley stayed near me, tracing patterns of muscles on my back through my shirt like she was solving a puzzle. She seemed perfectly content to wait, as though this was just any other day on the rock.

But that cold fear settled into my belly. The weather reflected my mood. Indecisive, tumultuous, cloudy. The head game had finally gotten to me.

What if we were forced to climb in bad conditions? What if it rained *again*? What if we got trapped here until we got so hungry we lost strength? The visit of the fetch had spooked me. I was scared for my friends. Beyond scared.

At the start of this climb, I'd felt like I was dancing with her. Even when the rain came last night and everything seemed to go to hell, I kept my calm because I let myself believe that the fetch was looking out for us. For all of us. That Winsley's quick-thinking quickdraws and Gage's last-minute grab were because all three of us were living inside my bubble of invincibility.

But that had been random luck, not the fetch. Gage could just as easily have fallen to his death.

I had to get myself into the headspace for climbing before we started up. Fear-stricken second-guessing wasn't going to get us up the cliff.

The skies continued to do their frustrating churning, clouds bunching, threatening to rain, then pulling back to reveal a little bit of sun. It was late afternoon when Winsley put a hand on the rock and said, "Decision time, boys. Rock's not great, but we're out of time. We go now, or we're going to have problems with nightfall."

"Let's do it. I've made airplanes out of all my paper," Gage said. "Only thing left is to start chucking pro over the edge."

Winsley looked at me, expecting me to chime in. When I didn't, she said, "Eric?"

"Yeah," I said, but I felt anything but ready. "Yeah, I guess we get to it."

She took my chin in her hand again and made me face her. "Hey," she whispered. "Bad dreams begone." And she winked.

I let out a breath and managed a smile. I told myself that it didn't matter if the fetch was looking after us. It didn't change what I had to do.

"I'll take the lead," Winsley said. "We can switch out later."

"Okay."

We clipped our sacks and our pro to our harnesses and started up, Winsley in the lead, Gage next, and me bringing up the rear. My fears bogged me down. I was worried about the stone, which had dried in some places but remained damp in others. I kept shouting up to Winsley and Gage, warning them to look for shadowed spots which might look dry but really weren't.

I also kept second-guessing Winsley's choice of route, though I didn't say anything to her. And I kept watching Gage's moves with a critical eye. I even made some suggestions to him.

After maybe the third suggestion, Gage stopped and leaned way out like a flag in the wind.

My heart flipped in my chest.

"Gage!" I shouted, thinking he was about to fall.

"Hey numbnuts," he said, looking down at me calmly. "I don't need you feeding me your beta. Knock it off or I'm gonna kick your skinny ass when we reach the top of this bitch. Got it?"

"Sorry, man."

And we continued on.

My next panic moment happened when we hit a substantial overhang. Just the slightest slip would put a climber into a free fall. No chance for a slide or a second grab.

Winsley went up and over it like a ballet dancer. Gage went next, and I tensed. But his superior arm strength served him well. He muscled up and around.

I went next, still thinking about Gage. I got up underneath it and, as I was reaching for a nice ridge with my right hand, my foot slipped where I had pushed it against a micro ledge. Without the pressure, my under-cling popped off, and the only thing attaching me to the rock were my two fingers on the ledge. I swung way out, and for a second, I thought those fingers were going to pop off too.

But they didn't.

I swung back in and snagged the under-cling again and pincered my arms so hard my pecs burned. I hefted myself up and over. There was a good spot on the other side, a nice little ledge. I stood there, face against the rock, and hyperventilated.

I found a good place for a cam, jammed it in, and I clipped in with shaky hands.

"Jesus," I murmured.

Gage was already clipped next to me, and Winsley on the other side of him.

I just breathed, in and out.

"That was close," he said. "Now are you going to stop fucking nannying me and concentrate on what *you're* doing?" he asked.

"Yeah," I said. "Yeah, I'm gonna do that."

"Last night freaked me out, okay?" Gage said. "But that was last night. I'm over it. I don't need your worry. You need to get your head straight or it's going to kill you."

I realized he was right. I wasn't feeling the rock.

"You okay, Thor?" Winsley asked.

"He's fine," Gage said. "He's just suffering from mother hen syndrome."

"But he's such a cute mother hen," she said.

Gage rolled his eyes. "Maybe I'll just throw myself over the edge right now and save myself from the flirting," he grumbled to himself.

I forced myself to let go of all my fears and expectations. I'd come here to free solo Half Dome or die trying. From now on, it was going to just be about the climbing. I had to become part of the rock. I couldn't climb for Gage and myself at the same time. Nobody could.

"You lead, Eric," Gage said. "I'm tired of having you staring at my ass."

Winsley chuckled, and we started off again. It took a little while, but not having Gage right in front of me did help. All I could see was the rock, and that's what I needed.

I re-discovered the rhythm I'd had yesterday, where everything in the whole world was just one move at a time. Slowly, it began to be fun again.

I got into the zone and I lost myself. Pull up, toe jam, pull up, hand jam, layback, push with the foot, pull up, crossover, pull up again. On and on.

The sun was going down when I heard someone calling for me. Dazed, I turned and looked down.

Gage and Winsley were a good thirty feet below me.

"Slow up there, Thor," Winsley shouted.

"Oh shit. Sorry!" I called down.

"That a good resting spot?" Gage said.

"No," I said. "But I'll find one."

"And slow the fuck down."

I looked around. There was a good spot a few feet above me.

"Roger that," I said. I worked my way up. My spot had a nice ledge to put my feet on, and there was the perfect crack next to it. I created an anchor for myself and clipped in.

"Got a tasty spot waiting for you," I called down.

Gage worked his way up to me, made his anchor, and clipped in. Winsley took a different route, climbed above me, and cammed into the same crack as me higher up. She rested her feet on my shoulders.

I looked appreciatively left and then right at the nice calves on either side of me.

We were hungry but we had no food, so we drank water. Winsley kept looking upward, then left and right. The sun was low on the horizon, and only the upper half of Half Dome was bathed in light. We still basked in that light, but the line was moving steadily closer. The valley below was already deep in shadow.

"About six o'clock?" I asked.

"Seven," she said, checking her watch. "We've got light for about another thirty minutes, then twilight for thirty more minutes."

"Oh," I said.

"Thing is," she said, scanning above us. "That's the Visor. Right there." She pointed to an overhang far above us.

I shifted, looked over my other shoulder. I'd assumed I couldn't see past that overhang because it was the only thing breaking the line of the flat face we were on. But the more I looked at it....

"I think you're right, that's the fucking Visor," I said, excited. The Visor was the last big overhang, that lip you saw from a distance at the top of the northwest face. It was wide and long, stretching almost as far as I could see. "How long you figure it will take us to reach it?"

She bit her lip. "The speed we've been going, an hour. Maybe. But maybe not. Some of the hardest pitches are next. The Zig Zags have a pair of 12A's until we hit the Thank God Ledge." She pointed. "Then another 12A and a 12C to cap it off. Big last push, then we're home free. Nothing but 5.8s from there all the way to the top. A bit of fun at the end."

"For someone who hates the numbers, you sure know them," I said.

"I'm a safety girl." She gave me a winsome smile.

"What do you think?" I asked.

She blew out a breath. "It's been slower today. I figured we'd hit the Thank God Ledge by now. We waited so long for the rock to clear, I don't know...."

"We're so close," Gage said. "I vote we go for it."

Winsley hesitated. "If we get bound up in the Zig Zags, it could take us past dark. And that's not where we want to spend the night."

"Let's do it," Gage said. "I'm not spending another night on the rock listening to you two whisper sappy bullshit to each other."

She chuckled and looked at me. "What do you say, fearless leader?"

I hesitated, then said, "Let's be fearless."

We headed up the Zig Zags with Winsley in the lead and Gage next. I took the rear and started to worry about Gage again now that I could see him. We'd been climbing hard, and he tended to spend his arm strength before the rest of us. But the more I watched him, the more I realized something had changed. I don't know if he was using his legs more, or if he had just kicked into a whole new gear. But he was more confident on the rock, seemingly through sheer force of will.

We made it past the Zig Zags, but it took longer than we'd hoped. It was twilight when we took a break on the Thank God Ledge, which wasn't nearly as welcoming as Big Sandy.

There was no pitching Winsley's imaginary tent here. The ledge was only a foot deep, though it was probably a hundred feet long.

"All right boys," Winsley said. "Decision time again. One more rough spot and we're home free. But we've run out of sun. This is actually a decent spot to spend the night if we have to."

I surveyed the slanted granite before us. The handholds looked minimal, the face smooth.

"It's mostly smearing," Winsley confirmed what I was thinking. "Thin and balance-y."

"Can we even do that in half an hour?" I asked.

She hesitated, then nodded. "Unless we fuck up. Probably be dark by the time we get past it, but by then who cares? The rest is cake. We can do it by moonlight."

"Then we're wasting time," Gage said.

"You sure?" I asked him.

"I'm good," he said.

He looked tired and hungry, but we were all tired and hungry. Part of me felt like it was a really bad idea to push it. But by morning we'd be starving. And we didn't have another rainstorm to stock up on water again.

One big challenge, and then we were through it.

"Winsley?" I asked.

"I'm dreaming of a shower," she said with a smile, then she nodded seriously. "Yeah. Let's do it."

"I'll lead," I said.

The chimney up from the ledge was almost relaxing, like it was preparing me with gentle hands for the next phase. It went by too quickly.

When I hit the smooth slope Winsley had said was "thin and balance-y," the hairs on the back of my neck stood on end. This was going to be a spot where we'd have to keep ourselves on the rock almost through sheer force of will, using the rubber on the shoes and the natural friction of our fingertips. Like Winsley said, there was the barest favorable slant to the rock, so if we fell, we'd slide for a second before going over the edge, rather than just pitching straight into a free fall. And the twilight made visibility crappy.

"Fun," I said. I chalked up good and headed onto it. Sweaty fingers could kill me.

I used all my concentration going up, then shimmying over. Once I felt my foot begin to slip, but I literally willed myself to stick to the rock, and it stopped slipping. Inch by inch, I went up and then up again and then...

It was done.

I reached the place Winsley had mentioned, a sweet little ledge about a foot deep. I looked at the next pitch above me— a bunch of jug work. I could see what she meant. It was practically a hike. We could almost run up that. As she'd said: a bit of fun before the end.

I turned my attention back to Gage. He'd made it past the 5.12A and was working on the 5.12C part, that tricky shimmy over.

I'd been mainlining adrenaline all day, but watching him now I got a new rush of it. He inched over, inched—

His foot slipped, and he went flat on his belly, sliding down the slope.

"Gage!" I screamed.

Flashes of the fetch went through my mind. She wasn't going to save him.

He was headed for the edge, his feet skidding, hands pressed on the rock.

I held my breath as he slowed, blood smears trailing from his fingertips.

He came to a stop, his heels only inches from the edge.

Winsley looked up in horror, frozen as she waited for the inevitable. One wrong move, and Gage would go over with nothing to catch him.

He stuck there, half a foot above the edge of oblivion. I could see his back pumping as he breathed. Slowly, carefully, he let go of the rock with one bloody hand and stuffed it in his chalk bag, then put it back on the rock. He stuck his other hand in, put it back. Painstakingly, he started back up.

Winsley and I just watched, transfixed and helpless, as he inched his way up the face. One hand. One foot. Another hand. Another foot.

He made it back to the regular route and got to the problem that had dislodged him.

And he made it past.

And then, suddenly, he was safe. He reached my ledge and I grabbed his arm, hauled him up.

"Jesus. Always gotta put on a show, don't you?" I said, and I hugged him.

"Fuck me, man," he breathed, hugging me back. "I thought I was gone."

"After you slipped and came back, I..." I said. "That was the best climbing I've ever seen."

"I'm just going wipe some of this water on my face..." He knelt next to a little pocket of water in a trench right along the edge of the ledge and splashed it on his face. "And then I'm going to lean against the wall here and try not to puke my guts up." He backed up and breathed hard.

I didn't have time to laugh. Instead, I turned my focus to Winsley. The light was bad now. It was almost full dark. The moon had only begun to rise, and she was just starting the climb.

Heart in my throat, I watched her move her way up. Gage had looked like a beetle scuttling, one jerky movement at a time, but Winsley seemed to melt onto the rock and ooze up it, defying gravity. She took this route with the grace she'd done everything else. In less than ten minutes, she pulled herself up to our little ledge like it had been no big thing.

"Boys," she said, breathing hard and smiling, standing right on the lip of the ledge.

"That was amazing," I said.

She gave a little curtsey, and I moved forward to kiss her.

That's when the front part of the ledge sheared off the cliff face without warning, taking Winsley with it.

CHAPTER 22

"Winsley!" I screamed, and time seemed to slow. Her mouth went wide with shock, her body hanging seemingly motionless, arms wide to catch her balance as she suddenly had nothing to stand on. My scream of anguish seemed to last forever, and it was like I was pulling my arms through sludge to get to her. I envisioned catching Winsley's hand, but I couldn't move fast enough.

She dropped.

"No!"

Without thinking, I leapt over the edge after her. Something scratched my ankle as I reached...reached for her. Rock dust billowed up, engulfing her as she fell. I could see nothing except her trailing ponytail and her arm reaching upward. I stretched to snatch her wrist.

I would have had her. I would have, but I was jerked to a sudden stop. My swipe missed her wrist by an inch, and I only caught the tip of her ponytail. I snatched it between thumb and forefinger. Hope surged in me as I felt the strain of arresting her body weight with two fingers. My muscles corded tight, and I yelled. I wasn't going to let go—

The hair slipped through my fingers, vanishing into the cloud of dust.

Winsley was gone.

"No!" I hung there upside down, helpless, the billowing rock-dust rising up to surround me. My mind froze, and a roar filled my ears. I couldn't think anything, couldn't feel anything.

It took a long anguished moment to realize that I *was* just hanging there, that I hadn't fallen even though I hadn't been tied into anything.

That's when I heard Gage's voice, and I realized he'd been talking for some time.

"Eric," he grunted. "C'mon, Eric, talk to me. You gotta help me man. You gotta grab on. I can't... It's slipping."

I came to my senses, and instead of the roaring in my ears, I heard the thunder of the rocks continuing down the mountain, taking Winsley with them. I was facing the drop and the cloud of rock dust that swirled around me. But I became aware that something had hooked into my climbing shoe, right next to my ankle. A finger. A single one of Gage's fingers was keeping me from falling. But he was slipping and the shoe was coming off.

"I can't...hold you, man," Gage said, his voice straining. He held tightly to a piece of webbing he'd secured in the wall above the ledge, but he was stretched to the limit.

My self-preservation instinct kicked in, and I doubled over, lifting myself up. I grabbed his wrist. He gasped in relief and hauled on me, pulling me up to the now half-sized shelf.

I turned, miserable, and stared into the gray cloud below.

"I tried," I whispered. "I tried to get her. I tried..."

"Nothing you could have done, man," he huffed, immediately clipping into his webbing. "Nothing anyone could have done. Now back the fuck up and clip in. Don't stand at the edge. More could still go."

"God, Gage. It's my fault."

"Shut the fuck up and clip in. I'm not kidding."

"She's dead, and it's my—"

"Hey," a voice called from below.

Winsley!

"Holy fuck!" Gage said, grabbing my arm as I leaned

dangerously over the edge, peering into the dust. A breeze cleared some of the cloud, and I saw Winsley clinging to the new, ragged rock face.

"Winsley!"

"Yeah," she called up. "I got a hand on."

I only hesitated a second, then my brain kicked in. I immediately started pulling quickdraws from my harness and making the Winsley-inspired quickdraw rope, snapping carabiners together like lightning. It only took Gage half a second to catch on, then he did the same. We used all of our quickdraws, then snapped our ends together and tossed the eight-foot make-shift rope down to her.

It came up about two feet short.

"We need more. Gage, we need more—"

"I can get it," Winsley said. "Give me a second." She drew a breath and started working the rock. Heel hook, lift up. Left leg to a new jagged slope, pull up. She moved as carefully and gracefully those last two feet to the end of the rope as if this was her first climb of the day. Then she clipped it into her harness.

"On belay?" she joked.

Gage and I hauled her up hand over hand until she came over the edge. I grabbed her arm, then her harness, and clipped her to me. Then I hugged her for all I was worth.

"God... Oh god," I murmured into her neck.

"Was that you?" she asked. "Pulling my hair?"

"I tried...to catch you. I just—"

"Pulling my hair." She shook her head. "You could just tell me you like me instead. What is this, grade school?"

I gave a short, relieved laugh. "Yeah..." I was crying now. "Yeah, that was me."

We all just clung to the side of the rock, breathing hard as the thunder of the falling rocks far below reverberated throughout the valley, and the rock dust moved down and out like some great billowing cloud.

I held Winsley's head between my hands, looking at her, disbelieving. She had a gash on her forehead that was bleeding pretty good, making a two-inch red stripe down the right side of her face.

I kissed her, then I kissed her again.

She laughed. "Enough, Romeo. Let's finish this thing."

"No," I said. "Let's just take a moment here."

"The rest of this could go any second," Gage said. "You don't know."

"It's a cakewalk from here," Winsley said. "Let's just go."

"You're sure?" I asked.

By way of an answer, she unclipped from me and started up the route.

Gage and I looked at her, then at each other.

"Girl's a beast," Gage said.

"Are your fingers okay?" I asked.

"Why, you got an ambulance in your pack?"

"I just mean..."

"You said you were going to stop the mother hen shit."

"I know."

He held his ravaged fingertips up, and somehow the bleeding had stopped. "Super Glued 'em while Winsley was climbing," he said. "They'll hold long enough."

I shook my head and chuckled, the nerves of everything making me feel jittery. He started up after Winsley, and she was right—total cakewalk.

I was the last to pull myself up and over the Visor. Winsley and Gage stood ready, peering over the ledge, and when I got close enough, they both extended hands. I grabbed on and they hoisted me up.

And then it was done. We'd made it to the top. We had free soloed Half Dome.

I couldn't believe it.

We all took a few healthy steps back from the edge and looked out over the valley.

"Holy crap," Gage said quietly.

Winsley didn't say anything, but we must have stood there for half an hour in silence. The moon came out, casting everything in a silver hue.

"Come on, boys," Winsley said. "Let's get gone. I'm still dreaming of a shower."

The route down the backside of Half Dome was made for tourists. We descended the piton ladders quickly and efficiently, then hiked down into the forest. When I finally put my feet on level ground, it was like visiting some alien world, after being on nothing but vertical surfaces for two days.

Once we hit the trees, we found a good spot and built a fire.

Our stomachs growled, so we just took sips of water for dinner.

We relaxed, gathered around the campfire. I sat behind Winsley, my legs outside hers, my chest against her back, and my arms wrapped around her. I didn't want to let her go, didn't want to lose contact with her even for a second. She didn't seem to mind and just held onto my hands, absently massaging my fingers.

As we all adjusted to the fact that we weren't in constant mortal danger, that we could actually let our guard down and not die, I asked Winsley the burning question.

"How did you do it?" I asked. "How did you...grab hold? The cloud of dust... You were falling."

"It was you," she said simply. "I didn't know until I asked you, but it was you. I mean, I was in a free fall. I was reaching out for anything I could touch, but there was only air and dust. Then it felt like a giant was yanking my hair—which, ouch, by the way. I wasn't even sure which way *was* up until that moment. But that little bit reoriented me, redirected my fall. I swung back toward the rock, hit it, and suddenly there were handholds. I don't know how I got one, but I did."

"Damn," Gage said.

"I tell you, I thought I was dead anyway," she said. "I thought the whole mountain was coming down. For those first few seconds, I just hung there, flinching. I expected a thousand tons of rock to scrape me off. But it didn't. And then I heard you guys talking. The rest you know."

"Whoa," I said.

"So thank you," she leaned her head back and kissed me on the cheek.

"It was Gage who saved us," I said. "We'd have both died. I didn't think, I just jumped after you. He's the one who grabbed my shoe."

"Who's your fetch?" Gage said, like he was saying "Who's your daddy?"

Winsley laughed, then said, "Your shoe?"

"With one finger," I said.

"It was two fingers," Gage said.

"Whatever," I said. "A hundred and eighty pounds on *two* fingers."

Gage did a quick flex.

We sat quietly, listening to the crackle of the fire.

"It's a story for the grandchildren," Gage said, shaking his head. "But I don't think I'll be doing that again anytime soon."

We chuckled.

With the adventure settling, our exhaustion took over. Ten minutes later, we doused the fire and lay down. Winsley snuggled in right next to me, right where she belonged.

CHAPTER 23

We woke up at first light, packed up our stuff, and headed back to Curry Village. It was a seventeen-mile hike, but nobody complained, even though we were sore and we had no food. Our water ran out when we were about five miles away, and we toughed it out until, finally, we were home.

"I'm having ten cheeseburgers," Gage said.

"And ten Cokes and ten baskets of fries," I added.

"Boys." Winsley rolled her eyes. "Your priorities are out of whack."

We both looked at her in surprise.

"The correct near-death-experience follow-up is...a shower. Shower first."

"After we drink our body weight in water," I said.

"Yes, after that," she said.

Winsley's tent cabin was on the far side of Curry Village at a site reserved for employees. We reached our tent cabin first and she stopped with us, hooked her arm into mine and pulled me into a kiss.

Gage rolled his eyes and went inside. The door slammed shut on its overzealous spring.

"Meet me at The Shack later?" she asked.

"Ten cheeseburgers," I breathed. "And all the whiskey. I

still can't believe we're alive. It's celebration time."

"And then some." She tipped her chin up the row. "I'm going to go wash." Her eyes turned mischievous. "And secure some pro."

"Pro?"

"Little round things wrapped in foil. I told you, I'm a safety girl."

"Oh!"

She winked and let go of me, sauntering away like she had that first day we'd climbed with her. Also like then, she waved over her shoulder like she knew I was watching her.

I went into the tent cabin to find Gage refilling his water bottle from a gallon jug by the side of the bed. I joined in. We drank the bottles dry, filled them again, and drank them dry a second time. Then we sat in silence.

"Dinner?" he offered, finally.

I looked at the grime on my dirt-smeared arm. "I'm starving but..."

"But Winsley's right?" Gage said.

"Yeah," I said. "I think Winsley's right."

"I fuckin' hate it when she's right."

Barely an hour later, showered and wearing clothes that were far cleaner than our climbing gear, we climbed the steps at The Shack. Lisa was there, and I suddenly remembered all of the awkwardness I'd left behind. But she had her normal gorgeous smile on, and she didn't say a thing about our last night together. She just seated us next to the rail and immediately brought three Cokes, even though Winsley hadn't arrived yet.

Fries came next, and we were halfway through the first basket when Winsley joined us. She was freshly scrubbed and the cut on her forehead had been cleaned and closed with butterfly bandages. She sat in the chair right next to mine and linked our fingers together. We'd ordered her a burger already, and it showed up just as she sat down.

We ate like starved rats. Gage and I split another burger. We ordered milk shakes and chomped through big chocolate chip cookies. And after that, we passed Gage's flask around, not even bothering to doctor the Cokes this time. We just lowered our heads and took surreptitious swigs straight from the bottle.

I felt on top of the world.

My arm was around Winsley, her leg on top of mine, my other arm resting on the wooden rail behind us.

Lisa's shift ended and she joined us just like before. I thought she might be jealous about how Winsley and I now sat together, but she was exactly the opposite. She just watched us with a "you guys are adorable" smile on her face and listened to us tell the story of the last three days.

Gage was laughing at my retelling of the rainstorm when I suddenly stopped talking in mid-sentence.

My father stepped up the stairs onto The Shack's deck, and the breath left my body. I couldn't think. I froze with my hand clenching Winsley's.

At first I thought I must be hallucinating. There was no way my dad would have come all the way back to the States to get me. That couldn't be real. Dad hadn't come back for Mom's funeral. No way he'd come all this distance just for me. I'd banked on that when I'd sped out of Durango spraying gravel.

His black eyes blazed, locked on me, like he wasn't going to look away from me for a second.

I felt like a boy again, like all of my adventures had been cookies stolen from a cookie jar and now my punishment had come due. Suddenly the road trip didn't matter. What I'd done on Half Dome didn't matter. Even the fetch seemed like a fanciful dream, too unreal and too far away to help me.

The real world had caught me, and I could see in my dad's eyes that it wasn't going to let me go this time.

I jerked to my feet, but my leg was tangled with Winsley's. The table jumped mightily, tipping plastic cups and scattering fries. My surprise turned to panic, and all I could think of was escape. Winsley looked up sharply, confused, as I disentangled myself from her, leaning on the rail.

"Wait," I said, holding up a hand like I could stop my dad

from coming, like he would see reason if I could just explain it to him.

I felt something cold and hard hit my other arm, the one on the rail.

"Holy fuck!" Gage staggered to his feet as handcuffs snapped into place around my wrist.

I spun to look into the eyes of Uncle Morty. He was on the other side of the rail, his head low because of the raised deck. He snapped the other half of the handcuffs on his own wrist and glared at me.

"You're not running anywhere this time, Eric," my Dad said. "You're coming with me."

Gage's chair spun and clattered on its side as he pivoted. His eyes flew wide when he saw my dad.

"What's going on?" Lisa demanded.

"What the hell?" Winsley shouted. She and Lisa both stood.

Uncle Morty vaulted the rail. "Chase is over, son." he said.

"You're going to do what I fucking tell you now," Dad said. "If I have to drag your ass to the airport in handcuffs, you're going to do what I tell you."

"Just let me explain—" I began, but Dad was already vehemently shaking his head.

"Nothing could explain this behavior," Dad said. "I'm livid."

Gage violently shoved the table over, getting everyone's attention. Gasps went up from the remaining patrons on the deck as our plates and cups crashed to the ground. Everyone went dead silent.

"You better let him go," Gage warned.

Uncle Morty held up his badge. "Gage Wilson," he said. "Seventeen years old. Son of Edward Wilson III, attorney at law in Durango, Colorado. You've stolen over $30,000 from your father. You're a minor without permission to be here, and you're drinking under age. You want to add assault to the list?"

"You're not a cop in California," Gage said.

"But you're a punk everywhere," Dad said.

"Fuck you, you deadbeat dickhead," Gage said. "You think

I'm going to shake in my boots because you mentioned my dad? I've already talked to him, and he's not the kind of asshole that puts his own son in handcuffs."

"You fucking little–"

"Don't fight, kid," Uncle Morty interrupted, deadly calm. "It's not going to go your way."

Gage's lips peeled back to reveal his shark's smile. His shoulders bunched, and his fists came up. I knew him, and I knew he would rather go down swinging than roll over. For a fleeting moment, I imagined us doing it, Gage and I just fighting our way out of this.

But then what? What happened after that?

Where would we run? And for how long? Even if Gage had somehow actually talked to his father about the money—even if that part was real—we'd broken other laws. Even if Uncle Morty couldn't arrest us, he could press charges.

Misery twisted in my chest. I remembered how I'd felt on the face of Half Dome after the fetch told me she wouldn't protect my friends. I'd been helpless to save them, to keep them from falling.

I wasn't helpless this time.

If I left quietly, Dad would have what he wanted: control. It'd pump up his ego. They'd let Gage's transgressions go. There would be no spillover onto Winsley or Lisa.

"Even if we win," I murmured. "We lose."

"What?" Gage said.

"Just...stop," I said.

"You're just going to let them take you?" Gage demanded. "After... After what we just did? Fuck them!"

"What is this all about?" Winsley asked, her eyes flicking from Dad to Uncle Morty and back again.

"I'll explain it to you later—" I said.

"No you won't," Dad said. "We're driving to San Francisco, and we are getting on a plane tonight."

"The fuck you are," Gage said, and his shoulders raised a little, like he was readying to lash out.

"Gage, stop," I said sharply, and that took the wind out of

his sails. A lump formed in my throat. "It's not... This isn't your fight."

"They gang up on you, I gang up on them," Gage said.

"Please don't," I said. "I got this."

Gage's chest pumped hard like he'd run a mile, but for the first time he took his gaze off Dad and Uncle Morty and looked at me.

"Don't let them take you," Gage said. "Not after...everything. It can't end this way."

"Maybe for me, it has to," I said.

Uncle Morty started around the fallen table toward Dad, hauling me behind him and coming easily within Gage's range. It was as though he was daring Gage to take a swing. For a second, I thought Gage would take the bait.

"Eric?" Gage asked rigidly, one last time.

"I got this," I repeated firmly. My heart ached, but I knew it was the right choice. At this fork in the river, I had to leave Gage behind.

He stood there, obviously hating every moment of it.

Winsley looked at me, confused. "Eric, I don't understand what's happening."

"I'll call you. I'll—"

"You don't have my number. Just...hang on." She frantically patted her jeans. "I need a pen."

Lisa ran for the waiters' station.

But Uncle Morty wasn't waiting. He hauled me down the steps and around The Shack with my Dad following closely, eyeing Gage like he expected him to start swinging. Together they took me up the path to a black Buick. Dad opened the passenger's door and Uncle Morty pushed me toward it.

"If you'll just give me a chance to explain—" I began.

"Nothing justifies what you've done," Dad said in his dark voice. "Get in."

"But, all of my stuff..."

"Should have thought of that before you wasted my money and my time," Dad said.

He shoved me at the open door. I ducked and climbed into

the passenger seat. Uncle Morty unlocked his side of the cuffs and locked them to the interior door handle, then slammed the door. Dad got into the back seat.

Uncle Morty climbed quickly into the driver's side and fired up the engine just as Winsley came running at the car, a flapping piece of paper in her hand.

"Just let me get her number!" I said, awkwardly trying to roll down the window with my free hand. "Can't you just wait a second?"

"Drive," Dad said.

Uncle Morty peeled out, spraying gravel just like I'd done when I'd left my old life behind in Durango.

"Eric!" Winsley shouted in a heartbreaking voice, but Uncle Morty drove right past her.

CHAPTER 24

The dark highway rushed at us, yellow lines zipping by like dots. Uncle Morty drove easily with one hand, his other hand resting on the console between us. He looked into the rearview mirror.

"Let me explain—" I began.

"Shut up," Dad cut me off from the back seat. "I want you to shut your mouth. All the way to Malaysia. I can't even describe how angry I am at you. You've wasted my time. My money. Do you know how much work I'm missing? It could cost me my job!"

"I didn't ask you to come—"

"You *forced* me to come!"

"Who gives a fuck about your job?" I shouted over the seat at him. "This is my *life* we're talking about!"

"You don't even know what life is yet," he hissed. "You're just a kid."

"You're not listening!" I said, tears standing in my eyes. "Everything I care about is back there. The things I've done this summer..." I wanted to tell him about everything. The road trip. The days of climbing. How good I got at it. The spiritual feeling I'd felt on the rock. How much I'd loved Winsley from the first moment I saw her. I'd been given the chance to face life on my own terms, and I'd done it. I'd been more than a match for it.

But none of this mattered to my dad. No matter how hard I argued, no matter how passionately I tried to make him see my side, he never would. In his eyes, I would never be good enough. I could never live up to his expectations. I was a fool to even try.

I'd started this journey because of the fetch, but maybe Gage had been right, that I drove myself hard partly because I was trying to prove to my dad I was good enough. I wanted him to look at what I was doing and say, "That's amazing, Eric! You're larger than life."

But he was never going to say that to me. Never.

Something broke inside me then, like I had been a ship tied to a dock in a storm, and the line had finally snapped. I looked at my dad with new eyes, with the eyes of an adult, not a child, and I saw a man so scared of losing control that he would try to stop me from growing just so he could feel better about himself. About *his* world.

"If you'd just done what I told you to do," Dad said. "None of this would have happened."

"Yeah Dad," I said. "You're right. None of this would have happened if I'd listened to you."

I turned to face forward and fell silent.

Dad mistook my silence for surrender, and he said, "Good. Now we can stop with all this nonsense."

I stayed implacably silent for the next half hour. Uncle Morty didn't say a word either.

Finally, it was my dad who spoke. "I'm going to catch a nap, Mort," he said. "Jetlag from chasing this damned kid."

Uncle Morty grunted, and I didn't respond at all to the jab. My dad settled himself in the back seat, but I didn't look at him. Whatever happened next, I was through listening to him.

When I heard him softly snoring in the back, I said to Uncle Morty, "You're not going to uncuff me, even in the car?"

"Nope."

"Is that really necessary? We're going fifty-five—"

"You jumped off a three-story balcony. Maybe you'd jump from a moving car going fifty-five. I gave you a second chance, son. You don't get a third chance with me."

"You can't take me to the airport," I said. "You can't put me on a plane with him."

"I can and I will."

"It doesn't even matter!" I practically shouted, then lowered my voice as my dad snorted in his sleep and shifted. "I'm going to be eighteen in twelve days," I said. "Twelve days! And then Dad can't tell me what to do with my life anymore. I could just get on a plane and fly back here."

"Then you do that. Until then, you're a minor and you're going with your dad."

"You don't even *like* my dad."

Uncle Morty didn't say anything to that.

"Please, Uncle Morty. I... I..." I wanted to tell him about Winsley. How perfect she was. "I'm in love."

"Are you now? That girl with the filed off fingernails and strong hands?"

"She's a climber."

"Is she?"

"I'm in love with her. Doesn't that count for something?"

Uncle Morty checked his mirrors again, but didn't say anything.

"She was... We were going to..." I felt my cheeks get hot.

"Gonna get laid tonight, were you?" he said.

"My first time," I said. "With the girl of my dreams."

"Bad timing for you, son. But you've been racking up quite a bill, and now it's time to pay up."

"I know I left a mess behind me. I know I ran from...everything. School. Dad. You. But...I had to."

"Did you now."

I hung my head. He wasn't going to listen to me, either.

"You don't even know what I've done," I murmured. "The things I've done. You wouldn't believe it."

He kept looking forward like he'd turned off his ears.

But I started talking anyway. I wanted him to know that the Eric who had ditched him in Durango wasn't the Eric sitting next to him now. I catalogued my summer of wonders, and what each part had done to me. Even as the story rolled out of me, I could barely believe it, and I'd lived it.

I started with Tina Cartwright, the PA speech, and my fight with the high school quarterback. I told him about my near-death fall in Canyonlands, but I didn't mention the fetch or the fact that I was going to die in twelve days, that this two last weeks of the summer were the only two weeks I had left. I just told him that the fall had made me realize how I was afraid of everything, and how I'd decided not to be that boy anymore.

I told him about Zion, about my awakening there, this newfound confidence that came from climbing. I skipped over the trip to L.A. since that was a sore spot, and I told him about Yosemite. About arriving with the eyes of a climber, looking up at the majesty of Half Dome for the first time. I told him about Winsley again, about each step of falling in love with her. I told him about the days of climbing with her and Gage, site after site, route after route, focusing our entire lives on feeling the rock, honing our abilities, learning what true friendship was.

And finally, I told him about the unbelievable trip up Half Dome, free soloing the whole thing. I told him how many times we'd almost died, and that we'd escaped and lived to celebrate.

"That's when you found me," I said. "It was our celebration, and everything was..."

I glanced over at him. He checked his mirrors, then put his gaze back on the road.

"I found this place inside myself," I murmured. "This...other me. I never even knew he was there. God, Uncle Morty, I turned into my own hero this summer. How many people ever do that in their entire lives? Everything I've ever wanted to do, I tried. Everything that scared the shit out of me, I faced it. I'm not that kid I was. Not anymore. Isn't that worth something? Isn't that worth more than you keeping a promise to a brother you hate, to do something that isn't going to matter in two weeks?"

He didn't look at me.

"It can't end like this," I said. "Can't you see that? It can't end with me taking a plane to a place I don't want to go for a father who doesn't care about what matters to me. Please, Uncle Morty. Please. I know it's twelve days before I'm an adult in the eyes of the law, but I already know who I am. Who I want to be. I don't need the law to tell me that."

His eyes tightened.

"Let this summer end the way it was meant to. Let it end in the arms of the woman I love. Let it end with me as the person I was meant to be, instead of who Dad thinks I ought to be."

He didn't say anything. I'd failed. He wasn't going to hear me any more than my father was going to hear me.

A calm descended on me then, and I set my jaw.

Ever since Uncle Morty threw the handcuffs on me, I'd slipped back into that scared teen I'd been three months ago. Through those eyes, Uncle Morty and my dad were Greek gods determining the course of my life. But the truth was this: they weren't gods.

And I wasn't a kid anymore.

I didn't need them to approve of what I was doing. And this predicament wasn't the end of the world. It was just another problem I was going to work out. I didn't want to make Uncle Morty my enemy, but if that's how it had to happen, so be it. No way were they putting me on a plane. I would do whatever I had to do to return to Winsley, to Gage. These were the last two weeks of my life, and I wasn't going to spend them with people who saw me as just a stupid kid.

Yeah, I had some difficult moves ahead. I couldn't get out of these handcuffs right now. I couldn't jump out of a moving car. But I was going to take it one move at a time. An opportunity would present itself. And when it did, I'd be ready.

I leaned back in my seat and looked over at Uncle Morty again. For the first time, I didn't see an invincible adult, a cop with a license to force me to do his will. The only power he had over me was the steel handcuffs.

"Didn't you ever want to be more than you were?" I asked, looking out at the road. "To be something different than what everyone saw when they looked at you? Didn't you ever say to yourself, 'I can be that thing. I can be more than even *I* thought I could be?'"

Uncle Morty took his foot off the accelerator. The engine softened, and the car slowed. He checked his mirrors and pulled over to the side of the road.

I tensed.

He turned the engine off, reached into his pocket and pulled out the handcuff keys.

Stunned, I watched as he leaned over me and unlocked the cuffs from my wrist. I didn't know if I should take this moment to lunge out the door or not. Was this some lapse of sanity that was only going to last a second? But his pale blue eyes were calm. The expression on his face was resigned, not ready-for-a-fight.

I hesitated. I could have flown out that door and he'd never have caught me. And I'd have made sure he wouldn't for the next twelve days. I could have, but I hesitated. I looked over my shoulder at my dad, still asleep.

Uncle Morty watched me like he knew the decision I was struggling with. When I settled back in my seat, he said, "Reporter."

"What?"

"I wanted to be a reporter. Travel the world. Witness history in the making. Write about it. I never did." There was no emotion to his voice, just a stiff statement of fact.

My mouth hung open. When I finally gathered my wits, I said, "I never knew that."

"Never told anyone," he said. "But I reckon if even half of your bullshit story is true, you did what I never could, son. Everything I've done in my life, I did for duty." He pressed his lips into a line, looked over his shoulder at Dad, then shook his head. "But not tonight. You're right, and he's wrong. Sending you with him just because. Well... You're not a boy anymore."

He reached across me and opened my door. It swung into the dark, empty night. The handcuffs rattled against the handle.

"Uncle Morty..."

"You go on, now," he said. "You go do...all those things you said you were going to do. Go kiss that pretty girl."

I looked at my dad in the back seat, still snoring softly, head on his arms. I wondered why he hadn't awakened when the car had come to a stop, when the door had opened. He should have, and I wondered if the fetch was at work again.

"I should say it to his face," I said, feeling the certainty in my belly. "I'm not running from him anymore."

Uncle Morty chuckled softly at that. "I see that you're not. You *have* changed, Eric."

I reached out and shook my dad. He roused, looking confused.

"Why are we stopped?" He sat up, dark eyebrows crouching down when he saw that my door was open. "What the fuck is happening here?"

"I'm leaving, Dad," I said. "I'm going back to my life."

"The hell you are."

"I am."

He ignored that, like I hadn't said anything worth hearing. "Mort, what the hell are you playing at?" he said as he yanked the rear door open and pulled himself out of the car.

I got out and closed the car door behind me.

"Get back in that car," Dad demanded in his dark tone, speaking through clenched teeth. He towered over me...

Except *no*. He didn't. Not anymore. My father had always been so tall, but now I was actually eye-to-eye with him. In fact, I was taller.

Dad flicked a glance at Uncle Morty, who had gotten out of his side of the car. "Dammit, Mort, get over here and help me."

"No," Uncle Morty said. "I don't think I will." He leaned his elbows on the roof of the cab, watching.

With a growl, Dad turned back to me. "Don't make this worse than it already is."

"It's already as bad as it gets," I said. "And I have something to say to you."

"Well, I'm not listening to anything you have to say until you get back in that car."

"Your choice. I'll keep it short. It's this: This is my life. Mine. And if you were inclined to listen, you'd understand why it's mine and not yours. You'd see what I'm doing here. You could even be a part of it. It's amazing. I made my choice at the fork in the river, and I'm not going back."

"Fork in the what?"

"The river."

"That makes no sense."

"It would if you'd listen."

"Get in the car, Eric," he demanded, and he grabbed my arm.

I didn't know what I was waiting for until it happened. But when his hand landed on me, I realized *this* was the new fork in the river. This was the threat Dad had always promised with his dark voice. This was what I'd always been afraid of.

He tried to shove me toward the car, and I didn't go. His brow furrowed. His strong hand clenched. I flexed my bicep in response. He tried to shove me again, and I stayed put.

I reached up with my other hand, grabbed his wrist, and slowly, forcibly removed his grip from my arm. He struggled to stop me but he couldn't. I was astonished at how much stronger I was now. His eyes went wide, and he tried to yank himself out of my grip, but I didn't let him go.

"*My* life," I said, giving one last squeeze of emphasis while looking into his fear-filled gaze. "Starting now."

I let him go.

He pulled his hand back, rubbing his wrist as he stared at me. I held his gaze for another moment, giving him every opportunity to try again. He didn't, and I realized it was over. There would be no grabbing, no throwing punches, no more demands.

Something wondrous fluttered inside me then, like a dozen pigeons loosed all at once. I wasn't afraid of Dad's dark tone, of his unspoken promise of some horrible fate. I wasn't afraid he wouldn't like me anymore, wouldn't approve of me.

I looked up the road the way we'd come. We'd been driving for most of an hour, and we were in the middle of nowhere. But that didn't scare me either. I'd walk back to Yosemite if I had to.

"If you're looking for a ride," Uncle Morty said, "That friend o' yours has been tailing us the whole way." He shook his head. "Idiot's been driving without his lights. Anyway, he's back there."

Surprised, I looked again, and this time I saw it. About a hundred yards back, the silhouette of The Pumpkin crouched on the side of the road. I laughed.

My dad watched me like he was seeing some alien thing, but he didn't say a word. I had no idea what was going on in his mind, but for the first time...I didn't care.

I looked over at Uncle Morty.

"Thank you, Uncle Morty," I said. "I mean that. Thank you."

"You're welcome, son. Good luck."

I walked past my stunned dad and headed for The Pumpkin.

CHAPTER 25

Gage got out of The Pumpkin as I neared. He had my wooden sword in one hand and glanced at the Buick up the road, then back at me, trying to decipher what had happened.

"You followed us?" I said.

"Like I'm just going to fucking let them take you," he said. He tossed the sword to me. "You said this helped you grow a pair when you were young. Thought you might need it."

I caught it and turned it over. The smooth, painted wood felt good in my hand. "I guess I didn't. Dad was my demon this time, but I guess I didn't need the sword to tell him what I needed to say." I thought of how I'd forcibly removed my dad's hand from my arm. "Or do what needed to be done."

"Fuckin' A," Gage said. "Well, keep it. Make for a good club if they come back."

"They're not coming back," I said.

"Oh?"

"No."

"Well get in the fucking car and tell me all about it."

I did, and as we sped down the highway back toward Yosemite I told him everything that had happened.

"The cop just let you *go*?" Gage said.

"Yeah."

"Well, maybe I'll change my opinion about cops," he said. "*Some* cops, anyway."

"Thanks for coming after me."

"You free soloed Half Dome, motherfucker. No way does that end in handcuffs. It's got to be some cosmic law or something. I'd'a broken you out of jail if I had to."

"Dad was determined to put me on that plane," I said. "But Uncle Morty... I didn't think he heard me when I told him all those things, but I guess he did."

"Wicked." He grinned.

"I guess it...resonated," I said. "Turns out he wanted to be a reporter when he was young, did you know that?"

"How the fuck would I know that?"

"I'm just saying. I don't think we're the only ones who dreamed of taking risks. Maybe everyone feels like that."

"No way, dude," Gage said. "Not everyone would do what we've done."

"Not climbing. But other things. Maybe everyone has that thing they always wished they could do, but they were too afraid. But we did it. This summer, that's what it was all about."

"And you popped your dad in the face?"

"No, I didn't hit him. He tried to shove me and I didn't let him. I think then... I think he just finally understood I'm not a kid anymore. He couldn't make me do what I didn't want to do."

"Fuckin' A."

We drove in silence for a while, and we soon entered the park just like we had almost a month ago. I climbed out the window and sat on the door.

Gage laughed. "You going surfing again?"

I didn't say anything. I smelled the pine trees on the wind, felt the warm night air rushing around me.

I tried not to think about the numbered days in front of me, tried to just be in that moment and not think about how it was all coming to an end.

I really tried, but as I looked at the hulking moonlit shape of Half Dome in the distance, tears prickled my eyes. I heard the soft voice of the fetch.

This is your moment. And it will never come again.

I let the tears come, let them stripe my cheeks, but they weren't entirely tears of sadness. God, what a summer. And though I had less than two weeks left, I could also look at it from the other side: I had almost two full weeks left, and I knew how to fit a lifetime in that span.

Live.

Gage pulled into the employee tent area and drove right down the dirt space between the tents, even though cars weren't supposed to go there. A few of the park employees were hanging out on the stoops of their tent cabins, and they stood up as The Pumpkin idled into their midst.

I dropped back into the passenger seat. "Gage, what are you—"

"I told her I'd bring you back," he said. "Promised I'd drop you off at her door, and I'm not going to start breaking promises now."

Winsley's door opened, and she stepped onto the wooden stairs that led down to the ground from her tent cabin. The Pumpkin rolled to a soft stop. A wide smile spread across her face when she saw me. God, she glowed.

"Go on," Gage said.

"Fuck me, I think I'm scared," I said.

He laughed and shoved me at the door. I got out of the car. He shut the door behind me and backed slowly away.

"Of course he'd drive down the center of the tents," Winsley said.

"It's Gage," I said.

She watched me like she could barely believe I was here. "How did he get you away from your dad?"

"He didn't," I said.

She looked confused. "Then how did you get free?"

"I flexed."

She laughed. "Seriously?"

"Uncle Morty let me go."

"And your dad?"

"Didn't agree with Uncle Morty. So I...persuaded him."

She narrowed her eyes, looking for the lie. "I bet you did." She shook her head. "You live a charmed life, Thor."

"I'm here with you. That's proof enough." I stepped up the first step, putting us eye to eye.

"Silver-tongued devil," she murmured. She took a fistful of my shirt and pulled me into a kiss.

Butterflies fluttered in my stomach. These past months, I'd come into my confidence as a climber. I'd faced my dad down. But here, now, I suddenly felt nervous again.

She threaded her fingers between mine, clasped my hand. "You," she whispered. "Come with me." She opened the door and pulled me inside. Two of the people who'd been sitting on their stoops outside whooped. I could have sworn one of those voices was Lisa's.

The spring door banged shut behind us, and Winsley led me to the bed.

This was going to happen. It was actually going to happen. Me and Winsley. We were going to...

"I've never done this before," I said.

She pulled my shirt over my head, kissed me. "I won't let you fall, I promise." She whispered the exact words she'd said the first time she'd belayed me. She grinned, ran her fingers up the front of my stomach, my chest. "You don't even have to talk."

"Just climb?" I asked.

"Mmmm hmmm."

"And the boobs?"

"Are gonna get in the way."

She pulled me onto the bed.

CHAPTER 26

The next week and a half was heaven. It was life as I'd always imagined it could be. I was the man I wanted to be, and I was in love with the woman of my dreams.

During the days, Winsley, Gage, and I climbed. With ropes. We'd had our fill of free soloing for the time being, and being roped-in made it play, like we were getting on a ride at Disneyland. In the evenings, we ate, drank, and talked shit at The Shack.

The nights belonged to Winsley and me. We didn't spend a single one apart. Mostly we'd bed down at her tent cabin, but a few nights we grabbed sleeping bags and snuck out to make love under the stars.

I didn't see the fetch a single time during that week and a half. But then, I wasn't looking for her.

However, I did do what she'd told me to do. I lived. I turned my face to what was facing me now, and I didn't look anywhere else.

But the morning finally came that we all had to leave. Winsley's job at Yosemite was ending, her flight back to Montana booked long ago. And Gage had to be back at CC for registration.

Winsley and I had taken every last moment we could get

last night, tumbling under the covers, talking, being together until the last possible second when the sun came up and she had to pack.

Most of the other employees had already left, but Lisa was still there. She lived in Sacramento and was going to give Winsley a ride to the airport in San Francisco.

Now all four of us stood in the dirt walkway between the staff tents, where Gage had driven The Pumpkin to drop me off at Winsley's threshold. Gage and I hugged Lisa, then Gage hugged Winsley. She gave him a long kiss on the cheek and whispered something in his ear I couldn't hear.

He smiled and nodded. She hugged him again, holding onto the back of his neck for a long moment, their foreheads touching, then she let him go. Gage backed up, and then it was my turn.

I swallowed. I could barely hold the doom away anymore. I was going to die. I only had a couple of days left, and I desperately wanted to spend them with Winsley. But she was focused on leaving, getting ready for college. She seemed to have forgotten the fetch's warning about summer's end, and I wasn't going to remind her. I wanted to leave her with the memories of a perfect summer. I didn't want her to feel my fear. But I also didn't want her to go.

I took a step toward her. "We could take you to the airport," I said. "Plenty of room for your stuff. You could sit between us." *Please*, I thought. *Don't say goodbye yet.*

She put her hands on my cheeks. "I know. But I...I want to think about everything that happened here. I've been ignoring Lisa for a week and a half. We're going to girl-talk all the way to San Fran." She held me with her gaze. "Yes, mostly about you."

I tried to smile.

"Buck up," she said. "I'll see you at CC. One short week." She got that mischievous look in her eyes that I loved so much. "You can...build up your anticipation and we'll work the problem together."

"Okay," I murmured.

After she'd mentioned she was going to CC, I'd only told her that I'd been accepted there, too. I'd never told her I wasn't actually going to attend, that even if I survived my eighteenth birthday, I didn't have the money for college.

She kissed me, and the electricity raced through my body. Every time it was the same. I kept waiting for it to fade, but it never had. It was the magic of our first kiss every single time.

We came up for air, and she held onto my face. "We said our goodbyes last night. *And* this morning." She laughed. "So I'm going to keep it short and sweet. I'm so glad...this happened. That we free soloed Half Dome and threw off the fetch's curse."

Curse? I suddenly realized that she hadn't brought up the fetch's "curse" because she'd thought we'd somehow beaten it. I swallowed hard. "Yeah."

"Hey...." She frowned, then she leaned in and whispered. "Bad dreams begone."

She kissed me again, long and lingering, then she let me go. She walked toward Lisa's car, and she waved over her shoulder like she knew I was watching her.

They both got in Lisa's Datsun and drove away, dust billowing behind them. I waved. Winsley's hand poked out the window and waved back. Then it went back inside. She didn't wave again.

I watched her leave, the lump in my throat threatening to choke me.

Gage drew up alongside me, and we watched Lisa's car until there was nothing left except the cloud of dust kicked up by the tires.

"Threw off the curse of the fetch, eh?" he said.

"That's what she said," I replied.

"That what happened?"

I didn't answer. The fetch had delivered on everything she'd promised. I was sure a near-death experience wasn't going to count. No. My death was still coming, and there was nothing I could do about it. I might be able to run away from my dad, from my school, from Uncle Morty, but I couldn't outrun the fetch's promise.

"Let's go," I said.

We headed to The Pumpkin, which was packed up with all of our things, ready for the trip back to Colorado. Gage had even filled up the gas tank yesterday.

I watched Half Dome as we left, watched it grow smaller in the rearview mirror, then become obscured by trees and bends in the road until I couldn't see it anymore. The moment it vanished from sight, it felt like I'd left a piece of my soul behind, as though what had happened there was a fading dream.

I stayed pensive as we wound out of the park and got on the highway. Every mile closer to Colorado was one step toward the hangman's noose.

Gage looked over at me several times, but he seemed content to let the silence stand.

I thought about the bargain I'd made with the fetch, and I felt trapped. As much as I wanted to, I couldn't rail against it. Every time I thought it was unfair, that somehow I'd been tricked, I asked myself the simple question: was it worth it?

And it was. Every bit of it. Perhaps now at the end it seemed too short, but this summer had been mine in every way.

Gage drove, and I watched the road rush past like water. I began to think of it as a river, and that somehow made me feel better. No matter what else happened, the forks in the river the fetch had talked about...I'd made my own choices. Me and no one else.

I imagined having stayed that kid I was in high school— scared of my father, of asking out Tina Cartwright, breaking the rules, getting punched by a jock, rock climbing with Gage, and everything else...

No. I couldn't have stayed that person.

I'd ventured out into the world, learned how to climb, to love it, to be really good at it. Gage and I had become brothers. And I'd loved Winsley. Winsley....

Yeah. It was worth it.

We stopped for gas. We stopped for food. Sometimes we listened to music, but we didn't really talk. We pushed hard that first day, driving thirteen hours straight to western Colorado. We got a motel room in Grand Junction around one o'clock in the morning. I thought of Uncle Morty briefly, but I knew I didn't have to worry about him or my father anymore.

We got up with the sunrise on the last day of my life and we drove across northern Colorado on I-70, cutting south at Denver and then finally into Colorado Springs.

Gage parked The Pumpkin outside a restaurant near the college called Wooglin's Deli. The afternoon sun lit the mountains to the west. We both got out and stretched. The hot engine pinged as it cooled.

"I'm going to go register," he said, stamping the blacktop with his shoe. "Then we can hang in my dorm room."

I looked at the admin building across the street. "Okay."

"What're you going to do?" he asked in a monotone.

"I'll just...wait for you in the deli."

He went quiet for a moment, then said, "'Kay. See you when I'm done. Grab me a sandwich or something."

"Sure."

Gage hesitated a moment like he was going to say something else, but finally he turned and went across the street, heading for the admin building.

I figured I knew what he was thinking.

He was wondering if I was going be dead before he got back. Maybe he really did believe.

CHAPTER 27

I didn't go into Wooglin's. As soon as Gage disappeared around the corner of the four-story CC admin building, I walked toward it, sizing it up.

It was built with that style where the brick wall of the building not only had corners that were easy to scale, but every fifth row on the walls had protruding bricks. They stuck out about an inch. Bomber jugs.

It took me all of five minutes to climb it.

I sat down on the edge of the roof, looking over the campus. It really was beautiful, even more so than UCLA, the old buildings mixed with modern architecture. Gage said all college campuses were beautiful, but nothing compared to this. Pikes Peak loomed to the west against the blue sky, and I couldn't love a place more than this. Maybe because I could see me and Winsley walking across that green lawn, hand in hand.

"Heavy thoughts?" the soft voice came from behind me.

I'd always looked forward to my fetch's visits before, ever since that first time at Canyonlands. I'd even longed for her sometimes. But this time I didn't.

She came over and sat next to me on the ledge. As always, she was dressed in a different outfit. This one was fuchsia stirrup pants, white Keds, and a loose, long-sleeved black shirt. It said "Colorado College" in gold across the front with a stylized tiger beneath it. The neck of it slipped over one of her pale, lightly freckled shoulders as she pulled her knees up to her chin like mine.

"It's a beautiful campus," she said.

"Yeah," I said, and I hated how petulant I sounded. I shut my mouth.

I tried—I honestly tried—not to feel bitter. She'd given me the choice at the very beginning: to dance with her or not. I'd said yes, and she'd honored her part. She had made me legendary. I'd been the hero of my dreams for three months. I'd done more in that time than some people do in a lifetime.

"How is it going to happen?" I asked.

"Your death?" she asked.

"Yeah," I whispered. "Will it hurt?"

"At first," she said. "Some say it does. Though a few say it doesn't hurt at all, that it's a relief."

Some say... I wondered how many young men she'd taken. I almost asked her, but I didn't.

"It's different for everyone," she said.

"I..." I got a catch in my throat. I thought of Winsley, of how I was never going to see her again. Then I rallied, cleared my throat. "Look, I wanted to thank you. I..." I shook my head. "You changed my life. I'd rather have lived this one summer the way I did than a hundred years the way I was before. You opened my eyes. I saw the world in a way I never thought possible. I knew my own heart for the first time ever. And I fought for it, for myself and for what's important."

She watched me with those huge green eyes, and her expression was unreadable.

"I'm not afraid anymore," I said. "Of dying."

"I know," she said.

"I just... Now that I've seen what life can be, I don't want to leave it. There's so much more to do. So many things I can do now that I'm not afraid of...well, of everything. It just seems... It's sad that it took the certainty of my own death to see that."

She nodded.

"But you gave that to me," I continued. "And I can never thank you enough."

"But you did thank me," she said. "You inspired me, Eric. You upheld your end, as much as anyone I've ever bonded with." She smiled, and whimsy sparkled in her eyes.

"Everything you told me came true," I said. "Except one thing."

"Oh?"

"You said if I kissed a fetch, I'd never love a mortal woman, or something like that. I'd never love anyone else."

"Yes."

"But you were wrong. I fell in love with Winsley. I'm still in love with her."

"I know," she said.

For a heartbeat I allowed myself to imagine that my love for Winsley was so strong it had shattered the dire magic the fetch had spun around me. "Is what I have with Winsley... Was it something special?"

Her green gaze became direct, her face serious. "Of course it's special," she said. "The most special thing there is. But you don't need me to tell you that."

"But you said I'd never fall in love—"

"I know," she said. "I lied."

For a moment, I couldn't speak.

"You *lied*?" I finally said, stunned. "W-Why would you do that?"

"Young men need something to push against. A challenge. They have to know what they *don't* want before they can see what they *do* want. Your head was swimming with a dozen fictions about Gage and Winsley. You couldn't see past it. Angst. Guilt. What Gage would do. What Winsley would think." She waved her hand like she was shooing flies. "But after you kissed me, you became clear about who you are and what you wanted. You stopped making up fictions about Winsley. You got out of your own way so you two could get together."

I opened my mouth, but for a second I didn't speak. The fetch just waited patiently, watching me with those green eyes.

"You lied to me so I'd fall in love with Winsley?" I blurted.

"Oh please. You were already in love with her."

"How..." I could barely speak. "How can I trust anything you've told me?"

"Maybe you shouldn't. My purpose is to shape young men out of boys. To cut the boy away, I do whatever is necessary. I will lie anywhere and everywhere I must in order to accomplish my goal."

"Which is to kill them."

"Of course."

"But that's...it's cruel."

"A little. But necessary."

I felt ill and my head swam. *How was that necessary?*

Then a thought hit me like a lightning bolt out of the blue, and suddenly I couldn't think of anything else. I leapt to my feet, backing away from the edge as I faced her.

"You...."

She leaned back, legs crossed, holding onto her top knee with both hands. "Yes?" She bounced her free foot like a little girl.

"You lied to me about Winsley."

"Yes." Her emerald eyes glittered like she knew where I was going and couldn't wait for me to get there.

"What else did you lie about?" I asked.

Her sharp canine teeth appeared as she smiled. "That's my Eric."

A thin ray of hope lit my heart. "You said I was going to die. Before my eighteenth birthday, I was going to die."

"This is the part I like the best," she said.

"You lied," I breathed.

"Yes."

A cold wind rushed through me, and for a moment it seemed like I didn't have any lungs to breathe with, no heart to beat, no organs of any kind. I was just a hollow tunnel for the wind.

"Did you think this was some devil's bargain?" she asked. "Did you think I'd suck out your soul at the end of three months, make you pay for the beauty you've experienced?"

"I... Yes."

"True beauty doesn't work that way, Eric. I'm yours. I always have been. I would never hurt you."

"So I'm not going to die."

"You already did. Sort of," she said.

"What does 'sort of' mean?" I demanded.

"The boy you were is gone. And it's a little sad. And it's a little cruel, like you said. Boys are wonderful, but they can't live forever. It started the moment you left class to talk to Tina Cartwright. The little boy began sloughing off and falling away. A little bit at each point of your journey. But that frightened boy dropped stone dead the moment you faced your father. I don't think you could bring that boy back if you tried."

"But I thought I was going to *die*," I said. "Like, not just some metaphor of death, but actually die. Why would you tell me that?"

"A person who knows they're going to die in three months lives life differently than a person who believes they have all the time in the world, who puts off what they really want because they think they'll have another day to 'get around to it.' But that's the real lie. A hurtful, horrible lie. No one is guaranteed another day, let alone years. This moment is the only moment that matters." She shrugged and smiled. "Sometimes boys need a fetch to remind them to live right now. And, of course, some boys I approach choose not to dance with me. They may never open their eyes to how much they can live. But you did. You inspired me. You *fed* me."

I blinked, stunned, and I tried to take it all in. "I can't believe it." My inevitable end, my steady march to the gallows, it was suddenly...gone.

My fetch's slender finger touched my chin. Somehow she had crossed the distance to me. I hadn't even seen her move.

"You're enough, Eric," she said softly. The whimsy was

gone from her eyes. "You always were. You don't need a college to tell you that. Or your father. Or Winsley. Or even me. It's right here." She tapped lightly on my chest with two fingers. "What you did this summer...was you. You made those choices. You climbed those cliffs. You stood up to your father. You inspired your uncle to see through your eyes. If you ever forget that, all of this will have been for nothing."

I hugged her, picked her up off the ground. She was warm and soft and she wrapped her arms around me.

"What about the magic?" I asked as I set her down. "The magic you used on me?"

"If I gave you a lift here or there, it was only to get you started. The best of the magic was yours. *You* worked the problems. Gage followed *your* lead. Winsley fell in love with *you*. Your magic. Not mine."

"And... Is this how it's going to be for the rest of my life?"

"I hope so," she said.

"No, I mean... Will you stay with me? Are you going to be with me?"

She put a coquettish hand against her chest and batted her eyelashes. "Marry you? Oh Eric, this is so sudden. I just couldn't."

"No, really."

She dropped the dramatic pose and cocked her head. "Wasn't it enough, Eric?"

"Of course it was. It was more than I ever dreamed, but..."

"I will carry you with me forever," she said, holding my gaze. "The memory of our summer... I will never forget how you inspired me. But fetches come when they're needed." She smiled sadly. "And you don't need me anymore."

My heart lurched.

She pulled me in and kissed me on the lips, swift and soft, then backed away. Her hand lingered on my cheek, and her fingers fell away one at a time like traces of silk.

"I will always be your fetch," she said. "But you won't be seeing me anymore."

"I don't want you to go..." My voice caught in my throat

TODD FAHNESTOCK

and tears filled my eyes.

"You're enough, Eric. Never forget."

Sadness washed over me. I wanted to say something to change her mind, but I couldn't speak.

"It's time for me to go now," she said softly. "And it's time for you to *live*." She walked toward the edge of the building.

Another lightning bolt of realization hit me.

"Waitaminute. Are you lying to me again?" I said.

She turned her head, and I saw her beautiful profile against the setting sun, her lips curved in a mischievous smile.

Then she became a red fox. She flicked her tail and leapt over the edge. I raced after her, but by the time I got there, all that was left was her laughter, floating on the warm Colorado breeze.

CHAPTER 28

I climbed down off the building, and Gage was waiting by The Pumpkin. He leaned against the door, his muscular arms crossed.

"Talkin' to the fetch?" he guessed.

I still wasn't completely sure if he believed in her or not. Maybe he just thought "talking to the fetch" was me gathering my thoughts, talking to myself.

"Yeah," I said.

"What did she say?"

"That she's a liar."

He narrowed his eyes, then his shark's smile appeared. "You're *not* going to die," he guessed.

"Apparently that wasn't the point." I held my hands out helplessly.

"Well, fuck. World's going to shit. If you can't trust invisible magical fetches, who the hell can you trust?"

I laughed as the emotion of everything washed over me. The whole summer. Running from my uncle. The spiritual vigor I'd found on the rock. The near-death scrapes. Facing my dad. Falling in love with Winsley. I tried to keep the tears from coming, but I couldn't. Gage watched me and then— shockingly—he put his arms around me.

I stiffened in surprise. "Dude—"

"Don't be a pussy," he said, and he hugged me.

I relaxed, and it felt good. All the emotion came tumbling out.

"I don't know what the hell I'm going to do next," I said shakily. "God, it was so easy not to be scared when I knew I was going to die anyway. It was easier when I didn't have a choice. Now all I have are choices. Except I have no idea what to do. And I don't have a fetch to point the way anymore."

"One move at a time," he said.

My head jerked up, and I laughed.

"Right?" he said.

"Right."

He squeezed me one last time, then let me go.

I looked northward at the beautiful CC campus. "Yeah. I guess I just got to work the route I'm on. I'll figure something."

"I say stay in the Springs. Get a job waiting tables."

"Yeah," I said. I sure wasn't going back to Durango.

"You'll need a car, though. To get to work and stuff." He tossed me the keys to The Pumpkin, and I caught them reflexively.

"No, Gage." I shook my head. "The Pumpkin is yours. I meant for you to have it." I held the keys out.

He kept his arms crossed. "Yeah, it was a sweet note. But I ain't taking your fucking car."

"Gage..." I clenched the keys in my fist. Even when I had nothing—no family, no money, no place to live—I'd had The Pumpkin. It had faithfully taken me everywhere I needed to go. To Zion, Joshua Tree, L.A., Yosemite, and back to Colorado.

Now, to suddenly have Gage give it back to me felt like a missing piece of my heart had been put back into place. It felt like hope. If I had The Pumpkin, I could do anything. I could start a new life or, if worse came to worst, take to the road again.

"I...I really did want you to have it," I said hoarsely, having a hard time talking around the lump in my throat.

"I know."

"Thanks man," I said.

"Oh, and you'll need the pink slip." He pulled the yellowed envelope that contained the pink slip from his pocket, except it wasn't the paper-thin envelope I'd given to him. It was full to bursting with something else he'd stuffed in there. He handed it to me.

My jaw dropped as I opened it. Inside was a thick stack of hundred-dollar bills. It looked like everything we had left from the trip.

"What is this?" I breathed, thumbing through the bills.

"Enough to get you through your first year. After that, you're on your own."

My throat tightened. "Gage, I... I can't take this. It's..."

"Fuck you, you can't take it. Life dealt you a shit hand and you ran the table. And you took me along with you, you righteous bastard. You gave me something I never had before, something most people never even get to touch." He flicked the envelope. "This? This is just money. We took it to follow the fetch, and I say the fetch is telling you to go to college with me. So shut the fuck up and take it."

Tears stood in my eyes, but I couldn't stop smiling. After all this, not only was I *not* going to die, but I was going to my dream college.

And Winsley... I was going to see Winsley again. I felt that familiar electricity rush through me.

I wiped roughly at my eyes. "I don't... I don't know what to say."

"Maybe say that this time, we're following *my* fetch."

"Okay," I said. An unbidden laugh escaped my throat, and Gage laughed with me.

We walked together toward the admin building, toward a new future. I swore to myself that I was going to honor the fetch. To face life like I had only one summer to live. To work out the moves one handhold at a time.

"We skipped out on finals," I said as I began to think about this new possible future. All the paths opening up before me presented their own problems. "They're not going to let me

219

register."

"It'll work out," he said with a cryptic certainty. "Lucky fucker like you?"

I glanced sidelong at him. "Hey, how'd they let *you* register?"

"'Cause one of us has a brain, moron," he said.

"What?"

"I used the telephone."

"You called the school?"

"During a resupply in Zion. Ms. Ellsworth bent over backward to help. Woman's got a thing for you. She smoothed things out. You'll drop a grade in a couple classes. Nothing major."

"How the fuck?"

"I pulled the zombie mom card," he said. "Said you went crazy. I went to help, you know, good guy that I am. Make sure you didn't off yourself."

"That bullshit worked?"

"Psychological deferment, she called it," he said.

"I don't even know what that means."

"Nobody knows what that means," he said. "But in this case it means we graduated."

I went silent, stunned, then said, "Well shit. That's…" I didn't have the words, only a growing thrill.

"Dude, if things don't work out with Winsley, I say date Ms. Ellsworth. Chick totally wants to suck your dick."

I laughed, and we walked for a moment in silence.

"Is that when you called your dad, too? In Zion?"

He didn't say anything.

I looked over at him. "Back at The Shack when my dad and Uncle Morty showed up, you said you'd talked to him. Was that bullshit?"

"Am I a bullshitter?" he said.

"He was just okay with it?"

"Fuck no."

"He had to be pissing red. What did you say?"

"I told him that $33,000 was what it took to buy you a set

of balls to become a man."

"You did not."

He gave me an enigmatic smile.

"What really happened?" I asked.

He just shrugged, and I knew he wasn't going to tell me. And there was nothing I could do to force him. This was Gage.

We walked a little more.

"So all this time we could register *and* you were going to give me the money?" I said. "And you didn't tell me? Dude, we were in the car for twenty hours!"

"I figured I'd wait until you pulled your head out of your ass."

I started laughing. "That's fucked up, man."

"What are you gonna do?" He shrugged unapologetically.

As we walked, he glanced over at the on-campus church. Shove Chapel, I remembered from the brochure. His eyes lingered there like they had lingered on many a rock face.

"I want to climb that," he said predictably.

By then I was looking at it too. My gaze roved over the beige stone blocks, looking for handholds. The stained-glass façade had two spires on either side, ending in cones made of stone shingles. It would be totally cool to hang off one of those.

"The spires?" I said.

"What I was thinking."

"One for each of us?"

"What else?"

"Let's do it tonight."

He glanced over at me. "Fuck tonight."

Our gazes locked, and we sprinted for the church.

Mailing List/Social Media

MAILING LIST
Don't miss out on the latest news and information about all of
my books. Join my Readers Group

FACEBOOK GROUP

AMAZON AUTHOR PAGE

AUTHOR LETTER

Summer of the Fetch is an anomaly amidst my collection of epic fantasy novels, and it was born in a whirlwind of unexpected inspiration.

It is the only book I've ever written that includes multiple authentic details from my own life. I'd been wanting to write something semi-autobiographical for about thirty years, all the way back to my college days. But whenever I'd try, I'd get about three or four chapters in before I'd scrap the whole project. I'd get to a point and think, "Ugh! This is my boring old life. Who wants to read this crap?" And in the trash it would go.

Summer of the Fetch started exactly like this, an attempt at something semi-autobiographical.

Now let me qualify that: this is a work of fiction. Most of it is pure fantasy, and the more I worked it, the more fictional it became. But there are some details from my own life. I did, in fact, graduate from Durango High School in 1988. There was a car called The Pumpkin, a 1967 El Camino with a Corvette engine and a short-throw racing shifter. I did go on a number of road trips which took me to Zion and Joshua Tree and Yosemite and many other places, not to mention Vegas and L.A. And I did do some rock climbing (though not nearly as much as my friends who helped me shape the details of this story). I also did some crazy dangerous shit that went along with that rock climbing. But I never free soloed Half Dome (nobody had in 1988). And The Pumpkin was not my car; it was my brother's.

So this idea of incorporating some of my real life into a modern day fantasy is how *Summer of the Fetch* started.

I went to bed on May 19 hankering for freedom. This was during the latter days of the first COVID quarantine order, and I was tired of being cooped up in my house. I was also feeling nostalgic about my high school days and the subsequent road trips, about how lucky I'd been in so many of those dangerous situations. And then I started thinking about the fetch...

The fetch is a concept I've held dear for decades. It was first brought to my attention by a college friend back in the 1990s. She'd described it to me was as an avatar of luck that attached itself to specific people, and she told me, "I think you have a fetch." (I was generally considered a ridiculously lucky bastard in those days.)

Her words rang true. I'd always felt like some benevolent force assisted me at the most important moments of my life, and that force had always felt distinctly female to me. So the fetch concept dazzled me. She felt right from the first moment, and I longed to put her into a story. But as I said before, whenever I tried to create something even partly autobiographical, I met with dismal failure.

But flush with this need for freedom and the sparkle of the fetch in my mind, I woke up on May 20 and gave it a try. I began with a bit of research. I knew the fetch came from Irish folklore, but I'd never seriously dug into it. So I looked to see if my college friend's definition matched up to the actual Irish definition.

To my dismay, it didn't.

The Irish fetch is bad news, an omen of death appearing as a doppleganger of the person it stalks. But I dug deeper and found, to my surprise, that the Irish fetch wasn't the original myth. The concept had crossed the North Sea much earlier, and in Norway the fetch was called a fylgjur, and it was different in some key aspects. The fylgjur is a spirit that appears in dreams as a guide or portent.

If the fylgjur steps out of your dreams into the real world—if you catch a glimpse of your guide while you're awake—there are varying results. If a male fylgjur appears, it's an omen of death just like the Irish fetch. But if a female fylgjur appears, it's quite different. She's a guardian spirit. She can make you, your family, even your entire clan, exceedingly lucky in all their endeavors. She will often take on the form of an animal. If she has a "tame" nature, she'll appear as a domesticated animal: ox, goat or boar. If she has a wild nature, it'll be a fox, deer, bear, wolf, eagle or some other wild animal.

Bang! That was my fetch. I latched onto her immediately. I kept the name fetch—rather than fylgjar—because I didn't want my readers spending time screwing up their faces and thinking "File-guh-jar? Fill-jure? File-gar?"

So with my mythology firmly in mind, I wrote chapter one.

It sucked.

I sighed. Same as it ever was... I was deflated. I could see it all happening in my mind's eye, just as it always did. I'd get pumped about chapters 1 and 2, maybe, then my interest would wane and I'd struggle through chapter 3. Then I'd realize just how boring the whole story was and I'd quit. A monstrous cynicism reared up inside me and I wandered around the house, trying to shake the whole stupid idea and get back to work on *Tower of the Four*.

But my dear fetch kept calling me back to the keyboard, and I finally decided to scrap my original chapter 1 and try again.

This time...magic.

The words poured out. I spent every waking moment writing. I became a slave to a force I'd never felt before. I sometimes forgot to eat. When I did eat, I shuffled into the kitchen in a daze—my mind still firmly in the story—grabbed food and went back to my office. At night, my wife Lara had to make me to go to bed. In the morning, I leapt up like I'd been electrified and went straight to the computer. Other commitments began to slide as I became obsessed. I didn't even stop to try to plot the story, to try to consciously organize the narrative; it just came out as though the whole thing had already been written in my head and it had chosen this moment to be born.

After the third day of this deluge as I blew past chapter 5, I dared to be optimistic. I might actually finish this!

By the seventh day, I was ecstatic; I could see the end.

By the tenth day, I was haggard, like this whole thing was beyond my control. Writing didn't even seem to be a choice anymore, like I was a passenger, an adjunct to the process, a mere doorway for the flood. I was a keyboard monkey whose only job was to keep typing while the fetch worked her will through me. Every time I sat at the computer, the inspiration returned and rushed out whether I wanted to write or not. It was almost painful.

By the thirteenth day, I finished. I sat back in a daze, blinking through my fatigue and not even sure what I had.

I left the keyboard, released for the first time in two weeks, and I slept for two days straight.

Months later, after the revision process and some awesome beta reader feedback, *Summer of the Fetch* became the story you are holding now. I hope you enjoy this trip back in time to the late 80s, and I hope you enjoy my fetch as much as I have.

Cheers! And happy reading.

-Todd

ALSO BY TODD FAHNESTOCK

Tower of the Four
Episode 1 – The Quad
Episode 2 – The Tower
Episode 3 – The Test
Episode 4 – The Nightmare
Episode 5 – The Resurrection
Episode 6 – The Reunion
The Champions Academy (Episodes 1-3 compilation)
The Dragon's War (Episodes 4-6 compilation)

Eldros Legacy (Legacy of Shadows)
Khyven the Unkillable
Lorelle of the Dark
Rhenn the Traveler (Forthcoming)

Threadweavers
Wildmane
The GodSpill
Threads of Amarion
God of Dragons

The Whisper Prince
Fairmist
The Undying Man
The Slate Wizards (Forthcoming)

The Wishing World
The Wishing World
Loremaster (Forthcoming)
Spheres of Magic (Forthcoming)

Standalone Novels
Charlie Fiction
Summer of the Fetch

Memoirs

Ordinary Magic

Short Stories

Urchin: A Tower of the Four Short Story
Royal: A Tower of the Four Short Story
Princess: A Tower of the Four Short Story
Pawns of Magic: A Tower of the Four Short Story
Here There Be Giants: *Fate's Dagger*
Talons & Talismans 2: *The Darkest Door*
Parallel Worlds Anthology: *Threshold*
Fantastic Realms Anthology: *Ten for Every One*
Dragonlance: The Cataclysm – *Seekers*
Dragonlance: Heroes & Fools – *Songsayer*
Dragonlance: The History of Krynn – *The Letters of Trayn Minaas*

ABOUT THE AUTHOR

TODD FAHNESTOCK is a writer of fantasy for all ages and winner of the New York Public Library's Books for the Teen Age Award. *Threadweavers* and *The Whisper Prince Trilogy* are two of his bestselling epic fantasy series. He is a finalist in the Colorado Authors League Writing Awards for the past two years, for *Charlie Fiction* and *The Undying Man*. His passions are fantasy and his quirky, fun-loving family. When he's not writing, he teaches Taekwondo, swaps middle grade humor with his son, plays Ticket to Ride with his wife, scribes modern slang from his daughter and goes on morning runs with Galahad the Weimaraner. **Visit Todd at** www.toddfahnestock.com.